THE HAUNTING OF ENGSTROM HOUSE

Nasser Rabadi

Paperback ISBN: 978-1-954931-00-8

Hardcover ISBN: 978-1-954931-01-5

Also by Nasser Rabadi

THE RAVEN HILL BUTCHER slasher novel series

Book one: The Christmas Morning Massacre

Book two: Return to Camp Solgohachia

Book three: Noel Hell

Book four: The Curse of Raven Hill

Book five: The Final Chapter

Book six (reboot of Return to Camp Solgohachia): A New Beginning

Book seven (reboot of The Christmas Morning Massacre and Noel Hell): Winter Graves

Book eight: Santa's Space Station of Slaughter

Book nine: Santa Goes to Hell

Book ten: Into the Santa-Verse

The ENGSTROM HOUSE series

Book one: The Haunting of Engstrom House

Book two: Return to Engstrom House

Book three: The Curse of Engstrom House

NASSER RABADI

The LOVE KILLS series of dark romance thrillers
Book one: Scarlet
Book two: Lust
Book three: Desire

Contents

1

ENGSTROM HOUSE WAS UNDER constant shadow, as if sunlight could not reach past its gate on its hill in Ashfall. Its windows—oversized, divided into many parts, and always shut—were always black. Stunted sickly trees grew prolifically in the forest behind it, and tangled vegetation was abundant at the house's sides.

Engstrom House was uninhabited for many years; its previous owners, who lived as recluses, and whose doors were seldom disturbed by the knock of any visitor, had disappeared. When the trouble began, it began slowly—soft knocks in the deep hours of night that gradually became frequent. Creeping unseen footsteps in all levels of the house. Moonlight shined through a window and rolled out in long stretches; the little boy who was looking over from his bed saw a silhouetted figure pass through the glow. On each occasion investigation revealed nothing, and all occurrences were ascribed to imagination alone.

There were curious whispers and rumors of ghouls seen around Engstrom House; figures that were seldom completely human, but often approaching humanity in varying degree. Most of the creatures were forward slumping with glaring red eyes. Some were nameless blasphemies with sharp horns that curved inward toward each other, bat wings whose beating made no noise, and ugly prehensile claws.

It was said that Engstrom House's trees swayed ominously at night, and it was sworn that they did so even when there was no wind, and that was said too of the misshapen weeds in the high terraced yard where birds never lingered.

In town there were odd conversations about what abnormal things had been seen or felt near Engstrom House; while it stood alone on its hill, people were careful never to pass by it. And it would not take long before travelers passing through Ashfall heard of things locked in the attic, and of strange amorphous shadows glimpsed in windows at all levels.

Everything that happened in Engstrom House's wide staircases, long eternally dark passages, and hidden doors in unusual corners is unknown. Cold wind chilled those who stood afar and watched the house; did something still walk its halls?

Within two years of Engstrom House's completion, every person in the Engstrom family was dead. The Engstrom children died of mysterious sicknesses. Body parts—but almost never whole bodies—of missing adults were discovered, and servants told incredible tales of voices and ominous sounds heard in walls and whispers they swore came from empty rooms.

Exactly one month after Engstrom House was completed, the youngest boy in the Engstrom family fell from the rooftop. He was found by a servant who told the family that John Engstrom had been pushed and had not fallen accidentally—but pushed by whom, the servant could not say. The same servant went missing before John's funeral.

A few months later, Helen Engstrom, the oldest of the Engstrom children, went up a staircase at night to find an extra blanket for one of her sisters. While Helen's footsteps were heard all the way to the storage closet and back to the stairs, she was never seen again. Sometimes, it was said, her footsteps still echoed through the halls.

Agatha was the first of the Engstrom children to die of sickness. Each child had different symptoms. Agatha suffered from dizziness which became so severe that she could not stand, and after putting up a desperate fight for three and a half weeks, she passed away in her sleep. Joyce suffered from an intense cough that caused her to spit up blood; Joyce died several months after Agatha, and when the doctors examined her corpse, they found maggots eating her lungs.

Timothy became ill one year after Agatha's passing, and was stuck in bed with what seemed to be a cold. He was only in bed for a few days, but as he was on the brink of recovery, he felt sharp pain pulsing in the back of his head. He was dead less than a day later. When the family's doctor examined Timothy's corpse, there was half of a needle stuck in the back of his skull; while it could not be determined if he passed away from the sickness or from the broken needle, nobody could be sure how the needle was put in his head in the first place.

Rapidly approaching the two year anniversary, the only remaining Engstrom child—Thaddeus—went mad, uttering shrieking horrors and screaming all through the night that he was not Thaddeus and did not belong in the house. Thaddeus screamed about unseen things in the air which he could not describe; something was fastening itself onto him that ought not to be. He screamed that nothing was ever still in the night—the walls and shadows shifted, things moved and changed and fluttered. The best doctors in Ashfall treated him, and for a while, it was suggested that he should be taken to Piedmont Wellness, a hospital in the neighboring town, but he died before that could be arranged.

Mrs. Engstrom starved herself to death. Her shriveled body was found collapsed at the base of the hill. The following day her husband vanished without a trace, and three months later Mr. Engstrom's dismembered corpse was found in only a few pieces scattered through unused rooms on every floor in Engstrom House. Nobody was charged with his murder.

The Bloch family moved in two decades after the Engstrom family's demise. There were eight of them: Mr. Bloch, his wife, his father, his three sons, and his two daughters. No member of the Bloch family was ever found.

The Bloch children told their friends of things they had heard or seen in all corners and levels of the house, and told about odd occurrences that happened in all hours of night. Sometimes they spoke of eyes at the bottom of stairways, or footsteps heard in halls. There had even been curious whispers about nightmarishly misshapen faces seen in dreams.

Just before the Bloch family had gone missing, Mrs. Bloch had given strange warnings to her relatives about the house. She had told friends in town that there were things in that house beyond any human understanding; things that were wholly unknown and indescribable to mankind.

When it was discovered that the Bloch family had gone missing, an investigation lasting one year was launched into their whereabouts. Nothing had been stolen from their home, and no trace of them was discovered in any neighboring town—all towns within a thirty mile radius were checked.

All that remained of the Bloch family was a single note in Mr. Bloch's handwriting, found in the pocket of one of his shirts. In hurried handwriting, it read: *I hear them in the walls, and I'm going to look for them.*

In Mr. Bloch's journal—of which several pages had been mysteriously torn and lost, and several remaining pages toward the end were entirely indecipherable—there were more references to voices and sounds hidden in walls. One such entry read: *I followed it for the first time today—that old familiar voice. I couldn't take more of the mystery, so I followed it. It's been on my mind every minute of every day. That little voice in the walls. I thought if I opened the wall I'd find it—whoever it really is—but there was nothing behind the portion of wall I broke open.*

Another entry in the journal recounted a dream of his: *The oaken door had fallen, and there I found a terrible row of ten stone cells with rusty bars. Three had tenants, all skeletons of very high grade, and on the bony forefinger of one I found a seal ring with unusual symbols carved into it. At the end of the cells I found a crypt with cases of formally arranged bones, some of them bearing terrible parallel inscriptions carved in Latin and Greek.*

In a prehistoric tumuli I brought to light skulls which were slightly more human than a gorilla's, and which bore indescribable ideographic carvings. Suddenly I found myself in a midnight cavern of boundless depth where no ray of light could penetrate. We will never know what sightless stygian worlds lay beyond the little distance I went.

After the Bloch family disappeared, their heirs kept the grass cut and took care of the garden; they did renovations in hopes that they could sell the house and pass on its curse to the next owner, whoever that may be.

The house never sold.

All of these years later, its creaking floors were never walked again by any permanent guests. Perhaps only spiders lived there now, and so many generations have gone by so that the spiders thought they had been the ones to build Engstrom House.

Dull and quiet, Engstrom House rested alone, and Ashfall children dared each other to go near its fence, unaware of its history that echoed within the walls. Somewhere inside was left the imprint of its many, many lives long lost and long forgotten, so that even the names of all the deceased were not known.

While most of what happened there was mystery, and would forever be unknown, there was one thing that everyone generally believed: that Engstrom House was *not* empty, that something unnatural was inside of it. Where the evilness had originated from would only be speculation. What caused all that trouble so long ago would all be a guess. The history of the house revealed no trace of the sinister either about its construction, or about the family who built it.

In the dead of night, formless shadows passed by Engstrom House's deepest window seats; Engstrom House watched every move that the sleeping town of Ashfall made. Unknown things stirred in empty halls and empty hidden doorways. Spiders crawled wickedly and freely up and down walls and beds; coldness spread through lonely rooms.

Engstrom House was alive tonight, because it knew that soon somebody would be visiting.

2

THE WELLHOUSE WAS MOSSY and grey, and it seemed to Helen that it had grown there like a weed in a flower garden that sprouted up on its own instead of having been purposely placed. The wellhouse had always been off limits—for reasons that her parents never told her—but whenever she passed by the wellhouse's sealed windows, as she was doing right now, she told herself, *Next time I'll peek in.*

The woods behind her new home spanned endlessly. Maybe there was no way out of them. The woods bent and twisted and anything could have been hidden within—but Helen knew her way to her hiding place well; she had marked a path with purple marbles just in case she should get lost. The hiding place was a little area between neighboring trees whose branches stretched and interlocked so tightly with each other that nobody could walk into the hiding space—any visitor had to crawl through an opening pressed extremely close to the ground.

The impossibly high branches were tangled so strongly that if she were sitting there right now in a storm, not a drop of rain would touch her—she had tried it before. And yet, sunlight still found a way to pass through the impossibly tight spaces that must have existed through the dense branches. It must have been magic.

Today her family was having a fire. It was her job to go into the woods with her red wagon and fill it with firewood, and she was careful not to dirty her brand new blue dress as she did so. Then, as she set a barren branch down into her growing pile, she heard somebody running up ahead.

It was her little brother Thaddeus. He was going deep into the woods.

"Thaddeus?" Helen dragged her wagon two steps toward him then let go of the handle and cupped her hands around her mouth. *"Where are you going? Thaddeus?"*

His footfalls raced distantly, and Helen moved quickly to follow him past the familiar river. But she lost sight of him as he moved between the trees. After a while of running, Helen stopped to catch her breath, and looked behind herself realizing that she had never been so deep into the woods before, and she could hear the warning her mother and father had given her a dozen times before about not wandering too far alone.

"Thaddeus, where are you? Can you hear me? Thaddeus? Thad-deuuuuuuuus? Come on, let's go. My new dress is getting dirty, and we have to start the fire."

Whippoorwills sang. Helen rested her hand against a tree and frowned. Where did he go? What was he doing here? She wanted desperately to turn back around, but if something happened to him… she couldn't stand knowing she could have stopped it. Immediately she thought about her little brother John, and how she wished so badly that she could have been around to prevent him from falling…

Helen didn't want to cry, but her tears erupted anyways. *"Thaddeus can't you come out already? I want to go home. Thaddeus you big dummy."*

Helen kept going, looking furtively over her shoulder, reminding herself all she had to do was move straight back and she'd be home, move straight back and she'd be okay, she couldn't get lost if she were this deep in the forest.

A jolt of terror pulsed through Helen's body when she heard the screeching—a sharp noise pierced the normally silent woods.

Helen came to a tree that had fallen over early in life and died, rotting slowly over a span of time that, as far as Helen knew, could have been anywhere between one year and ten thousand years. She went around it, and her continual search grew.

"Thaddeus please…"

Helen checked over her shoulder again, and the ground under her feet rose, and when she climbed up, it dipped down suddenly, and so fast that the world seemed to have been shaken in the hands of giants, because Helen was thrown down the slight rise and crashed into her brother.

When the pain receded slightly and she sat up, looking around, she saw what was making the screeching: rusted and bent chimes hung over the low fence of the cemetery. The cemetery must have been fresh and new once, but had been overtaken with sickly trees that seemed to have grown up from the ground along with the gravestones and decaying wooden crosses.

"Are you okay Helen?"

"What are you doing here?"

"Agatha dared me to see how far I could go into the woods."

"That's dumb." Helen hit her brother. "Are you hurt?"

"No." Thaddeus stood up then gave her a hand.

Helen said a silent prayer and tiptoed closer to the strange sur-roundings, careful not to make too much noise and raise the dead. The gate was eternally open—its doorway was completely missing, and so were the hinges. On the ground was a metal sign that read in big letters: ENGSTROM FAMILY CEMETERY.

Her heart beat so hard it was going to pop out of her throat. She went around the cemetery reading the names of people she had never known, reading dates of times her parents must not have existed in, and attempted to decipher some stones that had been so withered that nothing could be read, and it was a mystery who was buried inside.

Clouds covered the sun, and the graveyard was cast in ugly shad-ows.

Her guts twisted. She was going to be sick. She staggered back-wards and felt soft earth giving way under her feet—she jolted for-ward and looked down to see one of the graves, a small one for a little baby, had been halfway uncovered.

Thaddeus grabbed her hand. "Did you know this graveyard was back here?"

"Nuh-uh."

"I'm scared." His hold on her hand tightened. "Do you know the way back? Are we lost?"

"No, no." Helen hugged him. "We aren't lost at all."

"Helen?"

"Yes?"

"Do you think… is John… did John go to heaven?" Thaddeus asked, his voice barely above a whisper.

"Of course he did," Helen said, leading him past the decrepit gate.

The clouds parted away from the sun and prolific light spread over the woods again. Above them was a canopy of branches, and a particular ray of light slipped through the canopy and rested on a nest that must have belonged to a whippoorwill.

"Look at that nest."

"I can't see."

She pointed.

"I don't see it."

"I wanna bring it home and show Father."

"Leave it, Helen. Helen, leave it."

She ignored him. The nearby branches were low and she had climbed one hundred trees before. Maybe, she thought, there were already baby birds in it—birds were her favorite animal, especially the whippoorwills that lived all around these woods. She held on tight to a branch and pulled herself up.

"Helen let's go. It's almost time for the fire."

"I wanna see the baby birds. Quit yelling at me or I'll tell Father you were disobedient and I had to chase you."

"Helen don't tell Father."

"I'm gonna tell."

"Don't tell."

"Then shut up Thaddeus."

Helen's eyes were level with the nest; its thin branch must have been five feet off the ground. Seven eggs lay against each other—blue and green with freckles and spots, they were much different than the whippoorwill eggs she had seen before. They were mystical and enchanting, and Helen couldn't help but reach for one of them.

She turned, pivoting on one foot, her left arm wrapped around the branch that held the nest, while in her right hand she held the egg up for her little brother to see from the ground. "Look what I found."

"Look out."

Something flashed so quickly in Helen's peripheral vision that it was almost subliminal; in the split second that it happened, all that Helen saw were the hideously black unblinking eyes of a mother raven.

CAW! CAW!

Screams left her lips and strained her throat; it felt like pieces of glass cutting her up inside. The bony hand of a stranger was wrapped around her ankle; she screamed louder, pain pulsing through every inch of her body, and kicked it away to find that it wasn't the hand of a stranger at all but the tree branch. Five thin fragments extended from the stump-like end… and while it stayed still, she could have sworn that for a second—or maybe even less—it had been wrapped tight around her, pulling her down, and it had been warm and strong.

Thaddeus grabbed her hand again. *"Yuck, yuck, yuck. I've got it on me too now."*

"Huh?"

"Yuck."

Her heart sank. She let go of her brother's hand then let out another cry. She was covered in egg yolks. Across from her the mother raven stood on the grass and cawed. Helen wanted to apologize, but all she could manage to do was cry.

The bird stepped forward, flapped its wings, then flew away.

Thaddeus gave her his hand once more. Helen picked up the branch and dragged it behind her all the way home; her sobs didn't stop at all, and they became a million times worse when she found her father near the wellhouse. She yelled for him.

Father hugged her. He didn't seem to care about the yolks that stained his clothes. "Don't cry, don't cry. What happened, darling?"

"I wanted to look—at—at the nest and I fell and—and—and cracked the eggs."

"Come on, let's get you and your new dress cleaned up. Thaddeus, were you looking out for your big sister?"

"Yes, sir," Thaddeus said. "I told her not to and she didn't listen."

"Shut up." Helen wiped her eyes.

After she cleaned herself up and put on one of her old dresses, Helen warmed herself by the fire. Across from her, her mother was praying the rosary for John. Helen shuddered recollecting her mother's cries that sometimes drifted through the halls up to Helen's room. Sometimes Mother still screamed as badly as she had on the day John died, and the sound of her mother's cries made her sick.

Hot tears rolled down Helen's cheeks in crooked slants. She wiped them away.

Agatha came to Helen's side and handed her a glass jar with a few pieces of grass and a little twig in the bottom. Agatha was holding a jar of her own; one with the glow of lightning bugs flickering here and there inside around the edges.

"Do you want to catch lightning bugs with us?"

Helen took the jar from her little sister and stood up without saying a word. The warmth of the fire stretched through the night as she went off near the outskirt of the woods, studying the steady gleam and the slow movements of the lightning bugs. She crept up to one and caught it in her jar.

Joyce, the youngest child now that John had passed away, shoved her own jar into Helen's hands. "Can you help me catch one? Please Helen? Please?"

"Okay." Helen gave her own jar—which now possessed one lightning bug—to Joyce, opened the lid of Joyce's jar, and lurked for another bug to catch.

A little while later, Helen snuck away from the fire and returned to her room. She sat at the foot of her bed with her legs crossed, holding the wooden toy bird her father had made her a couple years ago; the crack on its wing was growing wider with age.

Helen's guts were twisted at the permanent thought of the broken eggs; she was so torn up by the thought of the dead birds that she couldn't enjoy the fire tonight. All her siblings were still catching lightning bugs, roasting bread over the fire, and playing games—but Helen couldn't enjoy any of the fun because she had broken the nest of eggs.

There was a knock on her door.

"Come in," she said.

Father opened the door then entered with his hands behind his back. "I've got something for you."

"What is it?"

"Guess which hand."

"Hmmm… right? No, left."

"Are you sure?"

"I pick… right hand."

Father extended his right hand. In it was a wooden pen with a thin strip of plastic making a window on one side to show her how much ink was left inside the pen. Then he extended his left hand; along with a shiny knife was a small section of the branch that had once held the nest, she could tell because the 'fingers' were still attached. He set the contents down between them.

"Your grandfather gave me this knife a long time ago. I used it to carve part of the branch you brought back with you into a pen. I wanted to show you that no matter how bad a situation might be, there's always a way to make it better."

Helen grabbed the remaining wood that was left from the branch. "I've seen you make sailboats and toys from wood, Daddy. Why did you make a pen?"

"So that the little birds can live in your imagination."

3

THE CORNERS OF ABIGAIL'S bedroom flexed; the darkened walls pressed in on each other so that the room shrunk. The shadowy outline of trees spread over her ceiling, and her eyes twitched from branch to branch.

Everything was collapsing. Perhaps she'd shrink so much that in another two months there'd be nothing left of her. She watched the pattern of shadows on the ceiling shake with the whistle of loud winds outside her window. How had things gotten so bad? For the past two months all color had been stripped from her world. All that remained was charcoal and dull.

She shut her eyes. Maybe she had been asleep for an hour, maybe for a day. When she opened them again the room flexed and coiled again and it was smaller now, and Abigail was shrinking along with it.

Abigail shivered with sudden coldness. It was one of the last things she could still feel.

Something whispered. Audible but wordless. Audible but distant.

Abigail, wrapped in the covers on her bed, turned toward the noise. The soft whispers continued but were indecipherable, and iciness wrapped tighter around Abigail so that she could never find warmth.

A chill slithered around her back like the invisible fingers of ghosts; it traced her soft skin slowly then climbed up to her throat and caressed her. The chill pressed tight against her body, sinking into her spirit.

The whispers were loud in her ear: *Today's the day, Abigail.*

Today, she thought. Yes.

Abigail pushed her covers away and sat up. She looked at her wrists. She had thought about doing it so much and had quit more times than she could count. It would be permanent and… and would it be worth it?

She went to her window and looked outside. The sun was setting, and the sky was streaked with what must have been pretty shades, but all she could see was eternal darkness.

The invisible chills caressed her again. Somebody whispered, *Yes, it will all be worth it to see colors again.*

Abigail sat at her desk. Her stomach clenched. There was only one escape from this ugly new world, wasn't there?

Think, think, where did it change? What happened?

Her mind was empty. Nothing. She could think of nothing.

You said it yourself, she thought, *today is the day.*

She opened her desk drawer to get her dream journal and her wooden pen with the plexiglass window. The letter was a paragraph. Maybe it needed to be longer. Three sentences were all she could think of.

In the bathroom she set her note on the sink with the wooden pen on top of it. Her hands trembled at the cold touch of the blade;

holding it tight, she stepped into the warm bath and stretched. Tears welled in her eyes and burned on their slow crawl down.

The room was abruptly cold, and she felt a chill trace her back like a spider dwindling down its web under a glossy sky. Through blurry vision she turned over the blade, raising it up to her eyes with her left hand to see it properly. She was right handed, yet somehow it felt more natural this way.

You can do it.

No, why should I?

Do it.

I don't want to do it.

Abigail pressed the edge of the razor to her right wrist. *What am I doing? I don't want to die.*

It lingered there, threatening to pull open the thin, thin veil between life and death; this side and that side. Where was she going to go when she died? What would happen to her soul? What did it feel like to be dead?

Pulling the blade away, she shuddered. She wiped her tears from her eyes then noticed the room was so cold she could see her breath.

Just do it then you'll be gone like you always wanted.

I don't want to kill myself.

You can see color again. Life won't be black anymore.

Abigail pressed the blade again to her wrist. Would it hurt?

The edge of the blade carefully opened a wound in her wrist; the pain was dull and warm at first, then a sudden jolt sent sparks of steely pain through her arm and into her body. Blood poured over the edges of her cut like water overflowing from a cup held under a faucet and colored the tub deep red.

She shut her eyes and she was plummeting under raging red waves—waves as red as decaying roses. Her lips stayed shut for as long as she could hold them, but they pulled apart and swallowed mouthfuls of bloody water. The tub must have been deeper than she thought, because she was continually falling with no end in sight, tumbling into the abyss of her own blood.

Descending into an eternity of red, she thought, *This is hell—I've gone to hell.*

Her stomach turned and her body convulsed, and she wished she had never done it. Wished she had never slit her wrist. Wished she had never—

Two hands wrapped around her and pulled. She had been falling so far that she was amazed there were hands long enough that could reach her at the bottom of her red tomb. The hands struggled and pulled and slipped but suddenly Abigail was sitting up, and a man was holding her. She opened her mouth to speak and coughed up mouthfuls of rosy water.

While Mother was making dinner, Abigail sat with her father in the living room. She wasn't sure how to ask him about it. Her mother had been the one to find her that day—her father hadn't been there. And the man in her memory… the man didn't even look like her dad. Yet she thought that he was.

"Dad?" Abigail said. For a brief moment she thought about asking about anything else, but she couldn't think of anything in the split second that she had. "I have a memory of somebody lifting me out of the tub. It was you, but it wasn't you. It did not look like you at all."

"Cariño, that must be a dream. Your mother found you. I was at work."

"What does that dream mean?"

"Maybe you resent me for not being there. God knows I resent myself. A man is supposed to protect his family."

"You've always been there for me. You couldn't have known."

4

THE SCARS ON ABIGAIL'S wrists would forever be a reminder of what she tried to do. As she reached from her bed to the floor she found that her dream journal and wooden pen with the plexiglass window had both fallen from her nightstand along with her little clown doll she had since childhood.

It was often that she thought about her wrists and about what happened, not with regret or loss but with emptiness. The memory was blurry, and only certain parts were clear; there was warm water, her eyes rolled back and she saw the ceiling, and fists slamming on the door. Something in her hands had fallen, and she was too weak to grab it. Something happened moments before that—but what had completely happened to her that day was unclear.

Her head ached like a hammer on a stubborn nail. She felt so guilty about hurting herself—not even remorseful, only guilty.

The red waters flowed when she shut her eyes. Sometimes if she thought about it hard enough, she'd be pulled back to the day, transported back into the tub, reaching down for the thing that fell from her fingertips and sank below the red surface, but she could not find it this time either.

The memory passed, and when she opened her eyes, both her hands were clenched together.

Abigail picked up her things and brought them to her desk. As she sat down, last night's dream came to her: she was running down a long unfamiliar hallway, the lights were off, she was barefoot, and looking over her shoulder all she saw was dense darkness. Something hideous was inside of it—even if she couldn't see who or what, she knew it was in there.

Abigail was chilled.

The dream was so clear, and Abigail felt as if she could transport herself into it like she could transport herself back into the tub. As she thought about it, her hands trembled; she was cold all over, as if the chilling primordial air in that unknown hallway had followed her all the way back into her bedroom. Abigail opened her window and stood in fresh sunlight; warmth overtook her gently.

Back at her desk, she opened her dream journal to the page that was marked with the red ribbon sewn into the spine. Below her entry from two nights ago was something scribbled in heavy handwriting, almost indecipherable: HELF

Who wrote in my dream journal?

Abigail slammed it shut. Did Mom and Dad absolutely not trust her at all? Was she never allowed to have privacy anymore? What were they doing going through her things? It was enough that they acted differently towards her since that day in the tub, and now they were spying on her?

She checked the clock. It was still early in the morning. She'd probably catch them before they left for work. She opened her journal back up again and went down the stairs, feet slamming loudly on every step of the way. In the kitchen her mother was dressed for work, washing dishes quickly before she left, and her father was opening cabinet drawers looking for his keys.

"Are you okay, querida?" Dad asked.

Abigail frowned. "How could you do this?"

"How could we do what, sweetie?" Mom asked, setting down a dish in the rack.

"I know what you did I saw it you guys clearly opened my book and wrote in it."

"What?" Mom said. She and Dad exchanged a worried look.

"What book are you talking about?" Dad asked.

Abigail opened her dream journal. "Why are you two going through my things? Look at this, who wrote this? Somebody wrote down 'help' in—"

"Does that say *helf?*" Mom asked. "What's *helf?*"

"Whatever. Just stop going through my things. Please."

"Querida, we did not write in your book," Dad said.

"Are you sure you're okay?" Mom said.

Abigail ignored her mother and ignored whatever else her dad said that she couldn't hear under her thudding steps back up the stairs.

She shut her bedroom door and locked it. She sat on her floor and crossed her arms around her knees and cried. Would anything be the same again? Would anybody ever treat her the same again? Couldn't everybody go back to being how they were before that awful, awful day?

I don't understand why I did it, Abigail thought. *I never wanted to kill myself. Why did I try...*

Abigail rubbed her eyes but the tears wouldn't stop spilling.

I wonder what things would have been like if I had succeeded.

She shuddered; chills slithered wickedly on her back in prodigious strokes like a snake stalking its prey. Before she could think again about that day, she was in that strange hallway again, her heart beating so hard that it was about to leap from her chest, her scream buried so deep in her throat that it would never reach her lips, and all she could hear were her own feet slamming on the cold floor.

Abigail went to her desk after she stopped crying, then opened her journal and looked for the pretty wooden pen. She had bought it about four months ago at a thrift store when she was shopping with her friend Beverly. There was something so unique about the little window carved into its side that she had to have it. But now at her desk she couldn't find it—so she grabbed another pen, pressed the button, and scribbled in the corner of the blank sheet. Her hand disagreed with her mind and flew of its own accord, spilling chaos across the page. What was her hand trying to do? Abigail moved the pen in ways that felt right, but nothing came out besides squiggles, as if she had completely forgotten how to write and needed to re-learn.

Abigail wondered what her room would be like without her, if she had succeeded that day in the tub; would it miss her, think about her, when she was some place far, far away?

Perhaps when she finally did die, and the rest of her family passed too, and the house was bought by somebody she had never existed at the same moment as, somebody new would move into her bedroom, and the walls would forget all about Abigail, and they'd become the walls of some new person, and then they would have similar thoughts as she did today, where they recalled a little nightmare about a girl who had done something in the tub, who had almost vanished, and the longer the walls thought about her, the more they'd just decide that it was only a dream—because walls did in fact dream—and as time went on, the walls would be more and more curious, and wonder about a girl they had known so long ago, whose pictures used to hang all over the house in hallways and in the kitchen, and after a while, when they still could not remember that her name was Abigail, the walls would think, *Well what did ever happen to that little girl anyways?*

But Abigail couldn't see that lasting for too long; the walls would have a new girl to watch over, to learn about, to keep all her secrets, and they would be so very happy with the brand new girl, until the cycle started all over again, and they forgot about her too.

RING! RING! RING!

Abigail picked up the phone and tangled the cord around her finger.

"Hey Abby did you forget all about me?"

"Sorry Bev I didn't realize what time it was. Guess I overslept. I'll be there soon."

Abigail brushed her shoulder-length hair. She was dressed in a pleated skirt, button-through shirt, and straw hat. Beverly lived a ten minute walk away. Abigail wondered what Beverly would have done if Abigail was not here anymore; if she had succeeded on that awful day in the tub.

Suddenly she noticed that her hands were reaching for something fallen—clutching at something that wasn't there; she heard pounding on a door, the sky became the bathroom ceiling, and she was chilled as she felt warm water around her body, as if she had reconstructed it from memory. Abigail shivered. Suddenly she heard her mother's voice: *Abigail open the door. Abigail, can you hear me?*

Why hadn't she opened the door? Why had she hurt herself? Why had she taken that blade and pulled it across her skin?

I've never wanted to kill myself. What made me do it?

Would Beverly have forgotten all about Abigail if Abigail had died? She wondered how Beverly would go on without her, if she would still remember her after a while. Abigail would have liked to think that she would be remembered just as she was, but she couldn't even remember her grandma's touch, and Abigail had only been fourteen when her grandma passed. That was an old enough age to remember details about a person—and yet, almost everything about the grandma she had known escaped her.

Grandma left her doll collection behind, but what would I leave behind? If I had died, what would Beverly have to remember me by? Will my memory last with any of my loved ones? Or will I be a picture? Will I be something you hang on a wall and every now and then the thought comes up?

Perhaps Beverly would find a picture they had taken together years ago, and Beverly would remember her because of that, unless Beverly lost it; then years from now, dozens and dozens of incomprehensible years into the future, since Beverly would have no picture of Abigail, she would think, *Certainly there was a girl I used to know, a friend I used to have—I think, at least, that she was real. Hmm... what ever happened to her? Oh, what was her name... Eleanor? Mary? Shirley? Natalie? Oh, who knows.*

Maybe if she had succeeded that day in the tub, maybe Beverly would be sad for a while, Abigail figured, but she couldn't see her friend being sad any longer than she had to be. She could see Beverly at the funeral, she could see Beverly mourning the next day, she could see Beverly mourning the following year—but then she saw Beverly getting over it. And Abigail saw herself ceasing to be a thought. Ceasing to be anything that mattered. Ceasing to be anything at all.

When Abigail was two blocks away on her walk to Beverly's house, her brain tried to make her remember something again—tried to bring out a memory that was long, long buried. Something inside her mind was trying to escape; her head pounded like a hammer on a stubborn nail once more. Leaning against a tree, she tried to remember. Everything was fuzzy—her head hurt and her thoughts jumbled. What was she trying to remember?

Beverly's house was a big and pretty redbrick house with a big American flag next to the front door. The grass had been cut earlier that morning, she noticed, and the black gate that led to the curving path that was recently recemented was open.

So many things had been fixed at Beverly's home that it looked as if the home had been built last month. Windows sparkled, the front door was freshly painted, leaves somehow avoided falling on the lawn.

A strong wind knocked Abigail's hat off; she took two or three big steps over the lawn to grab it, then she put it back on her head and straightened it out, and walked up to the front door and knocked. Just a second later, somebody answered.

Beverly moved a long strand of blonde hair out of her eyes, then looked Abigail up and down. "Hey you look fantastic."

Abigail shut the door behind herself. "So do you."

The house was pristine; the living room was spotless, happy pictures of a happy family were hung above the television, there probably wasn't a single crumb in the carpet. Beverly hugged Abigail so tightly that she was about to lose the ability to breathe; Beverly, with a big smile on her face, stood in the entryway to the dining room and kitchen while Abigail took a seat in the living room.

"Do you want ice cream?"

"No thanks."

"Cookies and cream, isn't that your favorite? We have strawberry too."

"No, it's okay. Really," Abigail said. Beverly had changed since the incident in the tub. She kept trying to baby her, to be too nice—if there were such a thing as too nice—and Abigail wanted to be treated like normal.

"I baked a pie yesterday, I picked the apples myself. Did you want any?"

"I'm not hungry, Bev."

"You're missing out." Beverly stepped through the living room toward the turntable. She stood on her tippytoes to reach the top shelf and find a Crosby, Stills, Nash & Young album. "Hey how about I put on a record?"

"Yeah sure okay," Abigail said. It wasn't exactly her favorite music but she knew Beverly was excited.

"My favorite track is *Our House,* I love that song so much. I don't know why the first two songs on either side skip, but it just makes me so happy." She sat next to Abigail. "Hey, are you okay? You look a little… a little pale."

Music played softly: *"Staring at the fire four hours and hours while I listen to you play your love songs all night long for me. Only for me."*

"Sorry, Bev. Today's been awful and it's hardly noon."

"Do you want to talk about it?"

"Could you believe my parents went through my dream journal?"

"What? Why'd they do that?"

"I don't know what they thought they'd find in there but they give me no privacy anymore. Why can't they just treat me like normal? Why can't they treat me like they used to? You know, they assigned me all these weekend chores trying to keep me busy, and I don't want to do any of it. I think they read about it in some book the doctor or somebody mentioned to them. I wish I could move out already."

"Well just think, we have one more year of high school left then you'll be off to college. Then you'll only have to see them on holidays."

"Whatever."

"So I've been reading this recipe book, I think I'm going to make these cookies tomorrow that you'll like. They're made with, let's see, there's—"

"Where do you put it?"

"Put what?"

"All these sweets, and you're thin as a twig," Abigail said. "Pies, cookies, and you don't gain an ounce of weight."

"A slice of pie or one little cookie never hurt anybody."

Abigail shrugged.

"Are you sure you're doing okay?"

"Yeah, I'm sure."

"Let's have fun today and forget about your parents and every-thing." Beverly stood up. "I'm gonna go grab my purse, I'll be right back."

Alone in the living room, Abigail wondered if when Beverly was an old woman, if she would make these sweets every day and only nibble at them, and whenever somebody came to visit Old Lady Beverly in her future apartment, if they would find it cramped full of sugary sweets. They probably would, and so much so that there'd be no room to maneuver, and they would have to yell at Bev from the doorway to make any sort of communication. The young boy that Abigail imagined—perhaps Beverly's future grandson—would shout at her from the one inch of space he was able to enter past the doorway, and Old Lady Beverly, a lady under a mountain of pies, would shout back that she could not hear him, could he come any closer?

A twenty minute walk away—it would have been much, much quick-er to drive but it was such a nice day, so walking was the thing to do—was the farm; Beverly's family had been friends with the farmer and his family for a long time, and so the farmer let Beverly walk through the orchard whenever she wanted.

"If it weren't for the shade of these trees, I'd be so sunburned," Beverly said. They were halfway to the farm. "I feel like I always need sunscreen on even when I'm making a run to the store."

Listening to Beverly ramble about sunburns was great; it felt like one of their normal conversations, before that awful day—

Don't think about it, don't think about it. Don't don't don't.

"Abby?"

"Huh?"

"You've been very quiet," Beverly said. Then, before Abigail could say a word, her friend added: "Sorry. I just wanted to be sure you're, you know, I just wanted to be sure you'd—you'd—you…. I just want to make sure you're okay."

Abigail tried not to laugh at her tongue-tied friend, or how goofy she looked when she was flustered. "I'm okay."

Past the orchard was a small lake where ducks swam.

The lake bordered the edge of the woods behind the old Engstrom place; flutters of wings echoed within its deeply cavernous expanse of branches. Abigail shuddered to think what was within those woods, or what was hiding behind the darkened Engstrom windows that immediately unnerved her.

The house stood alone on its hill. At the distance, it looked like a vague silhouette. Abigail had known the rumors of what happened there since she was a young girl. People disappeared there; whispers of hideous things seen in the windows circulated Ashfall. Abigail had never seen the place up close, but even from a distance it chilled her.

Beverly fed the core of her apple to a duck, and Abigail threw a pebble into the murky water. Ripples shook the surface then vanished after reaching the edges; Abigail wondered where the sound the pebble made went when it broke the surface.

PLOP!

Where did noise go? Abigail wondered if maybe all sounds were trapped in the air, and maybe one day they could be discovered again. She wondered if the sentences of all the people in the Ashfall cemetery were floating around her, and she was unaware; the words of the dead following her around forever.

She threw another pebble. "Where do you think it goes?"

"To the bottom, certainly."

Abigail shook her head. "I mean the sound. Where does the sound go?"

Beverly thought about it. "It disintegrates."

Abigail rolled another pebble between her pointer finger and her thumb. "The pebble goes to the bottom, and the waves ripple to the edges. It all goes somewhere, so why doesn't noise? Shouldn't it go somewhere?"

Beverly grabbed her own pebble then threw it. It sank, never to be seen again. "Because noise isn't solid, it's invisible. It's not made of anything."

"Hmmm... then how does it touch our eardrums? How should this sentence leave my lips and reach your brain?"

"Must be magic."

"Where do our sentences go when they're over?" Abigail asked.

"I dunno."

"What if one day they can find all the noises of history and write down all the lost conversations? Think of that, words would never be lost again."

"What an invasion of privacy."

"Do you ever think of all the memories that were taken to the grave? This memory between us, Bev, standing here, if we never tell anybody, and we both die a long time from now, and then nobody would know we were here."

"Why should they know about our conversations?"

"Right, Bev, why should they know all about your recipes? I still don't know where you put it all."

"Remember," Beverly said with a laugh, "when we were here and you wore your new pants and not even two minutes later you fell into the lake?"

Nothing could have wiped the newfound smile from Abigail's face. "Yeah, and how you laughed instead of helping me up."

"You should have seen the look on your face it was priceless. Ohmigod it was the funniest thing."

"Now see, wouldn't those sounds be worth finding?"

"Sure, if it's pleasant or relevant a thousand years from now to hear that *scream.*"

Abigail put her hands on Beverly's shoulders, smiling. "Then it would only be fair if they heard your scream too."

Beverly backed away. "Nuh-uh, no way."

Abigail jerked her an inch toward the water. "Your turn."

"No! Stop!"

Abigail pulled her hands away. "If they did find all the sounds, and you could relive those moments, would it make it less special? People always say going back in time would mean no moment would ever be special."

"I dunno. If you wouldn't relive it all, why live your life in the first place?"

"Hey, want to make a wish?"

A few feet away from the lake back toward the farm was a well; the well hadn't been used in decades, and the old wood boards that had been placed over it were decayed and fallen apart. Deep down in the unseen depths, which could have tunneled to the center of the earth, anything could have lived. When Abigail leaned close enough, she could have sworn soft whispers rose.

In her pocket, there were two cents. Abigail gave one to her friend, then tossed her own into the well; she listened for it to plunge into water, yet it did not make any sort of sound. Curiously she listened, as if the coin would not fall for another couple minutes.

"What did you wish for?"

"I'm still deciding."

"Abby, you're supposed to think of the wish before tossing it in."

"Is that so? What if it comes to me tonight as I sleep? Can I wish for it then?"

"Nope."

"Well then, I think it's unfortunate I don't have a wishing well with me at all times."

Beverly looked her cent over, shut her eyes, tossed it in. "I hope it comes true."

"What did you wish?"

"That your wish would come true, even if you wished for it at night while you slept."

Walking away from the farm on the bumpy path, Abigail avoided the cracks because of old superstitions. Hopefully soon, she thought, she could think of a wish. And hopefully it was a good wish, so that Beverly's wish was not wasted; if she wished for something dumb like a toothpick, it would all be wasted. Wishes had to be clever—and typically, they had to be big things, things easily forgotten, so that way she would not be upset if it did not come true.

Abigail couldn't remember what she had wished for at previous wishing wells or on birthdays. Maybe one day she would stumble upon a briefcase with twenty million dollars in it and say, *Aha! Just like I asked for when I was ten.*

Maybe she'd wish that *Beverly's* wish would come true instead, and their wishes would go through an endless cycle of perpetually demanding that the other's wish would come true instead; Abigail thought that eventually she would have to be the one to break the cycle. She would ask for that twenty million dollars and split it.

"Have you thought of a wish yet?" Beverly asked as if able to read Abigail's mind.

"No I have not. Any suggestions?"

"Nope."

"Very helpful. Hey, do you think if I wished for a unicorn, do you think that would come true?"

"Totally."

"And if I wished to know where all the noises go?"

"Obviously."

"Oh—what if I wished for a unicorn who could tell me where all the noises go?"

"Sure."

"A lot easier to come across than a briefcase of twenty million dollars," Abigail said, testing Beverly's ability to read her mind.

"Maybe you should wish for that."

"You know, I don't believe I could stand to have a well on my property. I think I'd drop coins in it hourly."

"Then I'd be there to fish them out."

"Of course you would."

"Need to make a living somehow."

Abigail looked down and realized she was forgetting to avoid the cracks. Part of her foot was dangerously close to one; and looking back at the path behind her, it was highly likely she had stepped on dozens of them, and when she arrived home there would be about one thousand messages waiting for her on the answering machine to let her know that her mother was in the hospital with a back broken many times over.

"Are you avoiding the cracks too?" Abigail asked.

"Nope."

"Bev, your mother will be *so* disappointed in you."

"I'll tell her it was Judy. They wouldn't be able to prove it either way."

"And if you're like me, without a little sister to blame it on?"

"She can't chase you with a broken back. You're safe from harm."

"Then you don't know my mother, the way she can throw a chan-cla like a major league pitcher throws a baseball."

5

HER SHOES WEREN'T UNDER her bed, so Helen opened the closet and moved around her piles of junk, but they weren't there either.

"Helen hurry! Mother and Father said we can't go without you."

I'm coming, Agatha, Helen thought. Gosh her voice is so loud that it reaches perfectly from downstairs.

"Hurry the corpses are in the lake! Helen you're gonna miss the corpses!"

"Blood Lake is flowing with corpses!"

"The corpses are overflowing Blood Lake! There are living brains everywhere."

I don't even want to go, Helen thought then left her room and went to the spiraling staircase. "I can't find my shoes."

"Down here," Joyce said. "You left them by the door."

Agatha and Joyce raced down the path while Thaddeus and Timothy grabbed branches and had a swordfight. When Timothy fell and scraped his knee, Helen picked him up and gave him a hug.

"You'll be okay," she said.

A moment later, when the children reached Blood Lake, he was over it.

An osage orange tree loomed over the lake from behind the dock; its shadow passed over the surface of gentle red ripples, and brain-fruit fell from its branches and rolled down the slight rise and into the bright red water.

Thin clouds slid across the sky; unseen whippoorwills chirped nearby. Helen stepped through a stretch of shadow off the path and into sunlight a few feet from the lake; warmth wrapped around her skin.

Joyce crept up behind Agatha, who was already a step deep into the water, and pushed her lower back with both of her hands. Agatha gasped and plunged into the red surface, flailing her arms until she realized she could stand up and she'd be fine. It was the shallow end.

"Be careful," Helen said. "You—"

"Helen can you help me untie my shoes?" Timothy asked.

Helen kneeled and untied them. "There you go."

"Thank you," Timothy said, then followed Helen to the deck where she sat with her book.

Thaddeus jumped from the dock into the lake. "Come on, Timothy."

Timothy stood at the edge, inching back. "I'm too scared to jump."

"Don't be a sissy."

Timothy plugged his nose and hopped in. When he resurfaced he grabbed a brainfruit and smashed the soft mushy green blob on top of Thaddeus's head. "Found your brain."

"Helen, Helen, can you take me to the deep end?" Joyce grabbed her hand. "Can you please? *Puh-lease.*"

"But I don't want to go in right now."

"Please? I want to go to the deep end, and you dressed to swim anyways."

"Because I wanted to lay on the dock and read a book first before swimming."

"Please big sister…"

"Fine." Helen put her book down, walked to the edge of the dock, and jumped in.

The water was lukewarm, perhaps a little more on the cooler side; quickly her body adjusted to the temperature. Helen dipped under then came back up, moving long strands of blonde hair from her eyes that had come loose from her bun. She took her baby sister in her arms and swam along the edge of the lake.

Halfway to the deep end, Helen stopped and said, "This is as far as I'll take you."

Joyce kicked Helen's stomach as she squirmed and shrieked, *"Monster! Monster! There's a monster behind you!"*

Suddenly big red splashes came down over them. Agatha swam up to them and stole Joyce from Helen's hands. *"Got you. Now you'll become a corpse just like me."*

"No don't take my brain! Helen! Helen! Help!"

Helen lowered her body below the surface so that only her face and hands pierced the sparkling surface. *"I can't reach you, Joyce. The corpses have got me too. They're pulling me under."*

"Nooooooo!"

Agatha carried Joyce near to the boys, who were throwing mushy brainfruits at each other. The storm yesterday must have shaken loose a hundred or more of them. Helen was so glad for rain—last summer there had been a drought, so the lake at their old home hadn't turned red when the fields were plowed because no dirt was carried down into the water.

Clouds passed over the sun, forming shadows that stretched as far as Helen could see; they lingered briefly then passed, bringing back bright prolific rays of sun that stretched over the surface of the water. Helen stretched in the warm rays then sunk under the water and swam to her brothers, who were wrestling against each other attempting to crush another mushy brainfruit on the other one's head. When she was near enough, she grabbed two brainfruits and smashed one on Thaddeus's head then one on Timothy's.

Thaddeus and Timothy looked at each other and nodded, then each of them grabbed one of Helen's arms and pulled her under. She shut her mouth and held her breath until they brought her back up to the surface, then she gasped and playfully hit them.

Helen scooped floating brainfruit goop and slammed it against Thaddeus's ear. "Your brain is leaking."

"It's more brains than you'll ever have."

"Yeah right." Helen floated on her back, watching the clouds move slowly across an endless horizon jagged with trees.

"Helen?" Joyce said. "Can you tell me the story of Blood Lake?"

"Sure," Helen said, eyes glued to the sky until her foot tapped against something soft. She looked down to see it was Agatha's arm. She was laying on her back too, floating happily along the pulsing red waves. Then Thaddeus joined them, floating on his back too. Timothy stayed near the dock, one arm around the wooden pole, the other holding Joyce. "It happened a very long, long time ago…"

Joyce gulped. *"I don't want to hear it. Never mind."*

"A long time ago at this very lake, a bride and—"

"I said never mind I said never mind."

"Too late, Joyce, I'm sorry. Have you ever heard what happens to the girls who die in water?"

"Nuh-no…" Joyce said. She was on the verge of tears.

"A long time ago, a bride and groom came down to this very lake. The night was very dark and the stars were shining to guide them, and they followed the soft glow. Together they stepped into the water, and—"

"Quit it, quit it, I've heard too much."

"Nuh-uh, I started now I have to finish, it's the rules, or else we'll be cursed. Do you want us to be cursed?"

"Nuh-no, Helen."

"The groom lost his bride under the surface of this lake and she drowned. The next day the lake was completely filled up with all of her blood, and her corpse was floating like we are now. The spirits of women who drown turn into evil little spirits like mermaids that live in water. And if she sees you, she's going to pull you under."

"Get out of the water, I don't want her to get you."

Helen swam gently backwards toward the deep end. "I can't help it, Joyce. I'm drifting… I can't move… I think there's something in the water with us…"

"Quit it, quit it."

Helen laughed. *"She's gonna get me, she's gonna get me."*

"Stop."

With a deep breath, Helen sunk into the murky depths, leaving one of her hands slightly above the surface to writhe back and forth—she imagined how terrified it might have made her baby sister. Then she pulled her hand below the surface, two seconds passed, and when she tried to break the surface, the bony hand that had once wrapped around her ankle in the graveyard deep in the woods wrapped around her ankle again and wouldn't let go.

She pushed her hand to her mouth and nose to stop air from leaving. Her lungs strained and she was desperate to take a breath—pain pulsed with the beat of her heart. She kicked to break free but the hand locked tighter around her ankle with its long slimy fingers coiling deep into her flesh.

Looking down into the maddening abyss her vision was completely obscured. Her body shivered as her heart beat so furiously that it was ready to pop out of her chest. The hand curled further up her leg and pulled her down. She kicked again, pushing with her other foot to break its grip, but all efforts to detach the grimy hand were useless.

Helen wasn't sure when her other foot was grabbed, but she did know that the distance between herself and the surface was growing. The two powerful hands wrapped serpent-like around her legs and dragged her down into its primal unseen depths.

Her lungs twisted; they burned with a desire for air. Her lips strained to part; with whatever power she had left in her body she forced her lips to shut. With what might be the last seconds of her life she prayed that God would rescue her, prayed God could get her away from the vicious hands pulling her further into the endless depths of hell.

Her breath passed her lips. A mouthful of disgusting muddy water fled into her mouth. She wanted to spit it out but was too scared to move; her prayers abruptly ended and her mind was blank. Helen was numb all over, and so devoid of feeling that she couldn't tell if there was one hand wrapped around her or one hundred.

For one short second her eyelids parted and through the darkened waters she saw the indistinct outline of her father. His arms wrapped around her and pulled.

Please don't let me die God—oh God I need to breathe I need to breathe it hurts it hurts it hurts it hurts it hurts—

Her father set her down on muddy ground. Helen coughed and choked and spit up water. Desperate breaths of air stung as they entered her lungs. She choked again, coughed, and sobbed. Her siblings stood around and watched her; her father told them to move back and give her space.

She thought she had to say something, but nothing came to mind.

Looking down at her feet she saw that prodigious strands of plants were tangled up and down her body. It hadn't been unseen hands at all…

"Helen? Are you okay?"

She coughed before saying, "Yes, Daddy."

He unwrapped the plants from her feet. "Have you seen these before?"

Helen shook her head.

"This is called a hydrilla. When I was a boy one of my neighbors went swimming and got caught just like you. Except his pa wasn't around to get him out."

6

A SLIGHT ORANGE TINT lingered in the sky; Abigail thought it was wonderful when pink or orange or any other color stuck to the horizon. Soft winds shook the surrounding trees; leaves tumbled. Heaven-bound birds sang to each other; maybe, Abigail thought, they liked it too when the sky was orange or pink or some other shade other than blue.

Nearby there was a bookstore, and Beverly looked at cookbooks while Abigail went up and down the other aisles. She had never been much of a reader, and none of the books she came across were appealing. When Beverly caught up with her, she was carrying two cookbooks in her hands.

"Find anything you like?"

"Nothing at all." Abigail shook her head.

"Pick a book, Abby."

"I don't like to read, I don't know."

"At least buy a bookmark."

"A bookmark for no book?"

"A bookmark's a good incentive to buy a book. Or maybe you have a book at home you could read."

"My parents have books. Big dusty boring ones."

"Don't judge a book by its cover."

"Can we judge them by their titles?"

"No, nor their page count, binding, or glossiness."

"Totally unfair, Bev."

"Want to have another look around?"

"No thanks, I'm good."

"You sure?"

"Yeah."

Beverly ignored her and went through the aisles again. Abigail found the discount section where damaged books were sold for two dollars and sometimes less, and a tiny purple pocketbook-sized journal caught her eye. It was pretty beat up but she couldn't help but be attracted to the whippoorwill that was drawn on the cover.

She flipped it open; the vintage pages smelled like an antiquarian library. There was no name written on the inside front cover. Somebody had filled out the first two pages of the old journal, but all the rest of it was blank.

"Oh hey what did you find?" Beverly asked when she caught up with her again. Now she was holding a third cookbook in her hands.

"This journal, it looks like somebody filled out the first couple pages then quit."

"You aren't buying that old thing, are you?"

"Why not?"

"Because it's ugly. Don't you want something else?"

The girls paid then left, and up at the corner Beverly pointed at the next street. "Pizza place is one block over I think. You know the one? We went there once with Judy."

"Ice cream, pizza, cookies, pies. Why, Beverly, if I didn't know any better I'd say you were trying to fatten me up, you wicked witch. If only left a trail of breadcrumbs all the way back home."

The pizza place smelled delicious; the girls ordered then sat down.

"How is Judy? I heard she's seeing somebody?"

"Gosh, gossip spreads faster than wind around here."

"Isn't she?"

"She is, his name's Oliver."

"What does he do?"

"I dunno, I've only met him once."

"She doesn't talk about him?"

"She does, I ignore her."

"Like we do about your recipes?"

Beverly wiped pizza sauce off her fingers with a napkin. "Ha, I guess so. So are there any other stores you want to go to? Mendy's Boutique isn't that far from here."

"Not really."

"Are you sure?"

Abigail nodded.

"Let's go anyways, I'll be quick."

As they walked down the sidewalk, Abigail's heart beat quickly. With one quick push of her left hand she shoved Beverly into the street. Her friend fell with all her bags, and the upcoming car honked and swerved narrowly getting around Beverly and avoiding running her over. The driver cursed at them from the open window.

Beverly was so shocked she couldn't move at first; neither could Abigail. She stood there dumbfounded at what she had done. Suddenly Abigail stepped into the street and extended her hand and helped Beverly up, then helped her pick up her bags.

"Abigail?" Beverly said when they had finished picking everything up off the street and were back on the sidewalk.

Abigail was quiet. She avoided Beverly's eyes.

"What the hell was that for?"

"I don't know what came over me."

"You could have killed me!"

Abigail didn't know what to say.

"Seriously. What the hell was that for?"

"I didn't want to push you. It was an accident."

"I can't stop shaking. God that was awful."

What is wrong with me?

Abigail couldn't stop thinking about what she had done. She had no idea why she had tried to hurt Beverly. Her friend's terrified face was stuck in her mind. And if that driver had been distracted then Beverly would have been struck.

Abigail shuddered.

Why did I do any of this? Why did I hurt myself? Why did I try to hurt Beverly? What's wrong with me?

She tried to remember what life was like before she had hurt herself in the tub. Maybe a time before the incident had never happened; maybe that day, that was the day she was born, and everything before that was only imagination. Abigail shivered. She wanted to go back to normal, back to a time before she had hurt herself, even if it was imaginary.

Abigail sat at her desk and opened the journal she bought today at the bookstore. The two entries were months in between.

The first entry read:

Today the builders put the finishing touches on our new home. I can't wait to see it. Father says I'm going to love it there, he helped design it, and he made a big room special for me. Mother is excited too, and all day we've been packing our things up. There's a farm by our new house, Mother says. I hope there are horses and I can pet them.

Father said that the land our new home is on has been in our family a long time. He says there already used to be a house there, but it was old so he hired people to tear it down.

Part of me is shy to move away from the place I've always known, and to leave all of my friends behind. What if my friends forget about me? Will I make new friends? And will I like the new friends as much as my old ones? What if I'm the one to forget my old friends? Part of me is excited for all the new things I will see, and everything my parents have told me about. Maybe my old friends will come over to visit me one day.

The second entry, dated months later, read:

I don't like thinking about it, but it's been on my mind ever since it happened. My little brother John died. He was the youngest of all of us, he was five years old, and now he's gone. No matter how much stuff we fit into this big new house of ours, it will always feel empty without him.

It was one month into our move, and none of us knew how he climbed up to the roof. My baby brother fell, maybe, I think, from the wind, but there was a servant in the back yard who said he saw everything. The servant said that John was pushed... but I can't believe that. Nobody was up there with him and... and who would push a baby boy?

Oh John, I pray for you every night. We all weep for you. I miss running up and down the path with you, and playing in the woods. It will never be the same without you.

Our servant who told us you were pushed went missing. Father told Mother (neither knows that I overheard them) that the man's family hasn't heard from him in all this time. Where could he have gone? There's something I don't like about that, and about some of the things I've heard around our house. There have been noises I can't explain. The other night, as I was trying to sleep, I thought I heard footsteps outside my bedroom door. Agatha dared me to look, so I did, and nobody was there.

7

AM I DREAMING?

Darkness stretched over Abigail's eyes and everything across from her was a blur. She was moving through an impossibly black hallway with something clutched in her left hand, something raised up above her head. She tiptoed quietly, afraid that whatever monstrosities were lurking in the cavernous shadows of the hall would grab her with prodigious claws if they should hear her.

Mindlessly she pushed open a shut door with her right hand, and stood at the side of the bed. Everything had stopped dead except for the beating of her own heart; it echoed so loud that it must have drawn every unblinking eye hiding in the depths of strange amorphous shadows toward her.

She brought her left hand halfway down to plunge the knife into her mother, then she shuddered and staggered away before the blade could pierce her mother's side. What was she doing in her parents' room? Why was she holding the knife in such a tight grip, ready to stab her mother?

Because I want my parents dead, Abigail thought, then forced the thought out of her mind momentarily. It resurfaced: *I want my parents dead.*

No. Don't think that way. I don't want them dead.

Her heart was about to rip from her chest and break into fifty pieces. Her hand suddenly unclenched and the knife fell between her feet. Abigail picked it up then tiptoed backwards to the door, and had never been more afraid than she was now ever in her life. What would she say if Mom and Dad awoke to find her here in their bedroom with a knife in her hands? And thank God she was back in the hallway without them waking.

What's happening to me? Did I want to hurt them? Did I want to do this?

Tiptoeing back to the kitchen she froze at the sound of bed-springs.

She waited.

Everything was still again.

Abigail slid the knife back into place. Carefully she crept up the stairs. Her bedroom was as black as a tomb, and that meant that everything took on a new shape. The pile of clothes on her chair was a contorted body whose head was fully turned backwards and stalked her with bulging eyes; its mouth was twisted open hideously, with a tongue licking jagged teeth.

Abigail laid under her covers praying. *What's happening to me? God help me. What am I doing?*

It was a while before she fell asleep, but when she did, she fell into a dream, and was back in that strange hallway with irregularly shaped shadows covering the walls. Abigail's own shadow was oddly elongated from the sourceless hints of light that gave her only vague vision in this dusty new world.

Where am I?

Heavy footsteps slammed behind her, echoes booming over each other, but it was the nightmare of all nightmares: running but not moving fast. One glimpse over her shoulder revealed nothing through the unnerving crypt of eternal darkness.

Up ahead was more blackness, and Abigail had an obscure compulsion that she'd be trapped in these amorphous shadows forever, always running, never stopping. When the hall curved she turned with it, and two hands grabbed her and dragged her away into endless shadows.

Abigail jolted awake. She couldn't tell the time because her eyes were still adjusting to darkness; a touch of soft light flowed past her partly open curtains into her room. It must have been about four in the morning. She rubbed her eyes then went across to her desk, moving the pile of clothes off her chair so that she could sit down to write about her dream before she forgot it.

In the first open space in her dream journal she wrote down the date, and every single detail she could remember about the place, like the high walls and how smooth the ground was under her bare feet. When she was done she returned to bed; she shut her eyes and drifted into dreamless sleep.

In the morning, her covers were like a bag of bricks holding her down, and she didn't want to move. Her eyes cracked open when sleep didn't surge back over her, and she looked up to see that it was still sort of dark outside her window. According to the clock it was twenty minutes past six.

She stretched, yawned, sat up, then went across her room. As she passed by her desk she noticed that the used journal, the one with the whippoorwill on the cover, was no longer in her desk drawer where she had left it but on top of her old journal. Her pen with the plexiglass window was edged between the pages like a bookmark. Had she been so tired last night that she wrote in the wrong book? With fragments of morning light, she opened the journal to read the new entry.

Thank you.

This is much better.

Your friend,

Helen.

P.S.

That house you dreamed about is where I grew up.

Abigail put her hands over her mouth so that she would not scream. Chills squirmed on her spine. She pulled her feet up onto her new chair and held herself tight into a ball. Who wrote in her book? Who knew she had written down a new dream two hours ago?

Nobody would know but me.

It couldn't be real.

She read it again. *That house you dreamed about is where I grew up.*

Where who grew up? Abigail thought. *Who's Helen?*

Below the new entry in the journal, Abigail wrote: *What's happening to me? Am I losing my mind? This is not real.*

Abigail switched the pen from her right hand to her left. Her left hand was guiding the pen along an empty line in the journal; the pen was leading and her hand was following. The words formed from the pen's own mind and her hand was there to assist it.

The words were in the same handwriting as before: This is my favorite pen. My father made it for me when I was fifteen years old.

Abigail threw the pen and journal across the room at the wall. She looked down at her hands; had she really written those words? Was she imagining it all? She was right handed; and yet her left hand perfectly mimicked the style of the other journal entries.

"I'm going crazy," she whispered.

She picked up the journal and pen and returned to her desk. She grabbed the pen in her left hand and brought it down to the paper, then pulled her hand back and paused to think about it. What was going on here? Abigail couldn't process what she had just seen her left hand do.

She hesitated a few moments longer then brought the tip of the pen back down to the page. You are not going crazy.

The pen wouldn't move again when Abigail tried to guide it with her right hand; when she switched it to her left hand, like last time, the pen wrote with its own mind and she led it down the page. It wrote: I miss my home.

Abigail put the pen back in her right hand and wrote: *Why have I had dreams about your home?*

Because you've been there before.

When?

In Engstrom House dark and deep, the answers to the questions you seek.

What will I find in the house?

Me.

Abigail shuddered. She grabbed another journal—her dream journal, that she had been filling up all year—and held the pen to an empty page. It didn't budge. It wanted to write—in her palm she felt an obscure urge to make the pen move, but it couldn't. Not on this paper. Not in this book.

She brought it back to the used purple journal from the bookstore. She held the pen in her left hand, and the writing continued: You'll find me.

Are you one of the Engstrom girls?

Yes.

Helen Engstrom.

Yes.

What is it like in the Engstrom place? Are any of the town legends true?

You should tell me, Abigail. You've been there before.

Abigail's hands twitched. A memory suddenly formed in her mind; hazy at first, then she was teleported into it as if it were happening all over again. She was kneeling in a bedroom, early morning sunlight filtering through the window and pressing down on her, and her fingernails were wedged between the seams of the floorboard in front of her. Abigail lifted the loose board and pulled it away to find a necklace. As she reached for it, she was brought out of the memory. She tried again to revisit, to figure out what had happened just before the memory and just after, but she couldn't bring it back as clearly as she once had—and, Abigail thought, she had never seen that room before. It was a big room, a room built for a princess, with a big bed and tall dressers and a closet. A chill crept over her spine. Something sinister was hiding just below the surface of the room. Something Abigail couldn't decipher in the brief moments that she was teleported away from the journal in front of her.

Abigail wrote: *What happened to you, Helen?*

She trembled as she switched the pen from her right hand to her left. Her left hand pushed it across the paper, and it wrote: It's so cold in here.

Abigail gulped. With the pen back in her right hand, she wrote: *Where are you?*

I can't tell. I'm scared and I'm cold. I want to get out of here. Please help me.

What can I do?

8

THE PETALS OF FLOWERS curled at their edges from the scorching summer weather; it must have been the hottest day of the year. The necklace was hardly changed over the course of the decades it must have spent in the graveyard coiled around the tree root near the withered stone that marked the grave of a person whose name had been partially eroded, and partially hidden by moss. The stone on the gold chain gleamed like a purple flame.

Helen had to unclasp it to get it out of the root.

She couldn't keep her eyes from the beautiful glow.

Passing through her home, she was sure she had seen this necklace before somewhere. And wondering how the root of a tree could bring this necklace from a grave, and wondering what else could be brought to the surface by those trees, she realized where she had seen it before. It was on the painting in the hallway outside of her father's library room.

A man and a woman under a tree were painted on the canvas. The woman wore a pretty white dress, and around her neck was an identical golden chain and purple jewel like what Helen found around the root in the graveyard.

There were footsteps at the other end of the hall. It was Father.

"Daddy? Who are these people?"

"Adolph Engstrom and his wife Mable Engstrom. This was all his land. Everything we have, it all came from him."

Helen went to her bedroom and pried up the loose floorboard that she had discovered on her first night in her new home. Inside was a secret hiding place. Helen tore a blank page from her journal and wrapped the necklace in it so that it would keep the dust away, then she put the floorboard back in place. A moment later, sitting on her bed, she opened her journal to the next page, and was about to write when Joyce came running into the room and put her arms around her for a hug.

"Do you want to play with me? Let's play hide and seek. I'm gonna hide where you'll never find me."

"You're easy to find. At our old home you always hid in the cupboard."

"Not this time. I found the bestest hiding spot and you're never gonna guess."

"I bet I'll find you in the first place I look."

"No you're not, quit it. You're not gonna find me Helen you're not gonna."

"Okay. Go hide and I'll count."

"And promise you won't cheat."

Helen put her hands over her eyes, pressing her fingers stiff against each other first, then pulling them apart so that Joyce could see Helen's eyes. "I promise."

"Quit it."

Helen extended her pinky finger. "I pink promise."

"Why do you use that hand? It's weird."

"Because I'm left handed."

Joyce wrapped her pinky against her sister's. "Okay now count."

"To what?"

"To… one million." Joyce ran away giggling. *"Count already."*

Helen closed her eyes. "One… two… three… four…" Somewhere along the countdown, Joyce's steps vanished around the closest corner, as if walking out of reality. This was the second floor, and if Helen had to guess, her little sister went to Father's library. "Five… six… seven… ten thousand… *one million. Joyce, watch out, here I come.*"

Father's library was impossibly filled with books; if she read ten books a day for the next year, she thought, she wouldn't make a dent in one shelf. Had Father actually read all these? Helen traced her left hand over a shelf of pristine spines as she walked across the red carpet that covered every inch of the wooden floor.

"Joyce? Joyce? Come out come out wherever you are. *Joooooooooyce I'm gonna find you.*"

Helen crept around the corner of the desk and ducked down into the space underneath it. Joyce wasn't there. After walking up and down the room, there were no more places that Joyce could be hiding in. Helen left her father's library and suddenly heard giggles and tiny feet running down a nearby staircase—there were so many staircases, and so many winding halls that it was difficult to pinpoint exactly where Joyce was going. Helen instinctively went for the main spiraling staircase.

Helen stepped through hallways on the ground floor. *"Joyce? Where are you?"*

She went to the closet by her parents' room, opened it, but Joyce wasn't there either.

"Joyce?"

Helen went through her new home opening doors and searching every room there was, looking up and down for her baby sister. Where was Joyce?

She kept saying I'd never find her...

"Joyce come out right now. Where are you? Jooooyce? Jooooyce?"

Helen walked through the hall on the far side of the house, ready to go back to the second floor and double check the library. Perhaps Joyce was trying to trick her, and had waited for Helen to check the library first. Maybe she went back up there to hide after all.

"Heeeelp!"

The shout cut through the air like a sharp blade ripping deeply into flesh. Helen was frozen.

"It's cold down here! Heeeelp!"

The screams came from behind the door across the stairway. Behind the door was a very narrow set of steps which took Helen to the basement. Descending, her hands searched the wall blindly for a light switch. How on earth did Joyce make it down here blind?

"Joyce I'm here, I'm here, where are you?"

"Help I'm cold Helen I'm cold!"

"I'm coming, I'm almost there, hold on."

In the months that they had been here, Helen hadn't been in the basement before. Through low windows of obscure glass she was granted some sunlight that pushed with great effort to fill the basement's hidden corners; it was like exploring a dream. She touched both her hands to the wall to keep her balance as she followed her baby sister's shouts, grimacing when she hit her ankle on an unseen object.

I wish there was a light switch. I wish I could see better.

The basement walls were strong grey rock like a castle, and everything that filled up the sprawling basement must have existed only in dreams; the formless shapes could have been anything, and the thought made shivers run up her back in chilling streaks. Helen was in a world that uniquely belonged to the basement.

"Helen where are you?"

Directly below a window up ahead, sunlight leaked down to illuminate a tile that had been pushed away to reveal a square entrance into the ground. The entrance into a cistern.

Helen kneeled. "You sure did hide well. Grab my hand."

Nobody reached. There was no reply.

"Are you down there?" Helen said. Her heart sank. *"Joyce?"*

All was still, then the waters were splashing. Goosepimples rose on Helen's arms. Suddenly dizziness ran lazily in her head, and she gripped the edges of the tile entrance to lower herself down into untold depths of the unknown.

Piercing cold water traced Helen's body. She fell face-first into the water and desperately reached for anything to grab onto; there was nothing but the numbing sting of icy water, and hydrillas wrapping sickeningly and grotesquely around her limbs. Helen jolted and struggled against the hydrillas; all she could see was red, and she was being pulled down...

And down...

And down...

Helen jolted away from her memory's grip, then stood up and braced herself on the wall. In an instant she was under the water again, pulling Joyce up and patting her back as she coughed up mouthfuls of water.

Helen felt the inside of the cistern shrinking. She couldn't stop shivering, holding her crying baby sister close.

"You're going to be okay, don't worry, it's all okay."

The cistern was divided by a low semipermeable wall into two chambers; on the other side of that wall, rainwater rolled in with sediments and debris. On this side, the quiet chamber, there was only water. Just above Helen's shoulder was a runoff pipe in the wall, reminiscent of the little hole in a sink, that prevented the quiet chamber from overflowing. It must've run off down the side of the hill and into the lake between her family's house and the farm.

Helen shifted Joyce in her arms then patted her back again as she coughed. Then she leaned against one of the walls and their sobs quieted down. Chills slithered up her back again, and white sparks of pain ran up her legs as she lost feeling in her toes.

"Joyce don't you ever do that again, okay? Don't you ever come down here again."

"Suh-sorry."

"Let's get you out of here, come on, can you reach up there?" Helen held her up as best she could. "Here, step on my shoulder, can you reach?"

Under the thin strip of light Helen watched Joyce's fingers grip the edges of tile. Her little sister climbed up and out.

"I made it."

"Is there a light switch up there?"

"I dunno."

Helen stood on her tiptoes and hopped, struggling to wrap her cold wet fingers around rough edges of tiles. Three or four attempts later she was able to hold on to the tile, but not for long; she was not strong enough to lift herself up out of the cistern.

"I'm stuck. Is there a ladder down here?"

"I dunno."

"What *do* you know? Joyce, look for a light switch so I can see."

Joyce's little footsteps passed through the basement.

Helen searched her hands along the walls looking for a ladder. She stepped carefully through the water, and all feeling was completely gone from her feet and working its way up her legs. It was unsettling to think that part of her body was completely devoid of feeling. What if her body got so cold that she could never feel anything ever again?

Helen wished the light from above did more than illuminate one small space down here in darkness. She wished its rays could have flowed all through the cistern to help her find a ladder, or to at least make her feel less scared. Anything could exist in the dark, anything could have been here with her...

She shuddered.

What if I never get out of here?

Helen leaned on the semipermeable wall that separated the quiet chamber from the chamber of sediment and debris. Curiously she peeked over the edge, and within the endless collections of residue and deposits, a decaying hand reached up desperately for Helen.

Endless screams painfully passed through her throat and escaped her lips. Helen staggered backwards from the decaying hand hopelessly outstretched with loose skin curled back from its bone.

What else was buried in those sickening deposits?

In her mind flashed the thought of a corpse with large blisters bursting on every inch of its skin; skin that was purpled and tearing, falling away and exposing bones. Grotesquely it rested with its head turned completely backwards, empty eye sockets two eternally staring black eyes darker than a doll's eyes.

Screaming endlessly she jumped again for the opening above her, praying that there was nothing else with her, praying nothing would rise from the grave of debris and sludge and wrap its bony rotten fingers around her.

The seconds that ticked by were maddening; the room was getting colder, the numbness in her feet was spreading up her legs, and she wished she could jump high enough to escape the dreaded cistern. Furtively she looked over her shoulder after every jump, anticipating the hand extending past the wall that kept it out of sight.

She jumped again and missed again, paused to catch her breath, and something splashed behind her. Carefully she turned, hands covering her mouth to prevent a deathly scream. She was all alone in the cistern.

I'll never get out of here.

Helen took shallow breaths. *You'll get out, you'll make it out, there's nothing with you, there's nothing with you, there's—there's nothing with you except that hideous hand.*

Helen tried to jump again but she was being held down as if hydrillas had coiled around her again to keep her from moving. She gave one desperate leap then wept again. *Joyce you idiot, why did you have to come down here?*

SPLASH!

Helen turned sharply. Again there was nothing.

She stared into the cavernous shadows and thought, *If I touch that shadow over there, I'll surely fall in.*

Helen had to be sure about the hand—if the splashes were only imagination, was the hand? She tiptoed to the wall, legs moving like legs made of bricks trying to walk on jelly, and leaned over the edge.

The hand twitched.

Helen screamed again and jumped for the exit; when the hand wrapped around her wrist she screamed again and pulled away, falling backwards under the water. She was back in the river again, all she could see was red, and the hydrillas tightened.

Stand up stand up...

Her body was completely alien to her, as if she were somebody operating a body for the first time; with no feeling in her legs she only hoped she was moving them correctly, and when she got up from the waters she saw that it was her father who had reached his hand for her.

"Grab my hand," he said.

Helen grabbed his hand and he pulled her through the opening. Without thinking about how wet she'd make his clothes, she wrapped her arms around him. Joyce, who had returned with him, put her little arms around them both.

"Helen," Father said, "are we making this a habit? Me pulling you out of water?"

"Daddy it's terrible, I saw something down there."

"Saw what?" Father put a hand on her shoulder.

"A hand," she said, barely louder than a whisper.

Father climbed down the entrance.

"Father don't go down there. Please don't."

"Where did you see the hand, Helen?"

"On the—on the other side of the wall."

Father climbed back up a few seconds later. "Helen, there's nothing down there."

9

Abigail wrote: *Tell me about your life.*

What do you want to know, Abigail?

I want you to prove you are who you say you are. How can I believe anything you're telling me?

What should I do to prove it?

I don't know…. Well let me ask you something, Helen. Do you remember if there's a necklace under a floorboard in your old home?

Yes.

Who put it there?

You did.

When did I do that?

I don't know exactly when.

Helen you need to give me something more than this. I am so confused. What is happening to me? None of this can be real.

I know you're confused. I've been with you a long time. I've been with you since you bought me from the thrift store. I know all about what happened to you a few months ago.

I never wanted to kill myself. I don't know why I did that. I don't know what came over me. Honest to God I don't know why I did it.

Don't worry, I believe you.

Why can't anyone else believe me?

I'm sorry.

It's okay.

Abigail, do you know anything about my family?

Nothing at all. I think my friend Beverly did a report about the Engstroms in junior high, but I don't remember it much.

Then let me tell you some things about my family. Things you wouldn't know otherwise. That would prove that I'm real and you're not imagining this. Okay?

Go ahead.

I was the oldest of all my siblings. I was fifteen when I died. My youngest sibling was John, and he died soon after we moved in. I was second to die. Then my siblings passed away one by one. Agatha, Joyce, Timothy, and Thaddeus. The house is five floors plus a basement. Behind the house is a wellhouse I was never allowed to go into as a kid, and a wide expanse of a forest that gave way to the lake by the farm.

There's something I don't understand. You said I've been there before. How would you know something like that? You died so long ago.

There are things I know and some things you know. Maybe if you help me we can piece it all together. Aren't you curious?

Yes I am.

Let's put our heads together. I need your help. I'm tired of being so cold and alone. I want to rest. Please help me rest.

I don't know if I can do this.

Abigail put the pen down. How could this be real? How could she hold the pen in her left hand, and the words of a dead girl come out? Carefully she rolled over the pen so that she could see the plexiglass window to the inside. Could a spirit really be in there? Abigail shivered.

Her left hand burned with a sensation to write. She picked the pen back up and guided it across the paper; with a mind of its own, the pen wrote: I need your help. You've got to believe me. I want to be put to rest.

Abigail didn't know what to think. She wanted to talk to Beverly about it but would Beverly believe her? What would Beverly think? If Beverly didn't already think Abigail was crazy after Abigail pushed her in front of an oncoming car, she certainly would after Abigail told her there was a dead girl in the pen who needed their help to be put to rest once and for all.

You can't be real.

Why not?

Abigail didn't write a reply.

Her hand hovered above the receiver. Should she call Beverly and tell her about Helen? Deep in her palms there was a pulsing urge to write something again to Helen, but she forced herself to keep away from the pen. Chills ran up her arms as she dialed Beverly.

"Hello?"

Abigail was unprepared for her friend to answer, thinking about everything Helen had written her. How could a soul linger behind inside of a pen? It wasn't possible.

"Hello?"

"Oh hey Bev."

"Abby hi how are you?"

"Is there something wrong with me?"

"What?"

Abigail was silent. She couldn't believe she blurted it out like that.

"Abigail? What's going on? Are you—are you okay?"

"I want to talk to you about something but I don't think you'd understand. I don't even think I understand."

"Talk to me. What's happening?"

"I shouldn't have called. I think I just need to be alone."

"Abby wait, is this about the car? Look, forget about it, I'm not mad, I'm fine. It was an accident, I know it was."

"I'll talk to you later."

"Abby."

"Please don't worry. I shouldn't have called. I'm sorry."

"Wait. Look. Are we friends?"

"What? Of course we are, Bev."

"I don't want you to hurt yourself again."

"Beverly, I can't understand why I hurt myself. It's like I wasn't in control. I can't understand why it happened. Every day I'm terrified it might happen again."

"I'm coming over," Beverly said. "Okay?"

"Okay."

After hanging up, Abigail returned to Helen's journal. She grabbed the pen with her left hand and guided it. It wrote: She pities you.

Beverly sat at the edge of Abigail's bed, and Abigail sat at her desk with the journal and pen.

"Do you remember that report you did about the Engstrom family in junior high? What do you remember about the house?"

"Huh? That was years ago."

"But tell me what you know?"

"Let me try to remember." Beverly crossed her arms and thought about it. "All I know is that there used to be another house there. It was knocked down and somebody built the one that's there now."

"The rumors about that place, do you think they're true? About the people that went missing or died up there?"

"You know that game in elementary school where you whisper something into the next student's ear and when the sentence has gone through the whole room it comes out completely different than whatever it first was? I wouldn't believe any of those rumors. Is that what's bothering you?"

"You know that journal I bought at the store?"

"That grimy old one?"

"Uh-huh. It belonged to somebody who lived there. It's been on my mind since I read it."

"Is it really? That thing could be worth money, aren't there people who dish out tons of cash for stuff like that?"

"I don't want to sell it, Bev. Look at this."

Beverly came over and leaned on the desk. "What am I looking at?"

"When I hold the pen in my left hand, the journal writes back to me. Look."

Hello Beverly. My name is Helen Engstrom. This is my journal.

Abigail wrote back: *Helen, tell her what you want from us.*

I want to be put to rest.

Beverly picked up the journal. "Wait, you're ambidextrous? I never knew that."

"No Beverly I'm not ambidextrous, it's this pen." Abigail held it out to her. "There's a girl in this pen. She needs our help."

Beverly grabbed the pen from Abigail. Despite being right handed, she tried to write with her left hand. In sloppy handwriting: *Hi I'm Beverly.*

"You weren't supposed to write down your own message, you were supposed to let it guide you." Abigail folded her hands together and put them under her desk. She could already feel Beverly's eyes wandering to her wrists.

Beverly held the pen there. "It isn't moving. Did Judy put you up to this or something?"

"You've known me all my life you know I'm not ambidextrous. I can't write cursive that well with my right hand even if I tried but you think I can do it with my left hand for a prank? Won't you listen to me? She needs our help."

"Let me ask Helen a question," Beverly said. She wrote down with her right hand: *How long have I to live?*

"Helen isn't a fortune teller."

"Abby I don't get it. What are you trying to show me?"

"I knew I shouldn't have called you. Helen's in this pen and she needs our help."

"Are you being serious?"

Tears were spilling suddenly from Abigail's eyes. "You need to believe me."

Beverly handed the pen back. "What do you mean there's a girl in this pen?"

Abigail adjusted the pen in her left hand then pressed it to the journal. The pen guided her hand to help it write: My spirit is in eternal pain.

"She needs our help."

"How do we help her?"

The pen guided Abigail's hand: Find my body.

Beverly watched Abigail with sullen eyes. "Stop writing that stuff down."

"It's not me it's Helen."

Before Abigail could lift her hand from the journal, it wrote: Release me from this torture.

The ancient dusty volumes collecting cobwebs at the topmost shelves in the back of the library must have been untouched for a lifetime, maybe more. Abigail had to have a worker climb up a ladder to reach the volume about Ashfall's history that fell within the years of the house's inception.

She and Beverly flipped through the book to the section titled "ENGSTROM HOUSE." There were pictures of the long tangled woods whose branches twisted like sickeningly contorted arms. Within the woods was a log cabin. According to the book, the Engstroms started out selling tobacco grown on their land.

More important to Abigail was a few pages later, where she saw the pictures of Engstrom children. Helen's smile was forever preserved in the black and white pictures. She had pretty blonde hair that fell straight past her shoulders.

"That's her," Abigail said.

The book read: Helen Engstrom disappeared from the second floor of her home. An extensive investigation revealed no evidence of Helen's location.

Abigail was chilled.

"What do you think happened to her?"

IO

"THERE'S SOMETHING ELSE I need to ask you about."

"What is it, Abby?"

"Do you think we've been there before?"

"The old Engstrom place? Have we been to the old Engstrom place before?"

"Ever since I found Helen's pen... I've had these strange dreams about a strange place. Helen said I was dreaming about the house where she grew up. I have this memory of a necklace with a purple stone. I think I hid it in the floorboards there."

A little path took Abigail and Beverly up the hill to the ancient house. It was set apart from the rest of Ashfall as if it had been cast out; it was grey and dull, as if it had *grown* out of the hill instead of being built. Its surrounding trees swayed gently, and Abigail pulled back her sleeves to feel the breeze, but there was no wind.

Its gate was tall and black and rusty; chipped paint littered the house's grass. Abigail had never in her life been this close to the old Engstrom place before, and yet it felt natural to her, as if returning to a place she had not visited in a long time, or as if finally visiting a place that she had only seen in her dreams.

Abigail dragged her hand along the fence. If the stories were true, and if something strange happened to her and Beverly at this place, and they should disappear together, then nobody would ever suspect that they were here, because no one ever came to visit this unnerving building.

Abigail bit her lip as she shivered from nerves.

"Can we turn back?"

Just as Abigail was about to answer her friend, something caught her peripheral; something moved so quickly that it was subliminal. Abigail and Beverly looked together at the house and the front door opened.

Cat was walking up to the building when she saw there were two girls at the gate. One was blonde and wearing flared jeans with a knit top. The other was brunette and wearing pocket shorts, a long sleeve shirt, and a straw hat.

When the front door opened both girls ran. Cat held in her laugh. She walked up to the front gate and met Bruno there. Bruno was carrying a dirty box full of things he found in the empty rooms in the Engstrom mansion.

"Sorry I was late, I ran into trouble."

"Trouble seems to have a way of finding you, doesn't it?"

Cat held the gate open for him. "You couldn't be more right. See you around."

As Bruno descended the slope, Cat walked over to where the two girls had hidden behind some trees. The girls watched her curiously, and for some reason that made Cat laugh.

"You didn't have to hide from Bruno. He doesn't bite unless I tell him to."

The girl had long black hair as dark as a crypt. It ended past her shoulders. Her lipstick and eyeshadow were equally dark; a pretty contrast from her pale skin. She wore a checkered skirt and a long sleeve black shirt. She opened the gate then shut it behind herself.

"Where are you going?" Abigail asked.

The girl crossed her arms. "Mexico."

"I just meant—you're going in there? Do you always go in there?"

"What business is it of yours?"

"Excuse my friend," Beverly said. "She's just curious about the house."

The girl came back to the gate and opened it. "Do you want to come in?"

Beverly and Abigail looked at each other then back to the girl. Could they trust her? What was that girl doing going into a place like this? Well, Abigail wanted answers, and now maybe she'd have them.

Abigail's hand burned with a desire to write. The pen and journal were in her purse. She didn't want to take them out in front of a stranger.

Her heart pounded. The Engstrom place was forbidden, and the fact that she and Beverly and the stranger were sneaking in here made her excited. As she came closer to the house, the more alive the house felt. She watched one of the dark windows, waiting for something to move, to pass by, but nothing did, and she looked away.

The stranger held the door open and Abigail reached it before Beverly. There was a brief second of hesitation when the door creaked on its hinges and Abigail stood in the doorway, but the eyes burrowing into the back of her skull made her move forward. The house was murky; sunlight ended at the doorframe and decided not to enter.

Right away Abigail sneezed; the room was covered with dust.

Inside the house was stranger than Abigail could have ever imagined; a place lost in time, as if some ancient day it was sealed up and unentered until now, a perfectly preserved species from a far away time. Long dark passages twisted in each direction. Abigail rested a hand on the icy grey stone wall; she looked at the terribly high and shadowy grand vaulted ceiling, and she wondered if there were any bulbs up there hiding, but she saw no switch to activate them if there were.

Some primordial feeling drifted about the house, as if its archaic evils came from a period beyond the house's construction.

It was *real,* all real, it was no longer just a place in a story. All the people who died here, the people who vanished, this was *actually* the place where it all happened.

Abigail stepped further into the front room; miraculously dust did not touch her. The couches were covered in white sheets. There was a fireplace on the first wall, and Abigail wished they had a few logs and a lighter to get warmed up in this chilly house.

"Pretty cool, isn't it?"

Abigail abruptly turned in a shock. She had forgotten about the stranger; and under the flow of shadows, her pale skin looked ghostly. For a moment Abigail wondered if the girl was alive or if she were...

"It's beautiful," Abigail said.

"In—in, well in an odd sort of way, I think so too," Beverly said.

"You know, I thought Ashfall lost interest in this old place. It was surprising to see you two at the gate. We never have visitors up here."

"I bought a journal that was recovered from this house. So I thought I'd see what this place was like."

"Bruno found that upstairs. I was with him when he did."

"Are you a squatter?"

The girl said nothing.

"My name is Abigail, by the way. This is Beverly."

"I'm Cat."

Beverly moved quietly around the front room. The floorboards creaking under every little step. "Geez this place is creepy."

At the mantelshelf, Abigail followed the neatly lined pictures of people; people who had lived here, all of them had suffered terrible fates. At the end, the final picture was a little girl with curly blonde hair in a blue dress on a swing. It was Helen.

Abigail's left hand moved on its own into her purse. She grabbed the pen and journal then looked furtively over her shoulder. Beverly and Cat were across the room talking, neither of them looking at what Abigail was doing. The pen guided her hand and it wrote: You are so close please help me Abigail.

I can't now. I will, but not now. Okay?

Please don't leave me I need your help please don't leave.

I'm scared. I'm sorry.

Abigail forced herself to put the pen and journal away. Part of her wanted to keep writing, and she struggled to resist. As she joined the others across the room, a chill wrapped around her back, and she had an obscure compulsion to leave Beverly and Cat behind and go off into the house.

"Are you ready to go?"

Abigail looked over her shoulder at the mantelshelf. Helen needed her—could she turn back now? Abigail was torn—she was getting involved with something unnatural. It was no wonder why Beverly had looked at her so strangely when she had suggested there was a spirit in the pen... a spirit that begged for their help.

"I don't know."

"Let's just go. I don't like it here one bit."

Abigail moved in short steps away from Beverly and Cat. "No. No, let's not go. I have to see if it's true."

"If what's true?"

"Remember what I told you?"

Cat crossed her arms. "What is going on here?"

"There's a necklace in here. One with a purple stone. You must not have seen it."

"I don't know what you're talking about. If there were any necklace in here, Bruno and I would have found it. We've found all the jewelry in this house, I'm sure."

Abigail went through the room and stood in the threshold between here and the rest of the house. "You didn't look under the floorboards."

"Huh?"

Beverly stood at her friend's side and held her by the hand. "You heard Cat, there's no jewelry left for you to find."

"But I know where I put it. It's under the floorboard."

Cat stayed in place, her arms still crossed. "Yeah right."

Beverly turned her attention to Car. "I'm sorry about this. I really don't know what she's talking about."

"I think I get it." Cat rolled her eyes. "One time this group of little boys came up here because they thought there was gold or something hidden in the walls. Everyone thinks old houses are full of little treasures, but all the relatives cleaned out this place decades ago. Lucky for me and Bruno they left a few things behind that we could flip. Not as valuable as jewels, but it makes us enough money…"

Abigail slipped her hand away from Beverly's and ran by instinct up the spiraling staircase to the second floor. Beverly and Cat's footsteps slammed behind her as they called her name. Abigail ignored them. She could see the memory clearly again in that moment as she turned through corners and came upon the door that she knew the necklace was hidden behind.

Its hinges squealed.

She kneeled down and her hands reached for the floorboard she had seen in her memory. She opened it just as Beverly and Cat stood in the doorway. Abigail reached her hand inside and pulled up the necklace. A streak of light from the window illuminated the precious jewel, and its glow flowed curiously around the room.

Cat snatched it from Abigail's hands.

"Hey, I don't know what the big idea is, but me and Bruno had dibs on everything that was in here."

Abigail stared up at Cat without a word.

"It's ours to sell."

Beverly was trembling in the doorway. She was trying to hide how bad her hands were shaking, but Abigail could still tell how frightened her friend was because Beverly was doing a bad job at pretending to be all right.

"Can we—can we go?"

Abigail stood up, walked past Cat, and joined Beverly in the doorway.

Cat lowered the necklace around her neck and admired herself. "Isn't it cute?"

"You shouldn't have worn that."

Cat pushed past them into the hallway. "And why not?"

Abigail was speechless. Why had she said that?

The girls all went down to the main floor, back to the sitting room, and were heading toward the door.

"I'm sorry about all this," Beverly said.

"Hey, it's no problem, you know? This necklace is so pretty."

Abigail's heart was pounding. This meant it was true—all true. Everything that Helen had told her. Everything Helen had said. It was all real.

Thick drops of blood leaked from the ceiling and spilled over Cat's left hand.

"They've marked you."

11

BEVERLY SHIVERED DESPITE THE warmth. She crossed her arms on the table and laid her head on top of them. Earlier that day she had been in the Engstrom place, and she couldn't shake the premonition she had in that building. She couldn't shake the feeling that things were going to go wrong—or that things were already very wrong.

She thought about leaving the graveyard, but Cat walked up the path and came over and sat across from her.

"I thought you weren't coming. And what a sick idea for a meeting place."

"I got lost."

"Really? Ashfall isn't that big."

"No."

"Whatever. Thanks for coming, Cat."

Cat didn't say anything.

"There's something wrong with Abigail. I don't know who she is anybody, but that's not my friend."

"Okay?"

"The way she looked at that place, and what she said to you…"

"Yeah, that was pretty weird."

"Cat, Abigail hasn't been normal in a long time. I don't know how she got like this, maybe I missed all the signs. You cannot tell her anything I'm about to tell you, all right?"

"Geez, I don't even know her."

"Sorry, but saying 'don't tell' is just something you *have* to say. So… she almost killed herself a few months ago. One day she was fine and the next it was like I didn't even recognize her. Sometimes I wonder if she died and came back a new person."

"Why did she do it?"

"I don't completely know. She had gotten depressed. She had been miserable for a little while before she cut her wrists. But I don't know what happened, because there were no signs before… before all this. She used to be happy. She used to be the happiest person I knew. Now she's different. Something changed, and I don't know what it is or how to help her."

"How is she different?"

"It's like she's not Abigail anymore, she's like a replacement."

"But how?"

"She keeps saying and doing things I know she'd never do. This morning, Cat you should have seen it. She kept trying to convince me—I really don't know what's gotten into her—she kept trying to convince me," Beverly shook her head, "that the spirit of a girl named Helen Engstrom lives in the pen she bought from the thrift store."

"Bruno sells all that junk he finds in the house. It could have been from the Engstrom place, sure."

"But she says a spirit lives in that pen. It's freaking me out, and—and that thing about the necklace. How could she possibly have known it was there?" Beverly paused. Cat was about to say something, but Beverly cut her off and continued: "When I look in her eyes I can't see my friend anymore. When Abigail was telling me about the pen, she told me if I held it in my left hand that I could *talk* to the spirit of this dead girl."

"What happened when you tried?"

"Nothing. I couldn't do it. But Abigail believes *she can*."

There was silence.

"Cat?"

"Yeah?"

"I tried playing it off this morning. Abigail's never been ambidextrous. Now she can write with both hands—she can write perfect cursive with her left hand, but she's right handed. You know how she knew it was Helen's journal? There were two entries at the beginning of the book when she bought it, and the handwriting matches up perfectly to what Abigail can do."

"I have a question."

"Yeah?"

"What do you think I can do about any of this?"

"I just want my friend to be normal again. Just the other day she pushed me in front of a car. Abigail has an obsession with that house, and I'm afraid she might hurt herself again."

"She pushed you in front of a car?"

"Yeah, and what's next? I don't know how to be a good friend to her anymore. I don't want her to hurt herself again."

Cat pulled back her long sleeve. Cuts all along her arm. "I'm not the best person to give you advice on this."

"I'm sorry."

Cat shrugged. "If you think your friend has a problem, you need to find her a doctor."

"Cat..."

"Like I said. What do you think I can do about any of this?"

"Why do you hurt yourself?"

"I hurt myself so I don't hurt others."

"What is that supposed to mean?"

"Because I'm in charge of my pain."

"What?"

"I'm sorry about your friend."

"What am I supposed to do?

Cat stood up from the table without a word.

"Wait, Cat." Beverly stood too.

"Yeah?"

"Never mind."

"Maybe I'll see you around."

"Yeah." Beverly frowned. "Maybe."

They split ways, and Beverly felt unblinking eyes watching her with every step she took through the graveyard. When she looked over her shoulder, Cat was gone, and Beverly was the only living person still in the graveyard.

As she walked to the big gated entrance, she noticed a raven's nest on a low branch. The raven watched her and never looked away. Even when Beverly was past the gate, the raven kept its deeply unnerving yellow eyes on her.

Beverly shuddered.

In her mind she saw the pretty necklace again, and Abigail pulling it out from the floorboards. She couldn't stop wondering how her friend knew about it. Once again, Beverly had a terrible feeling that everything was going to go wrong.

12

THE HOUSE WAS ESPECIALLY noisy today, Cat thought. As she ascended the main spiraling stairway she thought she heard footsteps above her; but when she stopped moving, the aforementioned footsteps also ceased.

"Bruno? That you?"

Silence. She was all alone on the second floor.

At the end of the short hallway was the red door. It was the only room in the building she had seen that was different from all the others; the others were made of thick wood that towered far over her head, constructed of four wide panels of vertical wood, and one wide panel running horizontal across the others. The other doors had shiny brass knobs but his one was silver.

The room was empty, except for the makeshift altar and a couple small windows that were high up on the wall. She set her purse down next to the altar then kneeled. She rolled back her left sleeve; each day she had to pull it further and further back to find new spaces. She was already feeling the rush before the cold edge of metal ever met her skin.

She pulled it across gently, slowly, taking her time to pull it across the width of her arm, and blood spilled warm over her skin. Rushes of pleasure spanned from her cut through her body, traveling further with every pulse.

Cat took deep breaths rolling back her right sleeve. It was harder to cut properly with her left hand, but it felt so good when her right arm was cut because her right arm was almost completely unblemished from previous scars.

In the middle of her right arm she pressed the razor blade, moving it quickly rather than slowly; she couldn't resist the high it gave her. She had gone two days without hurting herself to try and build back up tolerance, but it was an addiction, it was something she needed so bad that she couldn't give herself a break any longer.

Bruno opened the door, and when he saw what she was doing he immediately dropped his box and came down to the floor with her. He grabbed her by the wrists and she dropped the blade, accidentally staining his pants with a small streak of blood.

"I told you to stop doing this."

"Um, excuse me? You can tell me anything, doesn't mean I'll listen to you."

"You said you'd stop this."

"Yeah Bruno, here we go again. But you said, but I said, but you said."

"What the hell is wrong with you?"

"I didn't tell you to make what I do into your problem."

"You're screwed up in the head, Cat."

"Look you can stay mad at me or we can go into the bedroom in the next hall over and forget about it." Cat stood up and walked to the door. "I know you want to come with me to the bedroom, Bruno. Just come here."

Bruno stood up and followed Cat. The sheets and covers in the bedroom were all fresh sheets Bruno had brought in with him so that they wouldn't have to use the disgusting musty ones that had been left in this place.

Cat sat on the bed and pulled her shirt off; Bruno couldn't take his eyes off her.

"I knew you couldn't stay mad at me."

"Yeah," Bruno said, pushing her flat on her back. "Who could?"

"You're a peach."

He pulled her skirt off fast. His eyes traced each inch of her body from her eyes to her breasts to her legs. Cat's flesh shuddered under his touch. She slid on top of Bruno and kissed him, hands running up and down each other's bodies.

Cat wrapped her arms around Bruno. A moment later he pulled away.

"Where are you going?"

"I've got work to do."

"Can't it wait a few? You promised you'd take me out today. I thought we'd spend some time together."

"I'm already behind schedule. I've got a couple things to drop off but I'll be back in a little while."

Cat crossed her arms and rolled her eyes. "Okay. Go ahead."

Bruno left the room without replying.

She waited to hear him go downstairs before she left the bedroom and returned to the room with the red door. She pulled out a black candle from the hollow under the altar and pressed her lighter's flame to the wick.

An abrupt chill passed through the room and blew out the flame. The windows were shut. Cat turned and saw that the door was shut too. Where the soft gust of cold wind could have come from, she didn't know.

She lighted the candle again.

From her purse she grabbed her copy of *What Walks Unseen* by Dr. James McDowell. By candlelight she read:

Newspaper headlines:

ESTIMATED FIFTY CHILDREN FOUND IN EXPANSE OF SHALLOW GRAVES IN HOLLOW HILL!

SATANIC CULT BORE CHILDREN AS SACRIFICES TO THE DEVIL!

ADDITIONAL GRAVES DISCOVERED IN HOLLOW HILL!

WHAT ARE THE SECRETS OF THE HOLLOW HILL DEVIL CULT?

FORMER SATAN WORSHIPPER SPEAKS!

From an article: *An anonymous phone call was placed Wednesday morning at five o'clock leaving a tip for police about a devil cult who buried their children in hidden graves in the woods.*

From another article: *A couple who fled the cult are working closely with investigators to track down the others involved.*

More headlines:

BIZARRE DEATH OF PRIEST!

EXORCISM GONE WRONG!

PRIEST BURNED TO DEATH!

PRIEST'S FINAL DAYS DETAILED IN JOURNAL!

From an interview between Dr. James McDowell and his late mentor Dr. Holland:

Dr. McDowell: Who was the nameless couple? What happened to them?

Dr. Holland: During my research on this case I went right to the source. I scheduled a meeting with journalist Martin Lynch. Martin put me in contact with some officers from the Hollow Hill Police Department, but they wouldn't speak. All details about the fleeing couple were confidential.

Dr. McDowell: Why did Martin Lynch send you straight to the Hollow Hill PD? Didn't he have any information for you himself?

Dr. Holland: All he knew was that the couple came to Ashfall from Hollow Hill because that's where they had previously lived. Supposedly their family members had been trying to get them out of the cult before cutting off all contact.

Dr. McDowell: So what did you do next? What does a man do when all he's faced with are dead ends?

Dr. Holland: There was nothing left for me to piece together until I heard the story of a girl named Vanessa Gannon, and a priest named Father Lucas who died trying to save her soul. After Father Lucas died, somebody stole his belongings and published a copy of his journal. Although we know quite a bit about the final thirty days of his life leading to his demise, we may never completely know what happened on that final day, because everybody that was in Vanessa's home is either dead or missing.

From Father Lucas's journal: *This is not the first time this family has faced the devil before.*

Vanessa Gannon was twenty years old, the oldest of four children. If Mr. and Mrs. Gannon had in fact been the ones to leave the anonymous tip and flee the devil cult, then Vanessa had been born either just before they fled or just after. Could her possession have had something to do with the incomplete ritual her life had been created for, or was she only an innocent girl who became the victim of a demon?

Midnight-black hair, big blue eyes. Vanessa was beautiful. Slowly it all deteriorated until she was completely unrecognizable; her pretty eyes, in a way Father Lucas couldn't understand, contorted into a sickening misshapenness, as if her skull had been grotesquely reshaped into something less than human. Her mouth was crooked; it opened and her tongue writhed in a stream of foam. Her skin was leached of all color.

It all began, according to reports, on the day that Vanessa couldn't keep her secrets to herself any longer. She complained to her parents about hearing and seeing things that were not there—demonic faces and the faces of deceased family members were among the things she claimed to see. At night she told her parents that voices from the grave were whispering to her, telling her she was 'damned' and that she would 'rot in hell.'

When her family went to church, Vanessa was unable to walk past a crucifix. A month passed, and Vanessa's condition worsened to the point where she could not enter a church at all—its floors burned like fire and she could not stand it. She averted her eyes from all depictions of Christ and any paintings of saints; they sparkled so immensely that she could not stand to look at them.

From Father Lucas's journal: *The girl screams insanely tonight. She begged for help against the demons she was seeing. I hesitated to return to her bedroom, but I came to her bedside and her voice was changed. It became a cold dead voice carrying messages of Satan. Vanessa… believes that she is the devil in the flesh.*

In thirty days there were twenty exorcisms performed by Father Lucas. Some of these exorcisms lasted upwards of three hours. Nothing Father Lucas did had any effect on the girl. In the final five days leading up to his death, Father Lucas wrote extensively about the exorcisms and the things the girl would say.

From Father Lucas's journal: *Tonight Vanessa is repeating "You'll burn, Father Lucas. You'll melt under the grip of the devil."*

From Father Lucas's journal: *It was a hot summer day but when I stepped into that house there was only coldness, and I was welcomed by Vanessa's screams. Her eyes had once been soft blue and begging for release from the clutches of Satan. Now they were twisted and vile, and she yelled at me with a voice that was deep and guttural and full of malevolence. I stood at her bedside and read the fifth chapter of the book of Mark. Vanessa interrupted with continuous screams of pain, and when she didn't get me to stop, she shouted that I'd burn in hell—I'd burn in hell, she said, under the mighty grip of Satan.*

Newspaper headlines:

MYSTERIOUS FIRE AT THE HOME OF POSSESSED GIRL!
FATHER LUCAS IDENTIFIED BY DENTAL RECORDS!

Mrs. Gannon was found in a nearby room and had died from suffocation. Mr. Gannon and all four of the Gannon children were missing.

Newspaper headline:

SHALLOW GRAVE DISCOVERED IN ASHFALL!

A year later the dismembered body of the youngest Gannon child was found in a shallow grave in Ashfall—but what became of Vanessa Gannon and the rest of her family, and what had caused the fire in the first place, is entirely unknown.

Some say Vanessa was full with the power of Satan, and after killing Father Lucas sacrificed her family to begin another cult. Others say that Father Lucas's death, as well as Mrs. Gannon's death, were both accidental, and that Mr. Gannon fled Ashfall so that Vanessa would not be found guilty and sentenced to death.

Some have even suggested that Father Lucas was an agent of Satan.

Newspaper headline:

IS THE DEVIL CULT STILL OUT THERE?

Bruno picked up Cat from the Engstrom place in his red Volkswagen Beetle. There were dents in the sides and the paint was fading, and the license plate was halfway fallen off, but it was the car he could afford. He opened the passenger door for her and she thanked him.

She was beautiful; eyes as sparkling and blue as sun-lit waves that contrasted with her black eyeshadow. When he sat back in the driver's seat he reached over for a kiss, then he drove away from the house. Cat opened her purse and brought out a tin container that her pot was inside of. She rolled a joint and ran her thumb over her lighter's wheel four or five times; it wouldn't ignite so she set it back inside of the container.

Cat reached for the car's built-in lighter but the outlet was empty. "What happened to your lighter?"

"I don't know, I lost it."

"How do you lose your car lighter? It's not like something you just toss in your pocket. It's red-hot molten metal."

Bruno reached into his pocket and found his Zippo lighter and gave it to her. "Here you go."

"Thank you very much," she said. She took a hit then handed it to him. "Let's stop by the store later so I can get another one."

Bruno inhaled deep and coughed. Cat turned on the radio. The volume was too high so she lowered it. The music played: *Baby if I made you mad for somethin' I might have said, please let's forget the past, the future looks bright ahead.*

A little while later they came to Larkspur Highway.

"You used to drive around here often, yeah?" Cat asked.

"Yeah with my dad when I was like… ten."

"You don't like talking about him much, do you?"

"Best just to not say anything if you got nothing good to say, Cat."

"I know. I just feel like you bottle up your—"

"I ain't got nothing to say, okay?"

"All right, damn. Turn up here, Bruno. It's a good spot."

"This where you found that 'coon last month?"

"Yeah…. Plus the three rabbits," Cat said. Her eyes were sullen. The sparkle in them had dimmed significantly.

Bruno caught her expression as he parked his car where she had instructed him to. "Eh, I'll get you a live one, chin up."

"A white one."

"Yeah."

"With the lop ears."

"Yeah."

"And he'll be Mr. Harrington."

"Sure, whatever babe."

They stepped out of the car. Bruno opened the trunk; inside was an empty box next to the shovel that Cat grabbed and used to pick up a dead dog from the side of the road. Tire tracks were spread over its body; the dog had been split open and its mangled body was twisted in different directions. An eyeball grotesquely dangled out of its cracked skull.

"You know," Cat said, dumping the dog into the box in the trunk, "I used to catch rabbits all the time when I visited my grandpa's farm."

"Oh yeah? How big?"

"As big as that boulder you keep next to your shoebox."

"Yeah yeah, that boulder is bigger than your whole head, Cat."

"Hey, my head is perfectly cute and quaint."

"Mmhmm." Bruno ruffled her hair. "Hey, is that something you could use?"

Cat looked over to where Bruno was pointing. A dead bird covered in dirt. She knelt to examine it. "I dunno, can you get me the brush?"

Bruno opened the car's back door and found an old toothbrush on the floor that Cat sometimes used to clean up animals with. He brought it over to her and she used it to clean off the bird's feathers as much as she could; the bird was completely smashed in, hardly any of its bones left unbroken. And the feathers wouldn't get clean at all no matter how hard Cat scrubbed.

"Hmmm... no I don't think I can use this one. Thanks for looking out though."

"How about we get out of here?" Bruno said. "Want to catch a movie?"

"Sure."

13

ABIGAIL COULDN'T SLEEP. SHE laid in bed facing the partly open door; she was too comfortable to get up and close it completely. Chirping crickets echoed outside her window, and her covers were warm while the fan twirled cool air around her room. Music would've helped her sleep, but her record player was downstairs in the living room, and her room was unfortunately lacking a radio since her old hand-me-down broke and she hadn't replaced it yet.

With her eyes shut, and her mind and spirit rolling through darkness behind her eyes, she searched for the ledge of sleep so she could fall over the edge and be under sleep's magic spell. Falling asleep and being aware of it was like floating down a stream. Sleep dragged over her body in strong waves, pulling her further under.

As seconds ticked by waves moved over her faster, tighter, stronger, and she was drowning in sleep; its hypnotizing spell was about to be complete, until the whisper came softly from the hallway. It was so gentle that it passed almost unnoticed until she heard it again, and the soft wordless whispers pulled her out of the river of sleep.

Abigail's eyes opened, and she was fully awake, and she knew that she was not alone, and those familiar unblinking eyes that had watched her once were watching her again. She shut her eyes quickly, hoping that whoever it was would not catch her awake, but it was too late, and something whispered again; it was audible but wordless because of how low it was, and how far it was traveling, so that she could not tell what it was saying. All she could tell was that it was a girl's voice—a sweet, innocent, little girl.

She sounded afraid.

Abigail shuddered. Her heart raced, pounding like metal poles on concrete, and she wondered if the girl could hear its loud beating.

Abigail stayed still.

There was the whisper again; what was it saying?

All she wanted to do was curl into a ball and scream for Dad and Mom to come save her. That same scream she desperately thought about releasing built up in the depths of her body and inched upward, scraping against the walls of her throat, threatening to escape.

She did not want to believe that there was anybody in the hall, but the whispers were unmistakably somebody approaching her bedroom; the next whisper was closer, as if it were now in the room with her. Abigail shivered continuously; she bit her lips to keep them from separating. She breathed shallowly.

"Abigail..."

Behind shut eyes, Abigail pictured Helen, a little blonde girl, with a knife through her head.

"There you are..."

Abigail gasped, sat up, and pulled her covers to her chin. She scanned the room; empty... empty, except under the bed; she couldn't see under the bed. Suddenly she inched away from the edge, as if hands would burst up at any second and dirty long nails would sink into her skin.

"Help me…"

Abigail looked from one side of her room back to the other and met the deteriorating eyes of a decaying face; Helen Engstrom's grotesque and rotting corpse that was somehow animated with the touch of life. She reached her hand out for Abigail.

Abigail screamed and jumped from her bed and ran into the hallway and down the stairs. All the noise awoke her parents, who rushed to her side and asked her what was wrong. Abigail said nothing at first; after her parents asked her again what was wrong, she said it was a nightmare.

Her parents sat her down at the living room couch.

"Are you sure that's all it was? A nightmare?" Her mother asked.

"Yes ma'am."

Father went to the kitchen and came back with water. Abigail drank it.

"Thank you," she said, shifting the cup between her hands. "I'm sorry I woke you guys."

14

HELEN LEFT A TRAIL of purple marbles through the woods on her way to the cemetery. She went alone, carrying her notebook along with the new pen her father made for her. Tears couldn't help but come when she thought about the mother raven and her nest of eggs.

At the cemetery's edge she found the tree and looked for a new nest. There wasn't one. What had become of the mother raven, Helen wasn't sure. She was chilled remembering the way it had looked at her with its piercing eyes—eyes that wanted to see Helen dead.

Just inside the cemetery was a bench of splintery wood, decaying in areas around rusted screws, so Helen chose to sit on the patch of rocky ground instead, where grass couldn't completely grow. In her notebook she drew baby ravens. Baby ravens high in the clouds. Every space on the page was taken up with ravens soaked in vivid sunshine; and on the right side of the page, directly under the sun, was a branch with a big nest for them to go home to. Mother raven was waiting.

A sliver of wood from Helen's special pen loosened and poked her hand; a drop of blood welled at the rim of her cut and fell on her drawing of the nest. As she closed her notebook, the mother raven landed across from her, standing on a grave that had been overtaken with moss, and whose wooden cross had fallen and turned with the wind, so that from Helen's point of view it was inverted.

CAW! CAW!

"I'm sorry." The words softly left her lips.

Its deeply angry eyes never wavered. It stepped closer, passing over the upside down cross. The mother raven stood two or three feet away from Helen and leaned back, choking, writhing, crying until it heaved up a mess of chewed worms.

Helen screamed, running away with her pen and notebook gripped so tightly that the splinter pressed into her flesh again. When she was far over the slope that she had ascended to leave the cemetery, and the mother raven was no longer in sight, Helen stopped and rested against a tree to catch her breath. It was then that she was reminded of the burning in her hand; the splinter had gone into her palm again. She pulled it out and curiously saw that a thin trail of blood stained the glass window of the pen.

She passed the stream of water, came back to the edge of the woods, then went across the back yard and knocked on the door of her father's shed.

Father opened the door. "Why are you crying?"

Helen stepped past him into the shed. "Can you fix my pen?"

Father grabbed it from her hands. "Of course I can. What happened?"

"I poked myself on a splinter. See?"

Father looked over the pen then looked on the counter for a tool. "It'll only take a second."

"Really Daddy?"

"Sure, sure."

Father sat down in a chair at the work table and popped out the glass. Helen watched him clean out the blood. Then, just as he was about to say something to her, there was a knock on the shed door. Father opened it to find Mr. Carter and his daughter Julia. Mr. Carter had been one of Father's business partners for a long time, and Helen's family knew the Carter family well.

Father and Mr. Carter shook hands, exchanged hellos, and as Helen set off to show Julia around their new home, she saw Mr. Carter give her father a golden watch to repair. When light reflected off of the watch's band, it was practically blinding.

"I miss when you lived closer," Julia said. "I miss swimming together at the lake."

"I miss that too. But there's a lake down near the farm, and a little river in the woods. Do you want to see them? I don't know how long you're staying."

"My dad said we'd only be here a little while. He's got stuff to do in town. Woah this is house is so pretty. Hey, does your back yard go on forever?"

"Seems like it."

"I wish my back yard was this big."

"There's so much to see out there. I'm finding new things every day."

"Where's Agatha?"

"I think Agatha went with Mother somewhere. Hey Julia, you know what would be fun?"

"Huh?"

Standing by the back door into her new home, Helen pointed across the yard to the wellhouse. "My father told me it's off limits. What if we sneaked in?"

"I don't know but I've always been too scared to sneak on my own."

Their fathers were sitting at a table outside and looking over reports. They must have been more important than fixing Helen's pen, she thought. Neither of the men noticed that the girls were tiptoeing away from the house and to the wellhouse.

"Are you sure we should do this?"

"What's the worst that could happen, Julia?"

"I dunno."

The wellhouse was tall and grey, and two stone steps led up to it. The door into the wellhouse was on the right side of the circular structure, so that neither of their fathers could see them opening the door. Helen pulled on the handles and found that it was locked.

"Looks like we can't go in."

"No, there must be a way. There must. Oh, I know—the window."

There were two sets of windows, one on each side. The girls crept to the right of the doorway and together pressed their hands against the metal bars that were placed in front of the wooden window boards. The window was big and spanned from knee-height to a foot over their heads. Why had metal bars been placed in front of the windows?

Why do my parents want us to stay out of here so bad?

Helen pulled herself on to the little space there was in front of the metal bars, tucked her stomach in, and pulled herself through. It was a tight fit, but she was able to get in. Once she was past the bars she extended a hand to Julia.

"I'm scared. What if I get stuck?"

"Then you'll be stuck forever and ever." Helen rolled her eyes. "My dad put those bars there and he can take them off. Don't worry."

"But if I get stuck we'll be in trouble."

"We're already in trouble. Come on."

Julia frowned, stepping an inch closer and wrapping her hands around the bars. "You sure I will fit?"

"Are you kidding Julia?"

Julia slid her upper body through and grabbed Helen's hand. It was a tighter fit for her than for Helen, but they pulled her through.

For the first time, Helen had a look inside the wellhouse. It was as gray and dull on the inside as it was on the outside, but the strange pattern of ashen bricks against wooden benches and a wooden floor was beautiful. The well was in the center of the room; its stones came up to her waist. Because of the small amounts of light that the window let in, facing a forest whose branches obscured the sun, the depths of the well were completely unseen—there was no telling how deep it went.

Helen walked around the well then noticed there was a closet on the wall opposite the entrance; two wood doors locked with a padlock. She pulled on the handles anyways, trying to peek between the doors, but couldn't see anything.

Julia nervously bit her lip, sitting near the window. "Why would your mother and father tell you not to come in here?"

"Maybe they're scared one of us would fall in."

Julia gulped. "There's something wrong with the wellhouse."

"How do you mean?"

"It's freezing cold in here."

"I don't feel anything."

Helen walked over to her friend and accidentally kicked up a couple coins that were on the floor next to the well. She picked them up and put one in Julia's hand.

"Let's toss them in and make wishes."

She and Julia leaned over the side of the well. Below them was pure darkness; the well must have gone on for infinity. There was no end to its hidden depths. Helen rolled the coin around her fingers, carefully thinking over what she should wish for—and abruptly she was frozen. A whisper uprose from the crypt of impossible darkness.

"Do you hear that?"

Julia shook her head. "Hear what?"

Helen pressed her ear closer down, bracing her hands on the edges of the well so she wouldn't slip.

"Something's down there."

"Oh Helen I don't like this."

"Shush."

They were both still; all noises stopped dead. Helen waited for the whispers to come back.

"Helen?" Julia said faintly, almost scared to say anything.

"Yes?"

"Your eyes were black."

"What?"

"Your eyes—your eyes, they were completely black. For only a second."

"No they were not."

Julia took a small step back and dropped in her coin.

"What did you wish for?"

"To get out of here."

"I'm still deciding."

A chill and a distant whisper jolted Helen, and the coin dropped from her hand into the well of darkness.

"There's people down there, Julia."

Julia gulped and staggered backwards a step. "No. No Helen there's not."

Helen's eyes were black again.

Julia ran from the well but Helen wrapped her arms around her in a grip that dug painfully into her body. Julia's hands pushed feebly against her friend; she couldn't break free from Helen's hold. A scream formed deep down in Julia's throat, but Helen's hand against her bottom jaw kept it from releasing. Breaths came shallowly.

Helen carried Julia two steps back to the well and lifted her over the well's edge. She plummeted so fast that she couldn't scream; briefly she was aware of the falling, briefly she was aware she was going to plunge under the surface of the unseen water, then she was submerged in the blinding abyss.

Which way was up?

Julia struggled under the tangled blanket of black water, slamming her hands on the filthy edges of the well, pushing her body desperately upwards in hopes that she was moving the right way. It was freezing in the well.

And suddenly Julia realized she wasn't alone.

"Julia! Julia!" Helen lowered the bucket from the top of the well, cranking as fast as she could. *"Grab on."*

Perpetual screams erupted from down below, sending shudders up and down Helen's back. How had it happened? How had Julia fallen in? It happened so fast that Helen couldn't understand it—one second they were throwing in coins, the next her friend was plummeting...

There were shouts coming from outside the wellhouse too; their fathers must have heard. In an instant the door was unlocked and open, and Mr. Carter cranked for the bucket to be lowered. Both men tried to communicate with Julia but she wouldn't respond—endless screams drowned out all other voices.

"How did this happen?"

"She tripped. It was an accident."

When Julia was pulled up and out of the well she was shivering, and her wide terrified eyes wouldn't look at Helen directly. She was pale—as pale as a sickness that promised death. Mr. Carter hugged his daughter, but her terror never wavered.

Father went into the house and brought back towels, and Mr. Carter dried his daughter. Minutes later the screams stopped. Julia sat on one of the benches in the wellhouse, still avoiding Helen.

When Mr. Carter asked her what happened, she gave no answer. Instead, Julia said, *"There's people down there. They were pulling on me."*

15

Yesterday, upon the stair,
  I met a man who wasn't there
  He wasn't there again today
  I wish, I wish he'd go away...
  When I came home last night at three
  The man was waiting there for me
  But when I looked around the hall
  I couldn't see him there at all!
  Last night I saw upon the stair
  A little man who wasn't there
  He wasn't there again today
  Oh, how I wish he'd go away...
  That was lovely, Helen. Did you write that all by yourself?
  Yes I did. When I was alive I thought I'd grow up to be a poet.
  It was great. Maybe you can show me some others.
  Abigail? Can I ask you a question?
  Certainly, Helen.
  Why are you even friends with Beverly still? I saw everything that happened when you told her about me. She doesn't believe you at all. And she... she treats you like you're her little pet or something.

Abigail was hesitant to write back, but she switched the pen from her left hand to her right, and replied: *What are you talking about?*

Haven't you seen how she looks at you?

I don't know.

The pen abruptly switched from her right hand to her left before she could finish. The pen guided her hand, and Helen replied: I'm a better friend to you than she is. I believe you, Abigail. I know you were confused. I know you really didn't want to hurt yourself in the tub. Sometimes we do things and we don't even know why we did them. We need to help each other, me and you. It's what friends do. I know I've asked this a lot already, but I need your help Abby. I want to be at rest already.

I'll help you. I promise.

Thank you.

Abigail tapped the pen with the plexiglass window on the journal, wondering what to write back next. Then Helen wrote: I appreciate you. I'm sorry if I sounded mean at all.

It's okay. Really.

What did it feel like to revisit my home?

Being there was like returning to a place I've only seen in faded dreams. I don't think I liked it there.

But you can only put me to rest by going back there. You have to find where my body is hidden.

It's making me sick to keep talking about this.

But we need to talk about this to figure it out. My body is still in that house and needs to be laid to rest. Please.

My stomach is full of butterflies. You know why I'm so scared to talk to you about this? You know why I'm so scared about your old home?

Why, Abigail?

Because standing in that house felt so right. It felt like I belonged in that house.

I knew it would feel that way.

I felt like I was where I always belonged.

Let's put our heads together. There's something in that house for both of us. We can help each other. Isn't that what friends are for? Maybe with friends like Beverly, you wouldn't know that, would you?

Beverly is a good friend. I don't understand why don't you like her.

If she was a good friend she wouldn't be afraid of you.

Abigail put the pen down and closed the journal.

Chills pinched her skin. When she shut her eyes she was taken back to Helen's old home, taken back to the big open living room and the beautiful paintings on the walls, paintings she felt she had looked at a thousand times before. Amorphous shadows that filled the house's deep corners were comforting. She wanted to be back in that bedroom; Abigail wanted to see what else she might have hidden in a time long lost, in a time she could no longer remember. She wanted to follow Helen's words until she found the body.

How sad it was, Abigail thought, to be a spirit and not be at rest; to forever be cold, to be lonely in that house. What could have happened to Helen? The child she saw in that photograph, the wide smile, the freckles... what could happen to such an innocent child?

Abigail opened the journal again. She wanted to write first, but the pen was taken immediately into her left hand, and Helen's spirit guided her to help it write: Welcome back.

What makes a house evil?

Her left hand was still.

What is wrong with your old home? And who would want to hurt you?

Innocent blood was shed.

Yours?

A long time before me.

What happened there?

Helen was silent.

Abigail wrote: *Why you? Why did it want you?*

I don't know.

Abigail closed the journal again. She wasn't going to get anywhere with the answers Helen was giving. What *did* Helen know? Abigail had a suspicion that there was something Helen was keeping from her, but how could she know for sure? How could she trust the spirit in the pen?

What if I'm the one that's wrong? What if she really needs my help... Abigail wondered. A couple tears erupted in her eyes, and she rubbed them away. She got up from her desk and went downstairs. She needed to get out of her room—needed to get out of her house and think. She went to the kitchen and to the sink, grabbing a newly washed plastic cup from the dishrack. As she put it under the faucet she was blinded; she dropped the cup and blocked her eyes from the abundant flare of gold light.

Abigail leaned on the counter, her face burning, heat pulsing through her body with every beat of her heart. She took deep breaths and rubbed her eyes until the pain went away. When she peeked back at the window, she saw that the curtain was shut, but the picture of the Virgin Mary on the windowsill was still glistening. Dull paper with yellowed edges that had curled in over time; there was no reason on earth for it to sparkle so profoundly, but there was no denying it had blinded Abigail momentarily. Gooseflesh rose on her arms. Abigail filled her cup but couldn't look at the picture directly.

Abigail's hand shook as she put the cup back under the running faucet. At that same moment the front door opened, and her father walked in and hugged her.

"I didn't know you were coming home for lunch."

"Yeah, I forgot to grab my lunchbox."

Dad opened the fridge and grabbed it from the top shelf, then went into the dining room. Abigail watched him from the thin wall that hardly separated the kitchen from the dining room. Her hands clenched into tight fists, and the crescents of her nails burrowed into the soft palm of her flesh. She wanted to see him dead.

I want to stab him in the chest.

Abigail remembered a couple nights ago standing at the side of her parents' bed, attempting to plunge the knife into her mother's side, and the split second of realization when she pulled the knife away. She had been so scared about it that she hadn't even told Beverly what happened.

Without thinking about it, Abigail turned to stand in front of the Navaja knife resting on two metal pieces in the wall above a holy candle with the image of Our Lady of Guadalupe on it. The handle was made of sleek obsidian wood.

"What did you do today, mija?" Dad was coming back into the kitchen.

"Uh, nothing, Dad."

He came into the kitchen and saw her fingers hovering over the knife. Dad picked it up off the wall and looked it over, then put it back down.

"All of your tios have one too. It's a reminder of where we come from. When I came here from Mexico, I wanted something to remember home by. It makes me think of the life I experienced growing up, and the better life I wanted you to have."

Dad filled a cup with water then went back into the dining room. Abigail lifted the knife.

Abigail hid the knife behind her back. She moved slowly and silently forward, her heart beating at a thousand miles a minute. A voice in her head—a whisper, like she had heard last night—was telling her to do it, to plunge it deep into his skull.

"Maybe we will go out to dinner tonight."

Abigail leaned against the wall to watch her father. The fingers on her left hand curled around the knife handle and never wanted to let go.

He looked over his shoulder. "Any place you want to go, querida?"

Abigail shook her head. "Not really. It's up to you."

"Maybe to the Del Carmen."

She was glad when he turned back to his lunch. She couldn't stand looking him in the eye.

A silent step forward. She raised the knife above her head in a white-knuckled grip.

Do it, bring it down on his head. He deserves it.

No he doesn't. I shouldn't be doing this…. Do I really want him dead? Do I really want to hurt him?

Abigail caught herself with the knife inches from his skull. She brought it back down and trembled. She was sobbing. Dad turned to her and stood up, his eyes locked on the knife, putting a hand on her shoulder.

"I—I need to be alone." Abigail tiptoed backwards.

"Abigail. Give me the knife."

Her vision was completely obscured with tears that fell fast. All at once she was moving without realizing it, hurrying up the stairs and to the bathroom. Dad's slamming footsteps chased after her; he was yelling her name endlessly, and slamming his fists on the locked door demanding she open up.

"Open the door."

"No."

"Now. Open this door right now."

"No."

"Abigail don't do it! What is wrong with you?"

"Nothing. Go away."

"Maldita." Her dad slammed the door with his shoulder. *"Abre la puerta."*

Abigail shivered. She shut her eyes and rubbed her pounding temples. Behind her eyelids all she saw was red—she was drowning again, plunging deeper...

And deeper...

And deeper...

Dizziness pushed lazily through her head. Her knees wobbled and as she took small steps to the edge of the tub, then climbed in. Chilled porcelain raised goosepimples on her arms.

"Abre la maldita puerta."

"No."

Gripped in coiling vines, being pulled down into a sea of red. Abigail was taken back to that day months ago. Her tub was a big expanse of raging behemoth waves keeping her from ever reaching the surface. Her hands clenched for her blade that had fallen into the tub, shadowed by scarlet storms.

Suddenly she was somewhere else. Not a tub but a big dark room full of water. There was a little wall dividing her from something hidden; she desperately wanted to know what was on the other side, but was completely frozen in place when the little tile above her was pushed into place, completely blocking out any and all light from the hiding place.

Abigail's father shouldered the door again and it cracked. She was brought out of her daydream and back into the bathroom.

She hugged herself, knife pressing against her chest and grasped so tightly in her hand that it would hurt to let go. Her cries were endless; she was hyperventilating and couldn't stop, and when the door was completely broken open a scream left from deep within her throat.

Her father ripped the knife from her hand, threw it on the floor, then grabbed both of her wrists, searching them for cuts, then he pulled her sleeves back to inspect her arms. There was nothing to find.

He helped her out of the tub and hugged her. Minutes ticked by. Abigail wanted to stop crying but she couldn't at all. She cried so much that it made her body ache—but her tears and soft screams kept coming.

"I wasn't going to hurt myself." Abigail cried. *"I wasn't."*

Dad was quiet for a while, looking for something to say. *"Tell me what you were doing with the knife."*

There was silence as she cried loudly. Dad patted her back.

"I don't know."

Dad was crying too. *"Abigail."*

"I... I don't know."

16

Everything about the room felt fake. The walls were bright white, the paintings hung on them were ugly abstract polka dots, the spines of the books on the little shelf had not been broken, and the couches were not comfortable at all. Worst of all was the smile on the therapist's face.

Abigail despised the smile on therapist Megan Murphy's face. And she despised being here with her parents, but they dragged her. She didn't need to be here—she didn't need therapy, but after her dad found her with the Navaja knife in the bathroom a few days ago, they decided to set this arrangement up: once every two weeks they'd be here in Megan's office.

Abigail was zoned out after a little while; most of the conversation so far had been between Megan and her parents. She didn't realize until halfway through Megan's sentence that Megan was addressing her.

"Your parents are very concerned about you and something you… something that happened."

Abigail sat silently.

"Can you tell me about what happened a few days ago with you and your father."

Abigail looked from Megan to her parents then back to Megan. "He found me with a knife in the tub."

"Can you remember what else you were doing that day?"

"I was in my room, um, writing. Writing in my journal. That's all."

"What kind of things were you writing?"

"Poetry."

"Can you tell me what else you did that day?"

"I don't want to talk about it."

"Of course you don't," Mom said. "Megan we tried talking to her, we really tried, and this is all we get. It's like talking *through* her. She had no answers for us the other day and she has nothing to say now. I think I am losing my mind."

Dad turned to Abigail. "We only want the truth, mija."

"I've told you the damn truth a hundred damn times." Abigail screamed so loud that her throat was instantly sore. *"I wasn't going to kill myself. That's never what I wanted to do. I don't know what I was doing with the knife."*

Mom, Dad, and Megan were all quiet.

Abigail looked at her feet. Tears streaked her vision. *"I never wanted to kill myself."* The words left her lips softly. *"I wasn't going to hurt myself."*

"Don't you dare raise your voice like that again."

Dad put his hand on Abigail's shoulder. "Then please explain to me what you were doing in the bathroom with the knife."

"I..."

"We want to help you."

"I just don't know. Something came over me."

"Yeah right," Mom said.

"Shut up."

"What did you just say?"

"I said shut up. Can't you see you're what's making me upset? Why can't anyone believe that I... that I wasn't going to cut myself again? I don't know what I was doing. Sometimes we do things and we don't even know why we do them."

"I can't believe you because I found you bleeding to death in the bathtub."

Abigail said nothing. Felt nothing. She continued to stare at her feet and pretend nothing in the room really existed. She was tired of hearing it. Nobody would ever understand how she felt. Nobody would ever understand what she was going through. They could see fifty more therapists and none of them would get it.

"How did that happen?" Megan asked.

Abigail decided not to answer.

"I went to check on Abigail," Mom said. "I had come from work, and my husband was not home yet because he was on a double shift. I thought Abby was asleep because she did not come down to say hello like she always does. So... I went upstairs." Mom paused because she was sobbing. "Water was seeping out under the door of the bathroom. I couldn't get the door open so I found the key in a drawer and came back."

She was shaking and still sobbing at the end of her brief recap of the story, and she gripped Abigail's left hand tight. Abigail wanted to hit her away but decided to stay still. Maybe if she shut up for long enough the whole thing would be over and they could go home—*And kill me,* Abigail thought, *the car ride home is going to be hell.*

"That couldn't be an accident, Abigail," Megan said.

Abigail said nothing.

"Abigail?" Megan said.

Abigail looked up. "Yes?"

"Your mother found you in the bathtub. That couldn't be an accident. How did you end up there with cuts on your wrist if you didn't intend to harm yourself? You can be honest here. If there's something you want to say you can say it."

"I don't know what came over me. I told you this."

"Did you ever hurt yourself before that day?"

"No, Megan."

"What did you want to do with the knife when your dad found you a few days ago?"

"I don't know what came over me. I don't know what I was going to do with the knife."

"How did you get that knife?"

"From the kitchen."

"Walk me through what happened."

"I grabbed the knife and I don't know, I ran. I don't know what I was doing."

"Would you say that happens often? Doing things and not knowing the reason behind them?"

"No," Abigail said, thinking that maybe deep down she really did want all these things. Maybe she did want to kill herself that day. Maybe she really did want to hurt Beverly when she pushed her in front of that oncoming car. Maybe she wanted to kill her mother the other night when she snuck into her parents' bedroom. Maybe she really did want to kill her father with the Navaja knife a few days ago...

"Abigail," Megan said, "you know your parents love you, right? And I want to help you. We can't help you if we don't know what's going on in your head. So can't you—"

"What do any of you want from me?"

Her parents and Megan were talking, but her thoughts drowned them out. Desperately Abigail wanted to scream: *I ran away with the knife because I was stopping myself from hurting* you.

Suddenly Mom's hands were on her. *"Abigail."*

"Huh?" Abigail had been zoned out and missed something.

"Wait in the—"

"Wait in the lobby," Megan said. "I would like a few minutes alone with your parents."

"Hector, Sofia, the questions I need to ask you two is not easy, but I'm required to ask these things to figure out a way to help you and your daughter. Did Abigail ever show signs before recently that she was suicidal?"

"None," Sofia said.

Hector shook his head. "Never."

"You two have always been close with your daughter?"

"We, well, we were always close, very close," Sofia said. "Attached at the hip, I guess you could say."

"She was never like this until months ago," Hector said. "Our little girl has changed, and we don't know why."

"So distant it's like she's not my baby anymore."

"What do you two think it could be?" Megan asked. "Did anything happen to her?"

"You heard it all, you tell us," Hector said.

"Well," Megan leaned forward at her desk, "the leading causes of suicide among girls of your daughter's age are drug use and problems at school or home. And also some sort of loss or rejection. Those kinds of things. Let me ask you this, how are Abigail's grades?"

"Abigail has always been a good student," Sofia said.

"That's good to hear. So how are her grades?"

Sofia and Hector exchanged a cautious look.

"Well it's summer right now, you know?" Hector said. "Uh…"

"She just finished her junior year and I haven't seen her report card recently."

"Mhmm." Megan wrote some notes down on her steno pad. "Does Abigail have a boyfriend?"

"No," Hector said, "Abigail hasn't had a boyfriend since ninth grade."

Sofia put her hand on Hector's arm. "Remember that nice Reyes boy?"

"Who's Bruno?" Megan asked.

Hector raised an eyebrow. "What's a Bruno?"

Megan wrote more. "Just a friend that Abigail's mentioned. I thought you might know."

"What did she say about him?" Hector asked.

"When we talked in private I asked her about her friends. She mentioned a girl named Beverly and that she just made a couple new friends named Cat and Bruno."

128

"I never met any Cat or any Bruno," Sofia said. "What else did she tell you?"

"That's it."

"Are you sure?"

"Is there anything either of you want to tell me? Something that could have happened to Abigail at home?"

"What does that mean?" Sofia said. "Hmm?"

"Have there been a lot of fights at home? Has anybody—and I'm not saying it's either of you—ever hit her or hurt her in some way?"

"If we knew anything like that," Hector said, "we would have no reason to come to you."

Abigail took the journal and pen out of her purse as she sat in the lobby waiting for her parents. There were a few other people waiting to be next. The lobby was as ugly and pretentious as Megan's office was—ugly paintings on bright white walls, outdated magazines on the little glass table at the center of the room.

Abigail wrote: *Everything was easier before I hurt myself. I want to go back to that time. God, Helen, it doesn't even feel real anymore. It feels like there was never a time where my life was actually normal.*

It'll get better, I promise. Nothing lasts forever.

Can I be honest with you? Well, I've been wondering now if I really did want to kill myself. It's difficult for me to talk about, but I feel I can be honest with you Helen. I'm disgusted with myself. I'm disgusted about everything. I don't feel like a person anymore. I don't know what I feel like.

I just spent all that time trying to convince my parents and our therapist that I didn't want to commit suicide, but what if I was trying to convince myself? I think deep down… killing myself is what I really wanted. I feel so sick because I think I really did want to hurt my mom and dad.

You didn't want to hurt them. Nor did you want to hurt yourself. I know you didn't. You're a good person. We all make mistakes, Abigail. Everybody makes mistakes.

Helen? Can I ask you something personal?

Anything.

What is it really like to be dead? Abigail was about to switch the pen to her left hand, but she saw her parents coming from Megan Murphy's office. She wrote: *I'll talk to you later, here come my parents.*

Abigail stared out the window of her father's Station Wagon, thinking, *I wish I never went with them to therapy. If they make me go another time, I don't know what I'll do. Dr. Murphy is so stupid—and what did she need to say to them in private that she couldn't say in front of me?*

They weren't headed for home, Abigail noticed, which was on Merrimac Lane, but rather headed for State Street. Her dad turned the car on State and then turned into St. Dymphna Catholic Church's parking lot.

"Ahhh... *fuck off.*"

Mom looked at her through the rearview mirror. "We haven't been to confession as a family since Easter. It wouldn't hurt any of us to clean the slate."

Dad pulled the emergency brake while Mom opened the door and stepped out. Abigail crossed her arms defiantly.

"Mija, do this for your mother. You heard what Dr. Murphy said. We need to do more things together as a family."

"I don't think she meant confessing my sins to our friendly neighborhood—"

Dad put his hand on her knee. "Work with me. Por favor."

Abigail rolled her eyes, uncrossing her arms, then reached for the door.

St. Dymphna Catholic Church brooded between tall trees anchored at its sides. Past the heavy oak doors were dozens of hushed empty pews showered in a soft glow from stained glass paintings. Shadows clung to the corners of the room.

The confessional booth was a big walnut structure with tight doors that were typically stuck on their hinges. Abigail pulled twice on the door until it opened. There was barely enough space inside for her to close the door behind herself. She sat awkwardly on the little corner seat built into the wall.

"May the Lord help you to confess your sins."

"Forgive me Father for I have sinned. It's been... Easter since my last confession. I hurt myself." Abigail's body went slack. "I can't understand why I did it."

Silence.

Father Gutierrez slid open the screen. "How are you today Abigail?" Abigail noticed his eyes darting to her arms. He was trying to catch a glimpse of her wrists but couldn't because of her long sleeves. Then he continued: "You've been in my thoughts since I heard about your troubles."

"I'm tired of talking about it." Abigail leaned forward with an exasperated, raised whisper. "Can we just sit here in silence for a few minutes to make my mom happy?"

"Do you mind if I pray for you?"

She slumped again. "Go for it."

"Dear Heavenly Father, I pray that You forgive Abigail and that—"

"Do you have to do it out loud?"

Father Gutierrez looked up from the rosary wrapped around his hands. Obediently he continued in silence as his lips silently whispered his prayers.

Abigail opened the confessional door and left it wide open so that whoever went in next wouldn't struggle to open it. Mom and Dad were in a pew nearby, and when they saw her, Mom stood up to be next for confessional. Without making eye contact, Abigail walked past her parents while grazing her fingertips against the end of pews.

"I'm walking."

17

THE PIECE OF CAKE crumbled before Beverly could finish setting it down in Cat's plate. Beverly apologized. Cat, picking the strawberries out of the frosting, told her that it was okay. Beverly instinctively looked at Cat's arm then looked away; it was a long sleeve so that her scars were hidden. Beverly still couldn't understand how somebody could hurt themselves willingly. The image of the harrowing scars was burned into her mind.

"Tell me again what this was called?"

"Tres leches cake. Do you like it? Abby's mom taught me how to make it when I was a kid and I fell in love with it."

"I don't remember the last time I had anything this good."

"Cat, do you really live up there at the Engstrom place? Do you have a family?"

"You like getting pretty personal don't you?"

"I don't want you to stay the night there is all. Why don't you stay here? My room is next to the guest room. Won't you spend the night?"

"I dunno. I… I don't think so."

"That house was freezing and I was there during the *daytime*."

"Yeah, I guess everyone has a family. I don't live with mine."

"Is that why you hurt yourself?"

"I already told you why I cut. Do you still not understand?"

"I guess I don't. But I want to help." Beverly frowned, putting her hands on her face and looking down at the dining room table. "I heard something awful about Abigail today. Would I be a bad friend for telling you this? Mr. Martinez found her in the bathroom with a knife."

When the tears started to swell in Beverly's eyes, Cat came around and gave her a hug. She said, "Abigail will be okay, don't worry."

"Don't do it, Cat."

"Don't do what?" Cat broke off the hug.

Beverly looked at Cat's sleeved arm again. "Don't cut yourself. Don't do that."

"Look, are you going to spend this whole night lecturing me? Is this what I'm in for if I stay in your guest room? What's next, you're gonna try and make me—"

"I just want what's best for you."

"You don't even know me."

"We're friends," Beverly said. "We're friends, aren't we?"

Cat rolled her eyes. "I think I know what this is. You couldn't fix Abigail and now you're trying to fix me. Are me and Abigail your little projects?"

"Not at all." Beverly hit her hand on the table. She was shaking and tears were falling.

"You need to chill out Beverly. Not everything is worth spilling tears over."

Beverly didn't know what to say.

Cat stood with her hands on her hips. "You're obviously hurt. Maybe I shouldn't have been blunt or whatever."

"It's okay," Beverly said, although Cat hadn't given much of an apology.

Cat sat down. "I'm not used to anyone being... so nice."

Beverly wiped the last of her tears away. "I'm sorry."

"You shouldn't be the one apologizing. Here I am in your home and I was rude."

"I said it was okay."

"I'll tell you about my family, but please. No more tears. I can't stand it when people cry all over the place."

"Uh-huh."

"I'll probably need liquor to talk about this." Cat walked over to the liquor cabinet. "Do you mind if I—hey, it's locked."

"My parents hide the key in their bedroom. They don't know that I know it's in the sleeve of one of their records. They've got all these awful records of awful music from when they were kids."

Beverly went to her parents' room and retrieved the key. Then she poured whisky for Cat and herself. They sat together at the table and drank.

"You've got siblings, Beverly?"

"Just Judy."

"Well I have three sisters and I'm the youngest. My oldest sister is a nurse. I don't know what the other two are doing but I know they're both college graduates in the medical field somewhere. My parents are in a happy marriage and have been together for a long time."

"Uh-huh?"

"I haven't spoken to any of them in eleven months."

Beverly nodded. This didn't seem like the type of story somebody needed alcohol for.

"All my sisters, all of them are hard workers, and they had good jobs and when they were in college had good grades. Admirable, I guess. In high school I had the choice to either be just like them or be myself, and I knew there must have been more to life than being... than being like my sisters. More to life than just being..."

"Just a regular person?"

"Right. They're so vanilla. So I didn't know what I wanted to do with my life, I wasn't lucky like you are Bev, you already know you want to be a baker and you're good at it. That's a rare thing in a person, to know what you want to do when you're young and to be good at it. All my sisters wanted to be in the medical field but what if that's not what I wanted to do? What if I wanted to do something different? I wanted to figure it out for myself."

"And did you end up figuring it out?"

"Do I look like I figured it out?" Cat paused but Beverly said nothing. For the first time ever, Beverly saw a tear in Cat's eye. "Three years ago, when I was sixteen, I told my parents I was studying for an exam with a friend, but I went to a party. There was a boy I liked, he was a charmer, and we went up to a stranger's bedroom, and a few weeks later I found out I was pregnant.

"I was terrified of telling him, and I was terrified of telling my parents, and I—I was scared of telling anyone." Cat couldn't look Beverly in the eye as she told the story. "I killed my baby. I've regretted it every day that's passed. Every single day I've thought about my baby, and what it would be like if I hadn't... done what I did. How could I ever live with myself?"

"I'm so sorry," Beverly said. It was the only thing she could think of. "I'm—I'm—"

"I didn't want to live anymore. I wanted to die so bad that I didn't even wait to be home alone, I tied a rope and put it around my throat but I chickened out because I'm a coward, Beverly, and I could kill my poor baby but I couldn't do it to myself. I must have stood there for an hour on that chair, with the rope around my neck, trying to talk myself into it. And in the end I wasn't brave enough.

"That's when I started to cut myself. That's why I'm like the way I am. That's why I ran away from home and that's why I won't revisit a loving family who I know would forgive me. I don't deserve any of it. I don't deserve a good home. I don't deserve a friend like you. I killed my little baby—I don't deserve anything."

"That's not true. You were a kid. You... you..."

"You understand what I did, don't you? I killed my baby."

"Yes, I understand. But people change. You've changed. You're not the person that you were back then."

"Everything changes but there are things you can't ever leave behind. Some things will be part of you forever."

"Cat?"

"Yes?"

"Did you ever have a vigil for your baby?"

The blinds were pulled back to reveal a full moon on a starry night. Beverly lit candles below the window in the guest room then spread the petals from a dozen roses two at a time into a circle. As she finished, Cat entered with a picture frame.

"I couldn't find the one you told me to get, so your mom gave me this one." Cat shut the door then kneeled next to her and put the frame in the center of the rose petals and candles.

The drawing was truly beautiful.

"Woah. Cat that's breathtaking. Is she a girl?"

"I always thought my baby would have been a girl."

Shadows projected from the candles and ran across the pretty drawing Cat had created. Beverly had no idea that Cat was so talented. The girl that Cat had drawn in the picture was picking up a flower by a stream of water. A bumblebee was resting on one of the petals.

"Why didn't you tell me you could draw? You could be a professional artist."

"I dunno. It never came up."

"I think we should say a prayer," Beverly said, then the two girls closed their eyes and bowed their heads. Long silent moments passed without anybody saying anything out loud.

"Do my prayers even matter?" Cat whispered. "After what I did?"

"Of course your prayers matter."

They were silent again, then Cat said, "I asked her to forgive me."

Beverly stood up, grabbed a prayer card from her dresser, then came back and read from it. "Lord God, Who has graciously chosen Saint Dymphna to be the patroness of those afflicted with mental and nervous disorders..." Beverly stopped reading and locked eyes with Cat who was laughing. "Sorry, it was the only prayer card I had. Abigail gave it to me."

"Figures."

Beverly put the card down next to Cat's framed drawing.

"Can she forgive me?" Cat wiped away sudden tears.

"Oh Cat." Beverly gave her a big hug, then pulled away and slid her hands to Cat's shoulders. "You may have killed her out of fear, but your love made her an angel."

Cat couldn't sleep. She was lying on her side in bed in Beverly's guest room when she heard glass cracking. First she looked up at the window, and when she saw that it was untouched, she stepped out of bed and went over to the dresser where moonlight flowed to the framed drawing of her unborn child. The glass was broken. Cat turned the frame around and pulled the drawing out, then folded it up and put it in her pocket.

Underneath the guest bed was Cat's cigar case. She brought it out, opened it, and rolled a joint. As she ran her thumb over the wheel of her new lighter, she decided against smoking in the house. She didn't want to get Beverly in trouble if her parents found out. It was better to smoke outside.

Cat didn't try tiptoeing. She walked through the silent house and out the front door. As soon as the door was closed she put the flame to the end of her joint and smoked it. Ashfall was fast asleep and she was the only person who was wandering around in the dark.

After walking a couple blocks, Cat sat on a bench at a park. She wondered if she should bother going back to Beverly's. Was she a burden? Could anybody actually care about her, despite what she had done to her baby? Cat shuddered with the night chills that brought out goosepimples.

Cat reached into her back pocket and brought out her drawing. She ripped it up into six or eight pieces then dropped them into the public waste bin.

Maybe Beverly was wrong about everything. Maybe God didn't hear my prayers. Maybe my prayers didn't count.

Cat was half a block away when she changed her mind.

It was a nice thing that Beverly did for me. And it was a good drawing of my baby girl. Maybe I am *a good artist. Maybe I* can *turn things around.*

Back at the public waste bin, Cat reached in and found a piece of her drawing. Her child's face was stained with blood. She reached in again and brought out a segment of her picture that had been a stream of water; it was also stained with blood. Under moonlight, Cat saw that blood trickled from a black bag and leaked onto the fragments of her artwork.

She puffed her joint then reached for the bag. Inside was a fetus. Its crooked arms were tangled and held up in defense of its stiff body as if it had been struggling. Its face was scrunched and its mouth was partly open. It hadn't been quick or painless.

Cat dropped the bag back into the trash can and her joint fell in too. She ran away into endless stretches of night.

18

ABIGAIL AND BEVERLY SAT at the table in Abigail's back yard eating ice cream before it melted over the edge of their waffle cones and over their fingers. One of Abigail's neighbors was lighting fireworks. It was a beautiful cloudless day.

"Remember on the first day of school last year when I asked Mrs. Thompson how far along she was, and she said she wasn't pregnant? She *hated me.* She made last year *hell.* All the right answers on my tests that she marked wrong on 'accident', *yeah right.*"

"She was so red when you asked. You might've made her cry."

"Gosh, come on, you're gonna make me feel so bad."

"It's okay, she probably forgot by now," Abigail said. "Remember in seventh grade when we had to go to the boys' locker room to grab the volleyballs, then the boys all came in to change so we ran and hid under the desk?"

Beverly's smile widened. "Funniest thing that ever happened to us."

"Remember when Judy would slam her fists on your bedroom door and scream at us because we locked her out of our sleepovers?"

"And she cried and made my parents grab the key and unlock the door." Beverly rolled her eyes. "What a crybaby."

"To be fair there was the time you not only locked her out of the room but out of the house."

"She was annoying."

"She was seven years old."

"And? She was still annoying. Hey, remember Abby when Judy tried to throw that ball at you but you moved, and it hit the side of my house then came back to hit her in the face?"

Abigail almost dropped her ice cream from laughing so hard. "Remember when you convinced her she was adopted? What did you say to her again?"

"I told her she was adopted because her hair was a little darker than mine, and I told her nobody knew who her real parents were because they left her at our doorstep one night."

"Why were we so mean to her?"

Beverly shrugged. "I dunno but it was funny. Hey do you want to go for a walk?"

"Where to? I don't know if my parents will let me."

"Just around. Maybe we can catch a movie or something. Is there anything playing that you want to see? You can pick out whichever movie you want. I'll even pay for the tickets and drinks or whatever you want to get."

The over the top niceness that Abigail was tired of was back. She should've known that Beverly acting normal wouldn't last long.

"Will my parents even let me?"

"Ask them. I'm sure they'll say yes because—uh, because, uh… just ask."

Because you're with me Beverly and I won't kill myself if you're there, is that what you were going to say? She thought.

Abigail stood up. "Okay. Be right back."

Mom and Dad were in the living room watching TV; a movie was playing. A preacher man had L-O-V-E written on his right hand, and H-A-T-E written on the left. He was telling two children about Cain and Abel.

"Mom? Dad?" Abigail said, fidgeting with a hangnail on her right hand. They both looked up at her without a word. "Me and Beverly are gonna go to the movies—uh, if it's fine with the two of you, I mean."

Mom and Dad looked at each other as if communicating telepathically. Abigail was surprised when her father said yes, and when her mother went across the room to find her purse and gave Abigail spending money. She thanked them then returned to Beverly outside.

"They said we could go."

"Awesome."

It was hardly five o'clock but the sky was already broadening with dark blues and a streak of bright orange. The girls walked under the shadows of prolific trees, bees hummed, and fireworks continued to paint the sky over her neighbor's house.

"It's—it's so pretty. Uh, don't you think—don't you think so?" Beverly said. She was tongue tied. Abigail had the idea that her friend was thinking something she was too nervous to say.

Abigail went ahead and said it: "You want to know about the therapy thing, don't you?"

Beverly stopped walking and Abigail took a step past her.

"Well that's what's on your mind, isn't it? Doesn't gossip spread faster than wind around here?"

"I was curious."

"Who told you?"

"Um…"

"Oh I guess it doesn't matter. It sucked."

The girls stopped standing still and walked again.

"What happened?"

"It sucked. All we did was yell."

"I'm sorry Abby. I-I just wish I knew how to help."

"You can't help me. Nobody can."

"Don't say things like that."

Abigail didn't say another word, and Beverly went quiet, and awkwardly they went down Burroughs Avenue completely ignoring each other. Abigail almost completely forgot where they were going until she saw the movie theater's neon sign.

There were benches all along the theater. People were walking in and out with popcorn and drinks, holding hands or locking arms with their dates, but nobody was sitting on any benches. Abigail went over and sat in the one that was furthest from the building.

"You go in, Bev. I'm not watching a movie."

"What? Why not?"

"I don't feel like it anymore."

"Look forget I asked about therapy. I shouldn't have asked."

"You must think I'm crazy."

"No—no I-I—"

"Go ahead, Bev. Ever since I told you about Helen's spirit being in the pen you've looked at me differently. I know you don't believe me about anything. I was so glad today that for just a few minutes you seemed like your old self again but you're not." Abigail shook her head. "You're not. You act like you need to baby me because I hurt myself."

"I believe you, I believe you."

"Oh shut the hell up Beverly I know you don't. You don't believe me about the pen, you don't believe me that I didn't want to kill myself, you don't believe me about—"

"What would it take to convince you?"

Abigail was stumped. "I don't know."

Abigail opened her purse and took out the pen with the plexiglass window and Helen's journal.

"You brought those things with you?"

"Last thing I need is for my parents to find what Helen and I have talked about." Abigail shifted through the pages until she found a blank one.

"Just how much, uh, have you been talking to her?" Beverly eyed the growing amount of pages that Abigail had to skip through.

"A lot, okay? She's nice to me and she needs our help. We need to go back to the house to find her body. We need to put her to rest."

Beverly grabbed the pen from Abigail and wrote down: *Hello.*

Then she put the pen in her left hand and held it there, but nothing happened. "Why isn't she writing back to me?"

"Let me try." Abigail grabbed the pen in her left hand. It wrote: Hello Beverly.

Beverly took the pen from Abigail without asking. She wrote: *What do you want from us? What do you want us to do?*

Abigail took the pen immediately from Beverly and wrote: Abigail already told you everything. I want to be at rest. Can't you help me Beverly?

Where are you?

I'm somewhere dark and cold and I can't move. I want a way out. Please help me find a way out. Come find me. Set me free.

"Abigail I don't like this, stop it."

Before Abigail could put the pen away, the pen led her left hand to write: I'm begging.

Beverly inched back a little bit. She opened her mouth then shut it.

"We need to do something," Abigail said, "and if you don't help me I'll do it by myself."

"Hey Cat."

Abigail turned. Cat was standing behind her. "Hello," Abigail said, and immediately her eyes went to Cat's hand where the blood fell and marked her.

Cat sat in the open space on Beverly's right. "Did you two already catch a movie?"

"No," Abigail said.

"We just got here," Beverly said. "Not sure what we're going to see."

"Bruno was supposed to meet me here and of course he's thirty minutes late."

"Maybe he's stuck in traffic or something," Beverly said. "I'm sure he'll show."

Cat shrugged. "I don't think so."

Abigail stood up. "I'm going to the washroom, I'll be right back. Bev pick something out while I'm gone."

"How is she?"

Beverly wanted to burst into tears. "I don't know what to think. She's all over the place. You should have seen what she just had me do. She just tried to convince me—again—that the spirit of a girl lives in her pen."

"Where's the pen?"

"In her purse."

"Can I see it?"

"What? I can't go in her purse, she'll be back any second."

Cat picked up Abigail's purse and opened it. The pen and journal were the first things on top. "This it?"

"Yes but put it away, let's just ask her when she comes back."

"I want to try it out."

"It won't work. Helen only writes back when Abigail does it."

Cat looked through the pages. "So you're saying this right here, this is Abigail's print, and this handwriting here is 'Helen's' cursive that Abigail writes with her left hand."

"Yeah."

"But when you try to contact 'Helen' with your own left hand it doesn't work."

"Uh-huh."

Cat pulled up her left sleeve to test the pen on her skin; Beverly shuddered at the sight of her scars. Cat took the pen in her right hand and held it to an open space on a page. "Okay Helen, my name is Catherine Blackwell. Nice to meet you. Spooky pen, do your stuff."

The pen didn't move.

"Abigail says you have to hold it in your left hand."

"Uh-huh. Must be a left-handed ghost." Cat rolled up her right sleeve, switched the pen to her left hand, and held the nib to her right forearm. More scars. "Wait a sec."

"Huh?"

Cat's eyes went wide, staring through Beverly.

"What's wrong?"

Her hands opened and dropped the journal and pen. Her body convulsed and she reached a desperate hand to Beverly; as Beverly reached for Cat's hand, Cat fell off the bench at Beverly's feet. A powerful scream fled Beverly's lips; she knelt at Cat's side and held her.

"Cat. Cat."

Cat pushed Beverly away then sat up and laughed. "You should have seen your face. *The pen speaks.*"

"That's not funny." Beverly picked up the pen and journal and put them away in Abigail's purse.

Cat opened her own purse and brought out a green mass market paperback titled *What Walks Unseen* by Dr. James McDowell. There was a piece of newspaper used for a bookmark already stuck between pages. She handed it to Beverly.

"I marked a section for you about a girl named Vanessa Gannon. Ever heard of her?"

"No. Who is she?"

"A possessed girl who disappeared. She claimed to see and hear things, and she self-harmed herself. Sound familiar? Like at all?"

"What?"

"Things will only get worse from here."

"What are you saying?"

"Abigail's told you she's heard things. She's told you she's seen things. She's contacting a 'spirit' that lives in this pen. Next is either a seizure or not being able to walk past a crucifix."

"Are you kidding me, Cat?"

"Read it. Then we'll talk."

Beverly opened the book up to the marked page. The headline on the newspaper that Cat had used as a bookmark read: **DR. JAMES MCDOWELL'S CORPSE FOUND IN THE 'ENGSTROM HOUSE!'**

Suddenly Abigail was back. "Hey sorry I took so long, you two wouldn't believe the line."

Cat stood up from the bench. "Enjoy the movie. I'll see you two around."

After the movie, Abigail and Beverly went on their way back to Abigail's house.

"Beverly? Can I tell you something?"

"Uh-huh. Anything."

"I really wasn't going to hurt myself when my father caught me with the knife. I was going to hurt *him*."

"You were *what?*"

"I don't know what came over me. I came down to say hello to him, he was coming home from work because he forgot his lunch, and I... I grabbed the knife." Tears ran in hot slants down Abigail's face. "I don't know what came over me, but I stopped myself at the last second."

"Did you tell him that? Did you tell your therapist?"

"You're the only one who knows."

Beverly hugged her. "It'll be all right, it'll be all right."

"No it won't. What's wrong with me? I hurt myself then I hurt you, I almost hurt my mom the other night, then I tried to hurt my dad."

"Abigail I know you don't want to cause anyone any harm."

"Then why am I doing this?"

"Well I… well… I think that you—"

"Right before my dad came home, Beverly, I was at the kitchen sink. We've got that old picture of the Virgin Mary, the one with the curled and yellowed corners. That little piece of paper shined so bright I couldn't look at it."

19

As soon as Bruno saw Cat come through the front door into the Engstrom house he kissed her. Cat wrapped her arms tight around Bruno and they fell to the couch together; he kissed her neck up and down, then laid down on his back and pulled her on top of him. He put his hands inside her shirt then pulled it off and momentarily she was blinded when her hair became tangled in the shirt and blocked her vision. With a quick swipe she moved her hair out from her eyes.

"Bruno." Cat pulled away from his kisses. "Where were you?"

"What are you talking about?"

"We had a date yesterday. Where were you? I was waiting around outside the theater…"

"Oh hell. Can we talk about this some other time?"

"When something comes up I don't just leave you guessing where I am or who I'm with or what I'm up to."

"Well damn Catherine I'm sorry I didn't show up at the theater." Bruno gave her another kiss. "Forget about yesterday, all right?"

"Don't you like me? For some other reason besides sex?" Cat put her shirt on. Bruno was silent. Then Cat said: "Were you seeing somebody else?"

Bruno stood up from the couch. "Are you kidding me? You think I was seeing someone else?"

"Then where were you? You know what, never mind. I don't care where you were."

"I'm the only person who gives a damn about you Cat."

"Yeah right. You don't give a damn about me or anything."

"Get the hell out of here," Bruno said. He watched Cat walk away to the door, then he added: "Better not cut too deep this time."

"Go screw yourself." Cat slammed the front door. Bruno was yelling something at her, but she couldn't hear what, nor did she care.

It was a pretty day in Ashfall; clear blue skies and golden sunshine as far as her eyes could see. Tall trees covered her in shade, and bees flew from zinnia to zinnia. It must have been pressing eighty degrees. The day was perfect. Besides Bruno and his comments. It hurt to think about his words, but she couldn't stop hearing what he said: *Try not to cut too deep this time.*

She came to Beverly's house. It was a nice big house with a big lawn, a curving path that had been newly cemented, an American flag blowing in the wind. Beverly must have had it all, Cat thought. No gigantic mistakes in her past like Cat had made. A lot of friends. A future that seemed bright. Arms without cuts all over them.

Cat opened the little gate and went up to the door. Before she could knock the door swung open and a startled Beverly gasped and stepped backwards.

"You look like you've seen a ghost."

"It's Abby, she just called and told me to come quick. It's an emergency."

"What emergency? Is she okay?"

"I don't know."

There was no answer at the Martinez residence when Beverly knocked, but the door was unlocked so she let herself and Cat inside. The first thing she noticed was a sudden gust of cold; goosepimples rose across her arms. A sick feeling twisted in her stomach.

Sobs were coming from upstairs.

Beverly led Cat through the house to the stairs. "Up here."

"I can't see it."

A few steps up, Cat whispered, "What can't she see?"

Beverly wasn't sure.

At the top of the stairs Beverly thought about turning around; she had a sense that things were out of joint.

The door to Abigail's room was open. Beverly and Cat stepped inside to find Abigail sitting up on her bed cross-legged, her face buried in her palms. She didn't notice at first that Beverly and Cat were there, not until Beverly accidentally said: "Here we go again."

"I can't see it."

Beverly sat next to Abigail while Cat stayed in the doorway. "What can't you see? Huh?"

"I can't see it I can't see it I can't look at it I can't see it at all."

Beverly grabbed Abigail by the shoulders. "Get a hold on yourself."

Abigail wiped her tears; her attention quickly diverted from Beverly to Cat then back to Beverly. Something twitched in Abigail's eye;

something flashed in them for less than a second. Beverly couldn't tell what it was.

"Tell us what you can't see."

Abigail pointed past Beverly without breaking eye contact. *"The picture of the Virgin Mary. The one inside my closet."*

Cat crept a few steps to the open closet door. There was a picture taped there, accompanied by a prayer. "Is this it?"

Abigail buried her face in her palms again. *"Uh-huh."*

Cat ripped it from the door, leaving behind a corner under the scrap of tape.

"Cat put it back," Beverly said. "Can't you see she's—"

"Look at it, Abigail." Cat sat next to Beverly, holding the picture out. "What do you mean you can't see it?"

Abigail's hands tremored as she slowly removed them from her face then lowered them. Her eyes were closed. Her mouth opened slightly, taking in short breaths, her jaw clattering, then it closed in a tight frown when she found the strength to open her eyes and look at Virgin Mary.

Her eyes rolled back in her head so that they were predominantly white, her irises the color of fallen leaves burrowing into the back of her skull. Abruptly Abigail raised her hands to block her vision from the picture as if blocking her eyes from the sun. Cat was in a trance unable to move, so Beverly pulled her hands away, unaware at first the screams she was hearing were her own.

"I can't look at it."

Cat raised the picture again. Beverly wanted to rip it from Cat's hands but she couldn't; she was too curious as she watched Abigail attempt to set her eyes on Virgin Mary. Abigail shifted from left to right, adjusting herself to face the picture, her eyes straining to repel from Virgin Mary like two resisting magnets.

Cat lowered the picture.

"Why can't I look at it?"

Beverly slowly approached the door. None of it felt real. It all felt as if she were trapped in a wicked dream—a wicked dream that she couldn't wake from. She was trapped in here. She wished she could wake up from the nightmare that imprisoned her.

"I'll be right back, Cat."

"Where are you going?"

In the hallway was a crucifix with a depiction of Jesus Christ on it wearing a crown of thorns. Beverly removed it carefully from the wall and came back to Abigail with it. Cat was at Abigail's side consoling her, telling her it would be okay.

"Can you look at this?"

"What is it?" Abigail asked, then reached out her hand before Beverly could answer and she snatched it.

Abigail's fingers curled around the crucifix in a grip so powerful that her veins popped. Beverly stepped backwards, her lips pulling into a fake hopeful smile. Abigail opened her eyes carefully, her brown irises studying Beverly's frightened face.

Then in one swift motion Abigail looked at the cross. The thing on the bed was no long Beverly's friend—was no longer Abigail Martinez. Abigail's eyes were changed suddenly, so that they were two completely black orbs, two eyes as black as the bottom of a well.

Terror spread further through Beverly with every beat of her hammering heart; her heart beat so loud that it drowned out Cat's screams. Cat jumped from the bed and backed into the wall near

Abigail's window. For a moment, the thought crossed Beverly's mind to run; to run out of here and never come back. Instead Beverly grabbed the cross to pull it away from Abigail's paws—misshapen paws with spiked fingernails that threatened to pierce Beverly's flesh.

When the crucifix was back with Beverly, Abigail's hands were normal again, and her eyes were back to brown. She laid on her back, whimpering, hands convulsing. All of a sudden Cat was running out of Abigail's room.

Beverly dropped the crucifix and ran after Cat. *"Come back here."*

"What?"

"We can't leave her like this."

"I told you there was something wrong with her."

"Then let's help her."

Cat was shaking and could not stop. She grabbed one hand over the other to try and hold them still. "What should we do?"

"Abby's parents have Holy Bibles and crucifixes all over the house. Grab anything with Jesus or Mary on it—hell even grab anything with the donkey."

Beverly found a Holy Bible in the kitchen, found two in the living room, found one in Mr. and Mrs. Martinez's bedroom, and found another in the room of dolls that Abigail's grandmother had left behind. Cat checked the guest room and a few other places, and somehow came up with a few Bibles of her own—Beverly wondered why a family needed so many of them; in all they had thirteen Holy Bibles total.

Together they also gathered seven candles in thick glass jars with depictions of Virgin Mary, Jesus Christ, and various saints in them.

There were also pictures of saints in little picture frames in the living room, and rosaries scattered throughout the house. They grabbed any crucifix they could find, and brought everything of any religious significance to Abigail's room.

Abigail was laying on her back, eyes completely shut, and Beverly checked to see that Abigail's hands were back to normal, and were no longer the monstrous paws they had previously been when she held the crucifix. With everything gathered on top of Abigail's desk, Beverly and Cat sorted through it and laid everything out. First Beverly placed all the Bibles around Abigail as Cat handed them to her; six on each side of the floor next to her bed to form a type of circle. Then they placed the small green Bible at the foot of her bed.

Next Cat handed Beverly pictures of saints, as well as a couple statues, that they put around the bed. Abigail writhed with pain with every new item that was placed around her; the room was getting colder as well, but Abigail seemed not to be phased by it.

Beverly grabbed the next picture from Cat's hands then gave it back to her. "That's her grandma."

"I don't know. I thought it was a saint."

"Yeah. The patron saint of creepy dolls. The guest bedroom across the hall is practically a shrine. Give me another one."

Cat handed Beverly a dreamcatcher. "Here."

"This isn't a religious thing, we can't use it."

"Well we need all the help we can get."

When everything was laid out, Abigail was very still and relaxed and seemed somewhat peaceful; she hadn't said one word to her friends, and her tears had dried. Beverly stood at the foot of the bed with Cat at her side. Beverly picked up the small Bible.

"Do you think she's better now?" Cat asked.

Abigail opened her eyes and they rolled back in her head, and her lips twisted into a sardonic smile. She hissed.

"Bev do something."

"What part do exorcists read?" Beverly opened the Holy Bible. "In the beginning God created the heaven and the earth. And the earth was without form, and void, and darkness was upon the face of the deep. And the spirit of God moved—"

"No, no, I think it's supposed to be Revelation." Cat ripped it from Beverly's hands, turned pages, and read: "The Revelation of Jesus Christ, which God gave unto—"

"Read whatever's marked with that red ribbon."

"And as he was yet a coming, the devil threw him down, and tare him."

"Shut up shut up shut up." Abigail convulsed on her bed, gasping for air, and Beverly rushed to her side and grabbed her arms.

"And Jesus rebuked the unclean spirit, and healed the child, and delivered him again to his father."

"Stop reading it. Stop reading it or I'll kill you."

"And they were all amazed at the might power of God."

Abigail shook so furiously that she fell from her bed and landed on Holy Bibles. Her eyes turned completely black then they shut, and Abigail's body went slack in Beverly's hands. And for a moment, she wondered if her friend was dead. By instinct Beverly's hands felt Abigail's wrist for a pulse; there was a beating. She was alive. She was breathing.

"Help me lift her up."

Cat assisted Beverly to put Abigail back on her bed.

They exchanged an undecided look then picked up the Holy Bibles and candles and pictures and returned them to their original places. After one last check on Abigail to be sure that she was breathing, the girls went outside and sat in the back yard at the little table. They were silent for some time, processing the things they had seen, and hoped that whatever they had just done had helped.

"How do I know if it worked?"

Cat shrugged without making eye contact. "If it didn't, there's another way. You still have that book I gave you?"

"Uh-huh."

"At the end of the chapter I marked there's listed all the steps for a ritual to exorcise a demon."

"I'm a senior in high school, I'm not an exorcist."

"And I'm a drop out but you can't deny what we did up there had some effect."

Beverly said nothing.

"Don't you want to save her?"

"I do."

"It's still early. Remember Vanessa Gannon? I told you the next thing was that she couldn't walk past a crucifix, now look at her. Who knows how long until she's completely taken over..."

"She's not possessed."

"Don't be stupid. Get ahead of it. You've got the blueprints all laid out in that book in your purse."

"Cat no."

"You saw her eyes go black, you saw her hands turn into—into—"

"There's got to be a reason."

"*She's talking to an imaginary friend all day in her journal, her eyes can't look at a cross, and if that demon inside of her kills her then her blood is on your hands.*"

20

"IT'S BEVERLY."

Abigail shifted. She was too cold but when she wrapped herself in her covers she was too hot. Everything was a haze. She tried to open her mouth and talk to her friend, but no words came out. The last thing she could remember from today was crying, calling Beverly on the phone, but she couldn't even remember what for.

Beverly was sobbing. For what? Abigail wished she could move, wished she could sit up, wished she could talk to her, but her body didn't respond to any command that her brain sent down. She was a shell; a hollow silhouette. She was nothing.

There was no telling when Beverly left; Abigail floated in and out of the haze, completely blinded, with no idea what was happening around her. For all she knew she was dead, and this was death, and death meant having no body she could move and no senses she could feel, only a vague consciousness that would get smaller and smaller until it shrunk away for good. Then there was only darkness—darkness forever and ever, floating away in permanent eternal darkness.

Little by little, glimpses of vision returned; fragments of broken light pierced the black veil and Abigail could find glimpses of her bedroom. With each glimpse of light there was hope. Abigail struggled to break through the haze, trying to awaken, but there was something keeping her from moving.

All was still, all was darkness, and a vague wisp of red light cracked her vision and brought forth an image of a demon with two horns turned inward on each other, and deeply red unblinking eyes. It reached two impossibly long arms out to her, its filthy prehensile claws threatening to rip her skin, and Abigail jolted awake and out of the haze.

It was six PM. Abigail tried to remember what had happened today. Was Beverly here? What had happened? Chills wrapped tightly around her as she tried to remember. Abigail rubbed her eyes and stepped out of her bed, then she went into the hallway.

"Beverly? Beverly are you still here?"

There were only the natural noises of her home in response; Abigail was all alone. She went back into her room and took a seat at her desk then opened Helen's journal.

She wrote: *What happened?*

Beverly and Cat came to see you. You don't remember? You weren't feeling well.

No I don't remember a thing.

Maybe it's better that way, Abigail. So that you couldn't hear the things they were saying about you.

What did they say about me?

Nasty things.

They wouldn't do that.

Beverly is a fake friend and Cat thinks you're crazy.

Abigail didn't know what to write back. She had the pen in her right hand, thinking, when suddenly it switched over to her left hand, and Helen guided it to say: I'm your only friend and you don't even like me.

But I do like you.

Then why won't you help me?

I'm scared. So damn scared.

There's nothing to be afraid of.

Helen I just can't be sure that you're real. How can I believe anything you're telling me? What if Cat's right and I am crazy? Helen I've been doing bad things. There has to be something very wrong with my head. I want it to stop.

If you go put my body to rest I promise you it'll all stop.

How would that make it stop?

Because this happened to me before.

It has?

I'm just like you and you're just like me. We're kindred spirits, Abigail. You and me, that's how it was meant to be.

The sun was setting early in Ashfall so that prodigious shadows stretched and covered the world. Ashfall was different under shadow; darkness changed everything. Stepping out from her home felt like stepping into another land; a place that was not real. Abigail was an alien. A stranger in a strange land. Ashfall was no longer Ashfall at night, but some place else.

Night felt alive. As if things were moving unseen, lurking behind every tree, creeping behind every shadow. Chills slithered on her back viciously like serpents. She bit her lip. Soon she was past her house, past her block, and so far away that she could not glimpse her home anymore when she looked back.

She had to help Helen.

She had to put Helen's body to rest.

Accompanied only by leaves drifting on dry gusts of wind, Abigail passed through empty streets to get to the farm. The last remnants of sunlight dwindled between heavy tree branches on her way; she was guided vaguely by its stream. When trees parted she saw that the moon was already in the sky, and that it was full.

Arriving at the base of the Engstrom place's hill, she stood motionless. Nervously Abigail thought, *There's no going back.*

Slowly she ascended, then put her hands on the gate and lifted the latch. She pulled the gate back and stepped through. It shut with the breeze behind her. Abigail turned to look at it quickly then looked back to the house; there was something different about seeing it up close, rather than seeing it from below at the farm.

Her heart pounded. This house was forbidden. Winds wrapped around her, thrusting her forward as if pushing her over the edge. And the closer she came to the house, the more it felt alive. Abigail stopped a short distance from the front door and looked at one of the dark windows; she waited for something to move, to pass by, but nothing did, and suddenly she had the urge to look away. Now she regretting coming here, but she had already crossed the threshold; wind pushed against her back and forced her closer to the door.

Abigail put her hand on the knob—it was freezing, despite the warmth of night—and she pulled her hand abruptly back as if pulling it back from an engulfing fire. Then she reached for it again, turned the knob, and opened the door. A depth of murky darkness; Abigail imagined a hand with long filthy nails reaching through to grab her hand.

Inside the house was blindingly dark, and Abigail felt herself guided to a candlestick that was on the center of the living room table. Next to the candlestick were dozens of matches spilled from a little red and blue box. Abigail picked one up and struck it on the strip on the side of the box, then lowered the flame to the wick.

The candlelight projected strange cavernous shadows against the walls. Abigail passed through the living room through the doorway; for once in her life she was unafraid of what strange things might be lurking in darkness. She felt so comfortable in this house, as if it were a place she had always belonged to.

Up ahead was the main spiraling stairway. It looked like something out of a castle. Abigail dragged her left hand on the archaic railing, and a primordial chill wrapped around her body. She didn't know where she was going, she was following a vague sense of familiarity; a strange sense that she had been here before, a strange sense that she was going to a place she had seen a hundred times already.

Abigail couldn't be sure, but it seemed that the higher she went in the house, the less her candle had any effect on the things around her. Darkness pressed in closer, blocking her little flicker of vision. She squinted, passing around cabinets and statues and turning corners, walking through wide empty halls with warmth in her heart.

She was happy to be back.

I've missed being here.

Her hand pulsed with a desire to write.

She ascended to the next floor, then sat down at the top steps and set the candle down on her left. She opened her purse to get Helen's Engstrom's journal and the pen. She wanted to write something down first, but Helen took the pen before Abigail could.

Welcome back.

Where now? I want to find you. Let's end this tonight.

I hear water rushing.

Where does water run in an abandoned house?

Abigail. There's somebody in here with us.

Who's with us?

They're in the house. They're here right now.

Abigail shut the journal and put it and the pen away in her purse. She held the candlestick between sweaty palms. She continued up on her ascent. At the fifth and final floor of Helen's former home, Abigail listened carefully for sounds of anybody else, but there were no footsteps, no whispers, nothing that would indicate another human being; there were only the expected noises of a home: wind whistling through a cracked window, the flutter of a curtain, disturbing quietness.

Abigail turned a corner and without thinking twice went up the dropdown stairs that were fully extended. The stairs creaked under every step. Nervously she peaked over the attic floor and saw that a window at the far end let in a glow of moonlight. She climbed further up until she was completely in the attic. It was void except for a stack of moldy boxes far on her right. In certain spaces were imprints on the floor that indicated shelves or dressers had once been here—and had been here for a while, until they were recently moved.

Furtively Abigail looked over her shoulder, and a stretch of light reached to the other side of the attic where dozens of corpses of dead animals were nailed into the wall. Dead eyes of cats and birds followed her around the room. Below them were long black candles with dried wax dripped over the edges, arranged in a certain pattern. Underneath the candles were things written in chalk, but Abigail didn't take the time to study them. Instead she ran.

She ran for the dropdown steps and her hand *burned* with the urge to write—Helen wanted to tell her something. Abigail ignored it. She ran through the unending house too frightened to think about Helen or think about anything—she needed to get out of here.

Something itched in the back of her skull; something she was trying to remember. Abigail didn't have time to think about what it meant. She gasped for air as she ran, desperately wanting to stop, but Helen had told her there was somebody else in the house, and she didn't want to meet them.

You've got to help Helen you're so close, the thought suddenly came to her. Then: *If I stay here any longer I'll end up like those corpses in the attic.*

Abigail came off the final step of the main spiraling stairway then went through the living room and screamed when the pale figure, translucent under the feeble light of her candle, bumped into her. Abigail thought she was supposed to pass straight through the ghost but she did not; she smacked into the figure then jolted back, pushing herself against a wall, another scream fleeing her lips and echoing in the normally silent living room.

The ghost screamed too.

Abigail was about to scream again when the ghost, who had fallen, said, "Calm down."

"Oh, it's you."

"Yes, it's me, it's Cat. Is Beverly with you?"

"No she isn't. Cat don't go up to the attic, there are corpses up there—hell don't go anywhere in this house at all."

"I practically live in that attic. It's like my second home. And I wouldn't necessarily call my roadkill corpses."

"Your roadkill?"

"I use them as sacrifices in my rituals. You saw the pentagrams and candles, right?"

"Right."

"Are you feeling better? I was there today with Beverly—at your house, I mean. Is she meeting you here?"

"No she's not."

Cat was silent.

"Helen told me what you said."

"What do you—what? Who's Helen?"

"Helen Engstrom. She died in this house. She's my friend."

"Abigail you're not feeling good. I need to take you back to your home. Let's go, come on." Cat stood up, then took the candlestick from Abigail and placed it on the table. "Ready? I was waiting for Bruno but I think if I'm a few minutes late he'll understand."

"I'm not going." Abigail didn't know where the words came from. "Not yet."

"What are you waiting for?"

Abigail's fingers on her left hand tightened into a fist. Abigail clenched her right hand around it to stop it from shaking. Nerves bloomed in her stomach and spread through her body. The room was suddenly too hot, and Abigail was struggling to breathe.

"Abigail?"

Abigail looked up at Cat. She wanted to say something but couldn't find words.

"Let's get you home."

Her hand trembled; her fingers stretched and stiffened.

Cat put a hand on Abigail's shoulder. "Abigail?"

Abigail's left arm rose and her fingers tightened around Cat's throat; Cat was petrified without a moment to think or understand what was happening. Her eyes rolled back as Abigail's grip fastened, her fingers pressing deeper.

Cat's hands weakly lifted to her throat and curled around Abigail's hand. It was useless. Abigail raised her arm and Cat was lifted a few inches from the ground. With one last pleading look, Cat's eyes begged Abigail for freedom.

"What am I doing?" Abigail said. It was like a sudden nightmare—she hadn't wanted to do it.

Abigail commanded her left hand to let go but it wouldn't move; it wasn't in her control. It seemed as if the control she had over her left arm ended at the shoulder, and something *Other* had inhabited it.

Her fingers pressed through Cat's throat until they completely crushed it and met inside. Blood ran hot over's Abigail's hand and down her wrist, threatening to stain her shirt. With a powerful jolt of terror she let go of Cat.

Abigail stumbled backwards away from the corpse. Blood was flowing. It couldn't have been real—it had to be a nightmare. At any moment she knew she'd wake up. At any moment the terror would end, her heart would stop rushing, she'd be able to breathe again.

Seconds ticked by. Nothing was changing. She was not awakening. The corpse wasn't disappearing. The blood wasn't vaporizing. Morning wasn't coming in an instant. Abigail wasn't in her bedroom. She was in the Engstrom mansion with Cat's dead body across from her—and the blood, oh God, the damn blood.

Helen can help you, she thought.

Immediately Abigail opened her purse but there was no time to pull out the journal—she had to dispose of the body. Cat had mentioned that she was going to meet Bruno here—how much time did she have until he would come?

Abigail dragged the body out of the room, holding Cat's left hand with her own, and in her right hand holding the candlestick. Any familiarity that the house once held was now gone; Abigail didn't know where she was going, she had no sense of direction, she only wanted to escape this nightmare. A dead body on her hands—how could she keep Bruno from finding it? Bruno, who goes up and down houses like these all day looking for things to sell. He'd never leave any stone unturned. Looking through all the rooms, how long until he found Cat's corpse? Five floors, plus an attic, plus a basement. Was any hiding place good enough?

A trail of blood on the floor. Abigail shivered. Was there any way to clean it up?

Abigail collapsed in a hallway and kneeled over Cat's dead body.

"This can't be happening. This can't be happening."

Maybe now she could wake up from the nightmare, she hoped. Maybe now it could be morning, maybe now she could move on with her life.

You're not dreaming. Do something.

She opened the nearest door to a steep stairway that led into an abyss that must have been the basement. Abigail dragged Cat down the steps and paused to breathe when she came to the very bottom of the stairs. The candle reflected light off a bright surface that winked light back into Abigail's eyes; she lifted a hand to her eyes, shielding them, then moved it away when her vision adjusted. It was a full-body mirror with a thick layer of dust shrouding it.

Abigail didn't think she even looked like herself anymore. None of this could be real—she looked at herself holding the hand of a dead girl with a crushed neck, a neck she herself had crushed. Abigail felt her mind slipping; she was going to go crazy if she didn't die from a heart attack first.

She dragged Cat across the basement. Could she hide her in the chest? No, that's something a salvager like Bruno would open right away. Could she leave her under a pile of boxes? No, that would be too obvious. Could she hide her in the walls? No, she had no way to fit Cat through the vents.

Abigail ditched the body in the middle of the basement because she was tired of carrying around the weight, and walked the perimeter of the basement with her candlestick held out ahead of her. Hot wax was dripping then instantly solidifying. The candle was rapidly getting smaller, and she didn't realize how close it was to being finished. She had to rush.

Below one of the windows she found a tile that was pulled back to reveal a little room—it was wholly blinding, but when Abigail kicked a tiny pebble down into the entrance she heard water. What could be down there? She sat down and dangled her feet in. How deep was it? Abigail had a sense it wasn't too far.

She stood up and retraced her steps back to Cat's body, except it was missing.

A piercing scream emerged from behind her lips.

Abigail shuddered, stepping away from Cat's empty place on the floor, when she stepped on something soft. She turned and let out another scream. Cat's corpse. Abigail had been wrong about where she thought she had left the body.

She dragged Cat to the open tile. She stripped Cat down to her underwear—she'd need the shirt and skirt for cleaning up the trail of blood. Then, with tears blocking out whatever short vision the candlelight brought her, Abigail threw Cat into the hole. She put the tile back in place. Nobody would ever know.

Abigail kneeled and said a prayer—it was quick, only a sentence, but it was all she had time for. *"God rest her soul."*

Back in the living room, Abigail scrubbed the blood with Cat's clothes. While it worked and cleaned up some of it, the rags weren't as effective alone as they would be with water. Abigail gulped. She knew where she could find some at.

Her heart beat even louder than any of her screams that had torn at the walls of her throat today. She had to go under the tile.

The basement was getting darker, and her candle was dwindling to its end, and she couldn't stop thinking about Cat's mention of Bruno. There was only one thing she could think of that made her relax even slightly, and that was the fact that Bruno had stood Cat up at the theater the other day—would he do that again tonight? Abigail hoped he would. She needed more time.

Abigail moved the tile then looked over her shoulder. She had the sense that she was not alone.

Then she sat on the entrance to the tile, dangling her feet, and had a sensation that somebody was going to grab her. But nobody was down there except for Cat. And Cat was dead.

Abigail hopped in; the jump was short, and she gripped the candlestick tightly, afraid that it might fall and she'd be wholly drenched in the unknown. Water filled the small room up to her ankle; what was this place?

She shivered. She knelt with the remains of Cat's clothes and rinsed them off. Then she nervously looked straight ahead; there was a strange sort of wall, and she had an obscure compulsion to look over the low edge of it and see what was on the other side. Her heart beat so furiously that it was in her throat. What terrors lurked just beyond her reach?

Abigail felt eyes on her; felt that if she turned around Cat would grab her. Where was her body? Abigail tiptoed, turning slightly, a scream already burrowing in her throat waiting for any reason to escape.

TAP! TAP!

Another scream burned her throat. Footsteps in this hideous underworld. Cat was alive, Cat was going to grab her, Cat was going to—

A quick scan of the room revealed nothing. Cat wasn't down here. Had she escaped after Abigail? Where was she?

Abigail was completely frozen.

On her right was a pipe in the wall, about eight inches thick. Must have been an overflow pipe, she guessed, if the room got too full with water. Light reflected from her candle to the water below that pipe, and slumped in the corner was Cat's corpse.

Tears burned her eyes again.

Abigail wished there was a ladder to climb out of the floor, but there wasn't. She almost panicked but it was a short way up. She set the candle down through the hole then grabbed the tiles tight with her wet fingers. As she pulled her body up she felt a bony hand wrap around her ankle.

"I'm sorry cat."

She kicked and squealed and water splashed against cavernously black walls, and soon Abigail realized there had been no hand. Nobody had grabbed her. She was fine. She was all alone in the house, and Cat was dead.

I killed her. I killed somebody.

Abigail went back to the living room to the blood stains. She fell on her knees and scrubbed. She had to clean all the blood from the living room, had to clean any that had tracked into the hallway, and had to clean any that might've spilled when she dragged Cat down the steps and into the basement. It was going to be a long night.

As Abigail finished cleaning the last of the blood from the basement stairs, she heard the front door slam. That was when she remembered her purse was on the couch—if Bruno noticed it, if he opened it and found her ID card or her journal and the things she talked about with Helen, it would be the end of her life. He'd know she had something to do with Cat's disappearance.

Suddenly everything went quiet. What was Bruno doing? Was he standing there looking through her purse? Was he already figuring out who was in the house, and who must have been the last person to see Cat alive? Abigail guts twisted—all that hard work, making the body disappear, all the cleanup, all to get caught anyways.

She thought about running away and screaming—if it was too late for her, if Bruno knew everything, then who cared if he saw her. But she couldn't bring herself to run just yet. She had to be for sure if Bruno knew anything yet, or if he were distracted with something else. What could he be doing up there?

Now, Abigail thought, if he figures it all out she would have to move away. She would have to run away to another state, change her identity, become a completely different person. There was no getting out of this. She had killed somebody. There was nothing she could say or do to convince anybody otherwise.

Footsteps again. Coming closer. Did he know where she was? How could he know? Was he going to come down here? Abigail's thoughts raced—none of this could really be happening. She just wanted to be home, wanted to be in her bed, wanted to be away from this madhouse, wanted to wake up and for the calendar to be turned back a year ago—wanted the calendar to be turned back to a time before she had ever met Helen or bought the pen and the journal.

Suddenly she was crying again. Guilt was eating her alive. She was shaking and taking shallow breaths. She collapsed at the bottom of the stairs. She was a murderer, she thought, she didn't deserve to get out of this alive. She didn't deserve to cover up Cat's death. She was a murderer. She was guilty.

Abigail tried to collect herself. *You didn't want to kill Cat. Something else made you do it.*

No, it was my decision to kill her. I can't keep blaming these choices on anybody else.

Abigail waited a few more moments in silence.

How long have I been here? Hours? What are Mom and Dad gonna think? Oh God, what if they called Bev and Bev didn't cover for me? I'm gonna be in so much trouble.

The footsteps were nearing the doorway.

CREEEAAAAK! CREEEEEEEEAAAK!

Abigail pressed a hand hard over her mouth to keep her scream in. Part of her wanted to run and hide, but the other part of her thought he would hear her and come straight down. When suddenly there was the sound of a door opening and closing, Abigail bolted up the stairs, made it to the living room, and grabbed her purse from the couch. As best she could tell, it had been untouched.

"Cat? That you?" Bruno's voice made Abigail shudder. Just hearing Cat's name alone chilled her.

Abigail headed for the front door, carried by tired legs; she was exhausted from hauling Cat's body around, from dumping her into the little room under the tiles, and tired from going in and out of that same room herself. Cleaning had been tiresome, but she had done a decent enough job so that Bruno might not even notice that the floor had been cleaned—it was dark enough for him not to see anything… but it was also dark enough so that Abigail might have missed a spot. And tomorrow, in daylight, Bruno might see a speck of blood…

She gulped.

She was fleeing past the gate when Bruno came out the front door. Her feet ached but she managed to push herself past a tree and pressed her body completely against it, lowering herself slowly, carefully, while Bruno passed her.

"Cat is that you? Cat? Cat, come on, get back here, what's the matter with you?"

I'm never going to survive this night, Abigail thought.

Bruno went down a little ways then returned up the slope of the hill, and Abigail waited until several minutes until after she heard the gate close to feel safe enough to continue throughout the night. It was so dark. What time was it? What were her parents thinking? She prayed they called Beverly, and she prayed Beverly covered for her.

Attached lastingly to her mind, and to her shut eyes, was the vision of Cat dead. The short reflection Abigail saw of herself in Cat's eyes; the final thing Cat had ever seen. Abigail shuddered. She saw Cat in pain, being choked by Abigail's own hand. Then she saw her in the corner of that room, tossed away like garbage into the corner. Then she saw the blood—it hadn't seemed like a lot of blood at first, and Abigail had been surprised how much there really was to clean.

Were her own clothes dirty? Stained? Abigail studied her clothes as best she could without any light, and when she came a few blocks away from the farm she was able to see it better from a streetlight. Abigail batted away dust that clung to her like wet leaves. Her feet were soaked—she wanted to get these drenched socks and shoes off immediately—and there was a little water on her shirt as well. Abigail couldn't find one drop of blood.

Abigail was a five minute walk away from home when she saw the police car. It drove past her in the opposite direction, and she let out a sigh of relief. Then the lights went on, and the siren, and the cop turned the car around and pulled up next to her.

"Shit."

She stayed completely still. The window rolled down and she recognized him—she didn't know his name, but she recognized him. He had talked to her parents a few months ago when she was recovering in the hospital.

"Get in the car."

Abigail's knees shook. She took tiny steps to the car. In the back seat, she nervously put her seatbelt on. She couldn't find a word to say to him.

"Is everything okay Abigail?"

She was silent still.

"Home life all right?"

"Yuh-yes, sir."

"Is there anything you want to tell me about? Most kids who go missing are running away from something, or have something to hide."

"No, sir."

"Because if you have something to say, you can go ahead and say it."

"No, sir."

"It's not good to hide things, Abigail."

"I'm not hide—I'm not hiding anything." Abigail strained to get her voice above a whisper.

"Just went for a walk?"

"Yes, sir."

The cop pulled up to her home. "Is there anything you want to tell me about before we get down?"

"Nuh-no, sir."

Mom and Dad were waiting for her at the front door, running down to the car before the police officer could even open his own door. When Abigail was out of the car, her parents were hugging her, and then they were yelling at her.

"Don't go nowhere without telling us ever again."

"I was going to have a heart attack. Beverly hadn't heard from you, nobody knew where you were. You are going to be grounded until you're thirty."

Gee, thanks Beverly, Abigail thought. *Thanks a lot.*

Across the hall was the upstairs bathroom; Abigail locked the door then put her pajamas on the closet shelf. She was still shaking, and nothing could get her body to stop. Warm water rattled through the shower pipes.

Abigail undressed, tossing her clothes into a corner, then stepped in. Steam filled the small room; Abigail shut her eyes and put her head under the stream of scalding water. She saw it all happen again: Cat, concerned, only trying to help her. Her left arm had been completely out of her control; it wrapped around Cat's throat and she begged it not to, but it wouldn't respond. Everything after that happened so fast—her fingers poking holes into Cat's throat, the blood that spilled, dragging the body, hiding it, then cleaning up before Bruno could find her... and almost running into Bruno...

Abigail shuddered.

She didn't want to cry again but her tears came anyways. She was surprised she still had any tears left.

I didn't want to hurt you, Cat. I didn't.

21

It WAS A BRIGHT hot day, and now and then clouds massed in front of the sun and projected cooling shadows over Ashfall and the woods behind her home, and Helen led her little brother Timothy between trees.

"Snake! Look Helen a snake in the water, snake in the water."

"Where? I don't see it?" Helen leaned over the little stream.

Timothy stepped closer to her side. "It's gone."

"There was no snake."

"Yes there was."

"Nuh-uh."

Timothy pushed her in then stepped back and laughed while she angrily climbed out. Her hands were turned into two furious fists. Timothy backed away and ran through the clearing, but Helen was older and faster than he was and closing in on him.

"You can't catch me you can't catch me."

"Oh yes I will. Timothy Engstrom I will bury you alive."

"You can't catch me you can't catch me."

Timothy ducked under a low branch and turned around a tree, then turned around another one, and realized he didn't completely recognize where he was in the woods; but that was all right because they weren't deep into it at all, and if he kept going straight he might come out the woods and into the back yard; and if he went the other way, there was a chance he might end up near the stream.

He went to his right, pacing slowly, being careful to avoid fallen branches or crisp leaves, taking small breaths of air. He tiptoed, ducked under another branch, moved slowly, and almost shouted when he came across a couple bees pollinating zinnias; he was deathly afraid of bees and their awful stings.

Home was in sight. He was a few steps away from the back yard. He looked over his shoulder furtively, and not a sign of his sister in sight. Still, he thought, he needed to be careful. He sneaked out of the woods, into the back yard, and ran up to the home. Opening the door, an angry hand wrapped around his, and Helen looked down at him with eyes that he did not completely recognize; eyes that weren't Helen's own.

She turned him so quick and so powerfully that he lost balance and slipped, and her grip on his arm sent a wave of warm pain through his body when it jolted. She dragged him back to the woods, ignoring the little path, and bumping him over protruding roots of trees and over thorny plants.

"I'm sorry Helen—that hurts."

She didn't say a word.

She dragged him past the stream. He thought she was going to dump him in for payback, but she kept on going. Timothy thought his arm was going to be pulled out of its socket, the way she was yanking him through the woods.

He tried to hit her with his other hand but couldn't reach. It was useless. And all cries and begging were pointless—Helen didn't say a word to him until after she dragged him over the rotting trunk of a tree that must have fallen a long time ago.

"Almost there."

"Where are you taking me?"

No answer.

Timothy shut his eyes, and when he opened, they were in a strange place that he could only describe as a dream: a twisted graveyard with a broken gate, and at a short distance the expanse of trees reached at them like twisted hellish arms. He hardly had time to look at the nearby graves when his arm was tugged on again, and Helen pulled him through rocky dirt to a little grave marked with a wooden cross. It was shallow and freshly dug.

"Let me go."

"You've been a bad boy Timothy. You know what happens to bad little boys?"

"Helen stop it. Stop stop please."

She shook her head and flashed a devious smile. "Bad little boys get buried deep deep down in the ground."

"Helen stop it I'm telling Mom."

"You'll never see Mother again."

"Stop."

Helen pushed him over the grave, knocking him into the crucifix and sending it down with him. Timothy held the cross close to his heart. He looked up and was instantly blinded when a shovelful of dirt landed on his face. He squirmed and wiped it away. Then, as he looked up, another shovelful came down. Helen was laughing at him. What was wrong with his big sister? She had never acted like this before. He hit the dirt away again and adjusted himself, sitting up, when another shovelful poured in and landed on the head.

It wasn't a far climb up; he was only three feet down, he guessed. If he stood up he could climb up, but he was scared of his sister, scared of the horrific hellish laughs that weren't her own, scared of the look he saw in her eyes, scared of who the thing wearing her skin was. It wasn't Helen in that body but a monster wearing her skin, he was sure.

The cross was still in his hands, and when Helen came into view and shoveled more dirt in, he raised it up when he blocked his face. Helen screamed. Timothy couldn't believe it: Helen staggered back shielding her face as if he were about to be the one to throw dirt on *her*. What did she think he was going to do? Throw the cross at her? He was confused, but understood that now was the time to get moving.

Timothy climbed from the pit. Helen was directly across from him on the ground, holding her hands up over eyes and shouting.

"It burns it burns it burns."

Timothy gulped. What burned? He didn't understand.

"Helen? What's…"

He stood at her right side with the cross dangling in his right hand. She pulled her hands back and looked at the cross; her eyes changed in a sudden terrifying moment from pretty blue eyes to predominantly white as they rolled back in her head.

"Throw that crucifix away."

Her eyes could never look directly at it; they were repelled.

Timothy dropped the cross and ran as fast as he could away from his sister.

He never looked back.

Helen dried her eyes. What was she doing here?

Chilling winds wrapped around her despite the warmth of the sun directly overhead. Somewhere far away there was a raven cawing. Warm tears were running over Helen's eyes; she wiped them and looked around. How long had she been here? The very last thing she remembered, she and Timothy were near the water, he said there was a snake…

"Timothy? Where are you?"

She stood up then she caught a vague glimpse of it out of her peripheral: the cross.

Her eyes couldn't look upon it; as much as she tried, her eyes were pulled in the other direction. Knots pulled tight in her stomach. Helen collapsed and cried. When she looked at any other thing in her field of vision—a grave, a tree branch, a cloud, her hands—she could see it perfectly. But when she turned her attention to the cross, her eyes rolled up into her head.

Back home, Helen went up and down looking for Timothy, until she found him in his bedroom laying on his bed in pain. He was a filthy mess covered in pounds and pounds of dirt, and there were thorns sticking to his clothes. When he saw her he cried.

"Keep away from me."

"Timothy what—"

"Keep away I said."

"I can't remember anything. What happened?"

Timothy hurried off his bed and walked around the perimeter of the room, then ran out the door. Helen watched him leave and run around a corner. What had happened that freaked him out so bad? Had he seen her eyes? Did he know she couldn't look upon the cross?

Helen went to find her father. She found him when she went outside and he came out of the wellhouse and locked the padlock. He was breathing heavy, wiping sweat from his forehead. Going back toward the wellhouse made her nervous after what happened with Julia Carter the other day.

"Father?"

"Yes, darling?"

"Father pray for me. I need you to pray for me."

He kissed her forehead. "I already pray for you each and every day."

She hugged him. "Thank you Father."

For the next week Timothy stayed completely away from Helen, and Helen noticed that her other siblings had kept a little bit of distance too. She had drawn suspicious looks from them, and sometimes out the corner of her eye noticed them whispering, and occasionally pointing at her. Helen would have given anything to know what they were saying.

Over the course of that week, Helen urged her parents to have Julia Carter over again, but Julia never came, even when her parents said that they delivered the message to Mr. and Mrs. Carter. Helen supposed she'd never see Julia again after the incident in the wellhouse.

She shuddered. The wellhouse, then the graveyard. There was something terribly wrong.

Helen was sitting alone in one of the bay windows, reading—or at least trying to focus on reading—when she heard her sisters play hide and seek a hall over. Joyce was counting. Agatha was supposed to go hide.

Helen had gotten stuck when helping Joyce out of the cistern when they played hide and seek last time—what hell that was...

...but she missed her sisters, missed playing with them. It wasn't right that they should ignore her for a week. It wasn't right that they should listen to Timothy and think bad things about her. Sometimes she saw them turning crosses and Holy Bibles away from her when she entered rooms.

Helen discretely followed Agatha down a hallway and saw her open a door that led to one of the servants' rooms. Helen opened the door after her and found Agatha under the bed, where she was trying to adjust the covers so that they'd drape down and hide any visible space where she was hiding.

"What are you doing in here?" Agatha crawled out from her hiding spot nervously.

"I wanted to see you." Helen took a step forward. "Agatha you've all been ignoring me. What's Timothy been telling you?"

"Why should Timothy tell me anything?"

"I'm your big sister don't lie to me."

"Why would I lie to you?"

"At dinner yesterday you were staring at me while Father said Grace. What did you think you were going to see, Agatha?"

"Helen stop this, this is foolish. Joyce and I are trying to play a game."

"I know where you can hide. A place where Joyce will never find you. Where no one will ever find you."

"Don't say things like that."

Everything moved so fast that it felt as though Helen were watching it happen rather than actually doing it; Agatha was held under Helen's left arm, and Helen put her hand under her sister's jaw to keep her from screaming. She forced her across the servant's room to the door and opened it.

Nobody was in the hallway. Great. Nobody to see what she was going to do.

Helen dragged her sister to the stairs, taking her back to the ground floor. It was one of the side stairways and not the main one that spiraled, so Helen didn't worry about getting caught—seldom did anybody use this stairway.

Nearby they heard Joyce calling for Agatha.

Helen smiled.

They came to the basement entryway and Agatha struggled and kicked and Helen really thought they were going to slip, but she shut the door with no problem and brought her sister down effortlessly.

"I don't know why you're so mean to your big sister. We're supposed to love each other."

Even in daytime, the basement was still dark. Helen felt chills as she approached the cistern.

"You remember hearing about this, right? When I was playing hide and seek with Joyce and had to bring her out of there. There's things down there in the dark waters you wouldn't believe. It rained two days ago, who knows how much is left in there. Want to find out?"

Agatha whimpered, shook her head side to side, pleading with tearful eyes.

For one brief second Helen couldn't figure out what had come over her, couldn't figure out why she was holding her little sister over the entrance to the cistern. Then, suddenly, she forced Agatha down face-first into the darkened abyss that was the cistern.

Agatha screamed for help. *"Let me out let me out."*

"Nuh-uh."

"Helen please let me out help me out of here."

Helen picked up the tile and pushed it in place, sealing her little sister off. "You stay down here until you think about what you've done."

22

BEVERLY HAD NOT HEARD from either Cat or Abigail since that strange day in Abigail's home, when Abigail couldn't look at the picture of Virgin Mary in her closet. About four days had passed without a word from either one of them.

Beverly dialed Abigail's number. Abigail didn't answer. She didn't have a number to dial for Cat.

What's going on with everybody? Beverly wondered.

She went by to see how Abigail was doing. Abigail answered the door with a frown. She was pale and her eyes were dismal.

"Hey. You feeling better?"

Abigail didn't say anything.

"I called yesterday, your mom answered and said you were sick in bed."

"I guess I'm okay."

Beverly stepped into the house. "Why don't you get ready? There's nothing like fresh air to make you feel better."

"I don't feel like going anywhere."

"It'll do you some good."

"I don't think so."

"What if I made you a blueberry pie? With vanilla ice cream on top?"

Abigail rolled her eyes. "You're not gonna stop until I'm dressed, aren't you?"

"Yep."

"I'll be right back."

Abigail went upstairs. Beverly sat on one of the couches in the living room. Maybe they'd stop by the Engstrom place to see if Cat were around.

Abigail could hardly breathe. She couldn't stop thinking about Cat. Couldn't stop thinking about the terrible things she had done to her, and the awful feeling of power it had given her. Everybody was right. Abigail was crazy. Everybody was right to treat her different after she hurt herself.

Abigail and Beverly were on their way to the store when they saw Cat smiling at them.

The poster was stapled crookedly into a wooden pole. Abigail restrained herself from screaming. Cat's familiar face was immortalized on that sheet of paper; Beverly had no idea, Abigail thought, that she was standing next to Cat's killer.

MISSING

HAVE YOU SEEN CATHERINE BLACKWELL?

AGE: 19, HAIR COLOR: BLACK, EYE COLOR: BLUE, HEIGHT: FIVE-FOOT-FIVE.

LAST SEEN AT THE NEON THEATER

Beverly traced the edge of the poster with her hand. "Oh no…"

Abigail wanted to say something heartfelt to Beverly, but she had nothing to say. What could she possibly say? '*These posters are useless because she's dead.*'?

Abigail's hands trembled. She wanted to tear down the poster and throw it away. It didn't help that when they came to street light a block later, an identical missing poster was taped to it. Cat was following Abigail no matter where she went.

Guilt was building up inside of Abigail. She felt sick. How long could she keep up the lie? How long could she keep it secret? How long until everybody knew what she had done to Cat? Abigail wanted to scream.

Beverly had turned deep red. "I tried to warn Cat about Bruno. We should stay away from him."

"Maybe her family doesn't know she's always up at the Engstrom place. Maybe Cat doesn't even know they think she's missing." The words felt disgusting coming off Abigail's lips. "Maybe they just don't know…"

The girls were quiet, watching the poster as if expecting it to change.

"Something is *not* right, Abby."

"How do you mean that?" Abigail couldn't look her friend in the eye.

"Because I know her better than you do. She wouldn't run away, that's not something she'd do. Something bad happened, I know it."

"So what if you knew her better than I did? Maybe her family doesn't know she's—maybe she doesn't even know she's, uh, she's miss—"

"I wonder if anyone knows she was seeing Bruno. Maybe we should go to the police."

"But Bruno wasn't even…"

"Bruno wasn't even what?"

Abigail walked away. "I'm sorry Beverly, I need to go home. I don't feel good."

"But Abby…"

Abigail never turned back, never said a word to Beverly who was calling after her as she walked away with nervousness eating her alive.

The police station was a tiny building. There was nobody to see inside, and everything was a mess; some walls were torn down, ground was dug up, and tools were thrown in piles near stacks of wood and sheets of metal.

There was no receptionist at the front desk. Beverly had a little look around, debating to go off into the building all on her own.

"Hello?"

No response.

"Is anybody here?"

Walking around the other side of the desk to the hallway entrance, Beverly saw that there was a little sign hanging. Somebody wrote in black marker: UNDER RENOVATIONS, SORRY FOR THE MESS.

As Beverly stepped into the hall, a washroom door opened and a woman her mother's age who must have ben the receptionist almost bumped into her.

"Oh hi, sorry. The whole day's slow then as soon as I step away we get swarmed with walk-ins."

"My name's Beverly. I need to talk to somebody about my friend. She's gone missing."

"Down the hall there, Miss Beverly." The receptionist pointed to a room about six or seven feet down. "I'll send somebody in."

The door took all of Beverly's strength to get open. It shut with a powerful slam behind her. She noticed there was no doorknob on the inside of the room, so she couldn't get out on her own if she wanted to. The room was bleak and grey and empty besides the table, two chairs, and the single bulb hanging in the ceiling.

Beverly stared at her reflection in the one way mirror and didn't recognize the person standing in front of her. The carefully crafted girl-next-door persona was gone and in its place was suddenly a worried, overreacting busy-body.

A dark shadow moved on the other side of the mirror, or was it the reflection of a shadow moving in the room over her shoulder?

A security camera mounted in a dark corner of the ceiling panned the room. Its glowing red eye seemed to broadcast a nefarious purpose. With no doorknob available to exit the interrogation room on her own, Beverly began to second guess her own good intentions.

If every Good Samaritan is made to feel like a criminal then it's no wonder the world at large had grown so dark and cold.

Beverly crossed her arms. It was chilly in the room despite the hot summer day. She wondered what could have happened to her friend. Beverly's guts were twisting. Quickly she wiped away a tear as the door opened and Officer Daniels walked in.

"Sorry about the room. We're remodeling and this was the only quiet place where we could get away." He removed a note from his shirt pocket, then searched around until he found a pen. "Now Beverly, tell me about your friend."

"Her name is Catherine Blackwell. The last time I saw her was four days ago at..." Beverly wondered if she should mention Abigail's house.

"The Neon Theater?"

"How did you know that?"

Officer Daniels found a paper in his shirt pocket—his pocket seemed to hold an endless supply of convenient objects—and unfolded it. He slid Cat's missing poster across the table as if he were pushing evidence toward a suspect. "Catherine Blackwell. This is her, right?"

"Where did you get that?"

"A young man brought it in and asked for our help. He didn't have much information for us so there was nothing we could do. Perhaps you could tell me something more about the victim?"

"Victim?"

"Just a slip of the tongue."

Beverly opened her purse and brought out a tissue to wipe her tears away with.

"Usually when somebody goes missing… it's somebody who's close to them. A friend. A family member. A boyfriend."

"Uh-huh."

"Seems she knew you and Bruno pretty well. Did she have any other close friends?"

"Well she somewhat was friends with my friend Abigail but they weren't very close."

"Do you mean Abigail Martinez?"

"Yeah—how did you know her?"

"I talked to her parents in the hospital a few months ago. And just the other day I brought her back home after she ran away. Do you know when Abigail might've seen Cat last?"

The day she ran away, Beverly thought. *That was the last day I saw Cat. Where did Abigail go that night? What was she doing?*

"The Neon Theater. Neither of us saw her after that."

Officer Daniels tapped his pen on the notepad. "So tell me everything you know, no matter how small. Anything can be helpful when a person disappears."

What could she clue Officer Daniels in on? Beverly realized she didn't know much about her friend at all. She knew Cat had three sisters but didn't know their names—didn't even know anything about Cat's family outside of the vague things Cat mentioned on the night of the vigil. Catherine was dating Bruno, and Officer Daniels must have already known that. And Officer Daniels already had a picture of Cat on the poster, and all the details about her height and eye color.

"I know she was sleeping in the Engstrom place, and she was seeing the boy who gave you that poster. His name's Bruno. She... Cat hurts herself. She cuts herself up and down her arms."

"Do you know Bruno well?"

Beverly shook her head. "No, but I never liked him because he was going in and out of that house, flipping stolen belongings and making money while Cat didn't have a single cent. She had to resort to sleeping in one of those cold rooms while he went home every night. If he loved her, wouldn't he have taken care of her?" Then Beverly thought, *But he cared about her enough to come down here and give them a missing persons poster that he made...*

"That boy was roughly your age, maybe a little older, Beverly. I imagine he was living at home. Would your parents adopt a total stranger for more than a weekend?"

Beverly frowned. "I can't speak for my parents. But *I* would take somebody in."

"Well then you're special. Most people aren't like you. What else do you know about Catherine?"

"Nothing," Beverly said. She thought about Cat alone in that old dark house, and thought about Abigail running away from home. Who even knew how long Abigail had been gone, and what could be done in that long span of time... and there were so many rooms where a corpse could be hidden in the Engstrom place... "I can't think of any enemies, I can't think of anything that was wrong with her. She was turn—"

"She was a cutter. Do you think she might have taken it too far?"

"God no. She was turning things around. She was going to change her life for the better. We had a talk about it. She was going to get her life on track… and now… Officer Daniels, can I ask you something?"

Officer Daniels nodded.

"How often do you see these things work out? I'm scared. I'm terrified that somebody might have hurt her. What are the odds she'll be found?"

"The odds lessen with each day that goes by, that much I can say. Look, I wish I could give you a twenty-year detective but it's a rookie who gets the missing drifter cases."

In that moment when she had been with Cat at the Engstrom place, and had her hand around her throat, all Abigail wanted was to see Cat's body rot. She wanted to watch Cat die. But why? Why had her body taken control and viciously murdered Cat?

A little idea was forming in her mind, but she did not want to admit it.

Abigail had ignored Helen for a week, but it became unbearable not to talk to her about it. She opened the journal and wrote: *Everybody was right about me. I'm crazy.*

Everybody who said that is also a little bit crazy.

And you're not real, Helen.

If you're crazy then how could you tell if I'm real or not?

I don't like you anymore.

Why did you kill her?

You wanted Cat dead. Why?

If I'm not real then it's you who wanted her dead.

You tricked me into going into that house. You tricked me that I was there before. You tricked me into believing your lies. You're not real Helen you're not real.

Why are you talking to me if I'm not real?

I don't know.

I'm the only friend you've got and don't forget that. If Beverly knew what you did to Cat then she'd turn you in to the police in a heartbeat. You think anyone else would keep your secrets like I have? Go ahead, blame me. What else is new?

What is wrong with me?

Nothing is wrong with you.

Don't say that.

I told you I'd help you. Won't you finally listen to me?

You can't help. Nobody can. I'm crazy. I should have…

You should have what, Abigail?

I should have cut deeper that day in the tub.

Abigail slammed the journal shut. She put it and the special pen away in her purse, then she got dressed. She couldn't believe she was gonna go crawling back to the church, but she was all out of ideas. She needed help desperately. Needed God. God was the only person who could get her out of this mess.

As she dressed—putting on the first clothes her hands touched when she opened her drawer—she couldn't figure out how she got to this point, couldn't figure out what was real or not. Was she even still Abigail Martinez? Was she even still in control of anything in her life? She had so many questions and no answers.

Cat slumped into the corner suddenly popped into her mind again. She couldn't shake the image; it clung to her like ivy. She didn't want to believe she had done it but she had—she had killed somebody and she couldn't get over it, couldn't shake the images in her head, couldn't shake the guilt, couldn't feel any more worthless than she did now.

She went downstairs and was about to leave when she suddenly went to the kitchen. She tried to look at the holy candle of Our Lady of Guadeloupe, but her eyes rolled back in her head every time she tried. That was okay though, she thought, as her left hand reached for the Navaja.

There was a shadow over St. Dymphna Catholic Church. Abigail didn't like it. Its trees swayed ominously as she entered the empty church. The tip of her Navaja scraped lightly across the end of each pew as she passed down the center aisle to the confessional booth.

The door opened without sticking.

Abigail sat silently in the booth.

"May the Lord help you to confess your sins," Father Gutierrez said.

"So. I've always wondered, what kind of sick pleasures do you take from putting kids in a box and forcing them to tell their secrets?"

There was a pause before Father Gutierrez responded. "The Sacrament of Reconciliation is one of the most unique and beautiful aspects of our faith. This teaching was a part of your own Confirmation."

"Save it for the faithful, Padre."

Father Gutierrez leaned closer to the divider between them. His eyes met Abigail's. Quickly he blurted: *"Dios te salve, Maria. Llena eres de gracia, el Señor es contigo."*

"I can't see Him, but I can see you fine Raul. Even through this flimsy screen." Abigail briefly raked the knife's tip across the screen's geometric pattern.

"Bendita tú eres entre todas las mujeres, y bendito es el fruto de tu vientre, Jesús."

"Do you wear a condom to confession, Father? I've seen you touch yourself in here as they tell you the salacious details of their lives. I know what goes on under those vestments."

"Santa María, Madre de Dios, ruega por nosotros, pecadores, ahora y en la hora de nuestra muerte. Amen"

Leaning back in the cramped space, Abigail put one foot up against the divider and swirled the tip of the Navaja around her nipple through her shirt. "You may be free of sin, but how will you escape all the vicarious pleasures you relish? How arousing is it to lock me in this cell and have me all to yourself, in a tiny space where you make all the rules?"

Abigail seductively ran her tongue along the sharpened edge of the blade and leaned forward to the screen where Father Gutierrez lustfully stared at her. He was shaking. From shame? From fear? Abigail leaned in close to the screen, the tip of her Navaja resting at the center of one of the geometric shapes within the divider screen.

"Are you touching yourself right now, Father?"

"Si." He whispered weakly, maintaining eye contact.

"Go in peace."

Abigail lunged the Navaja through the screen into the priest's eye socket. He convulsed, and blood gushed in big spurts. Just as quick, she withdrew her knife back into her compartment, and Father Gutierrez fell over dead.

Standing, she reached through the divider and pulled up a length of Father Gutierrez's chasuble to wipe the blade clean.

"Forgive me Father for I have sinned."

23

ABIGAIL WANTED TO CONFESS to Beverly all she had done, but every time the words came close to leaving her lips, she stopped herself from letting anything slip. It was killing Abigail to keep the secret inside about Cat, and now Father Gutierrez...

They were in Beverly's house at the dining room table, and Abigail couldn't look her friend in the eye. Beverly was bringing a blueberry pie out of the oven. Abigail's stomach was in so many knots that it made her sick to think about eating.

"I wanted to surprise you with this but I'm glad you came over. What did you want to talk about?"

Abigail noticed that Beverly wasn't looking directly at her either when she spoke. Abigail said, "Well it's about Cat."

Beverly was shaking as she set the pie on the table. For the first time that day, their eyes met. Abigail could tell that Beverly wanted to say something but was resisting.

Here it is, Abigail thought. *I need to come clean. Beverly knows.*

Abigail opened her mouth, and the words that left her lips didn't match at all to the words she had planned to say; it wasn't the confession she had rehearsed in the bathroom mirror that day. "Can we make copies of the poster?"

Beverly looked a little relieved. She let out a deep breath. "Uh... uh, yeah, that sounds like a good idea. We can pass them out."

Abigail looked away from Beverly. How could she live with this secret? How could she live with the terrible things she had done?

Beverly opened a cabinet and was shifting things around. Abigail's hands were shaking hard, and she squeezed them to keep herself still. None of this could be real—maybe she had died that day in the tub and all this was a sick unreality; a demented, twisted afterlife.

"I need to tell you something."

Beverly stood still, turning her attention slowly to Abigail. Beverly's blue eyes were full of worry.

"Never mind," Abigail said. "I can't tell you."

"Abigail you can tell me anything. *Anything.*"

"Forget I said anything."

"Don't do that to me, Abby." Beverly had come away from the cabinet without grabbing anything. She sat in the chair next to Abigail and grabbed her hand. "You're my best friend. There's nothing you could do that would make me love you any less."

"I love you too, Bev."

Beverly let go of Abigail's hand. She avoided looking directly at her as she asked, "Where did you go when you ran away?"

"I just needed to be alone."

"Okay," Beverly said. Abigail didn't like that Beverly had asked that—why had she brought it up so suddenly? Before Abigail could think too much about it, Beverly added suddenly: "I went to the police."

"Huh?" Abigail inched away. She trembled. Her lungs couldn't take another breath. Her heart was about to stop.

"I think Bruno did something to Cat. That's the only explanation."

"'Missing' from Ashfall. Who goes missing here? Just drop it. She isn't missing."

"Do you hear yourself? She's my—she's *our* friend."

"We hardly knew her."

"But she's missing. This is a big deal. Wouldn't you want somebody to look for your if you were missing?"

Abigail frowned. "What, um, what did the police say?"

"Nothing. And nothing I told them was of any use anyways. The officer shook my hand and hoped for the best." Beverly frowned. "Come with me. Let's go see if Cat's okay. I want to see if she's there and I'm not going in there alone."

"But I'm scared of that place." Abigail's breaths were shallow. It was a mistake to come here, and a mistake to try to confess. This was serious. Helen could be right—if Beverly knew what Abigail had done, she'd turn Abigail in to the police. And murder was the most serious crime there was. Her whole life would be ruined over something she never had wanted to do; something that she couldn't even explain why she did it. But none of that mattered—it didn't matter than Abigail hadn't wanted to hurt Cat, it didn't matter that she couldn't understand her actions. She was the reason Cat was dead. She was absolutely guilty; the thought made her shudder. It felt as if all of existence was deteriorating around her.

"Do this for me. Please. I need to know she's okay. I don't know where else to look or who else to talk about this with."

It was a bleak day with grey clouds gathering in the sky. Abigail had brought her umbrella with her when she left from her home to Beverly's in case it rained, and now she nervously carried it with her to the Engstrom place.

"Thanks again," Beverly said.

Abigail couldn't find words.

Together they ascended the hill.

Abigail was chilled when she saw that one of the missing persons posters was stapled to the tree nearest the Engstrom place.

Abigail moved ahead of Beverly and opened the gate, eyeing the darkened windows, praying nothing would happen or go wrong—praying that her mind would stop imagining Beverly putting together the pieces. But that look in Beverly's eyes today told Abigail that Beverly already knew something—or at least *suspected* something.

The house was so cold that Abigail could see her breath. She rubbed her arms together, holding a flashlight from Beverly's house unsteadily in her right hand, and Beverly stepped up to the archway that led from the living room into the rest of the house.

"Catherine? Cat? You... home?"

She's not going to hear you. She can't *hear you. She's dead. She's dead Beverly, what don't you understand?*

Abigail went to a mantelshelf and found a place that was devoid of any pictures or candles. An urge to write was burning in her hand, and she thought she'd see what Helen had to say, but Beverly stepped back in from around the archway and Abigail decided it was best not to do it unless she was completely alone.

"Do you really think she's here, Bev? Maybe we should be looking somewhere else."

"Where else would she be? Huh? Well maybe the cemetery."

"The cemetery? Why would she be at the cemetery?"

"Because when I first hung out with her, that's where we went."

"Oh, uh, okay."

"Let's have a look around."

"Where, well, where should we look?" Abigail said, switching the flashlight from her right hand to her left. "If she was here she would have heard you yelling her name."

"She sleeps upstairs. If she's up there she couldn't hear me calling from down here."

"She's not here."

"I bet Bruno is involved. Gosh even *thinking* about him gives me goosebumps. Please, we owe it to her. Do it for me. I promise I'll be quick."

Abigail frowned. There was no getting out of it. They had gone this far. "I'll do it for you."

As they went up the spiraling stairway, with Abigail shining the light against darkness that seemed to be chained in place and impenetrable, Abigail noticed something flash within the expanse of primordial blackness; something subliminal that vanished in a sudden glance.

Cat's eyes.

Cat watching her through mysterious winding hallways.

Abigail shuddered.

"It's Beverly, Cat. I'm here with Abigail. We're here to check on you. Cat, people think you're missing."

Abigail's hand curled tight around the flashlight. "She's not going to answer you."

"Huh?"

Before Abigail could answer, the door below them opened. The girls stood motionless, Abigail's eyes glued to Beverly's, and when the thudding footsteps echoed loudly through the living room, the girls still dared not move.

"Is it Bruno?" Beverly whispered to Abigail.

"Hello?" A gruff voice called.

In a sudden flash of panic and worry Abigail and Beverly ran up the stairs, passed through the next floor with only a small glimpse ahead of themselves through the archaic spread of dense shadows. Whoever was below them was chasing them up the spiraling staircase wordlessly.

The girls stopped next to a big cabinet and caught their breath. Abigail held Beverly's hand, squeezed hard in fear, and shut her eyes; she saw Cat's dead body slumped in the Wet Room. It was never going to leave her; the memory clung to her like ivy and was wrapping around her, choking her, coiling tighter, never ceasing.

"Abigail." Beverly whispered, tugging her arm and leading her in another direction.

The footsteps were coming their way.

Abigail and Beverly left the cabinet and turned a corner. Maybe they could hide in a room, Abigail thought, since there were so many rooms and there was no way on earth anybody was going to check them all. Abigail reached for the first door she saw, pulled it open, and forced Beverly through the door. She shut it, feeling for a lock, but there was no lock.

It was a closet. Maybe it had cleaning supplies in it once, but the cabinets were rusted and empty. It was viciously cold in here; flashes of chilling air pinched Abigail's skin. The footsteps of the stranger were still audible, moving nearer and nearer to the closet, but Abigail smiled—she and Beverly were safe in here away from the stranger who was out there searching for them.

Abigail wanted to whisper to Beverly and discuss their plan of escape, but she was worried about being too loud, and the nerves in her stomach were on fire because the stranger's footsteps were much louder now, and closer...

And closer...

And closer...

This is how I die, Abigail thought. *Locked in a closet with Beverly in the Engstrom place. Nobody will know where to look for us. Nobody will know where to find our bodies. We'll be corpses before we're found.*

And Abigail prayed God would have mercy on her soul when she died.

The closet was getting tighter and shrinking. Abigail couldn't breathe. Couldn't think. All she knew was she needed out of this house and bad. She needed to see the house burn to the ground. Needed to be free of its grip once and for all.

The footsteps died down, and Abigail let out a sigh of relief, then the door was pulled wide open with a burst of bright light momentarily blinding her; she turned her head and raised a hand, and through her fingers pieced together a mouth and a gun.

Her eyes adjusted. It was Officer Daniels.

He lowered the gun. "Get out of the closet."

Abigail and Beverly obeyed. They stood outside the closet and he shut the door. Abigail aimed the flashlight at the officer's feet, and his light was split between both of their faces. Abigail figured that at any moment he'd pull out his handcuffs and arrest her for Cat's murder.

"You girls shouldn't be here."

Abigail and Beverly looked at each other, then back to Officer Daniels.

"Look, I know you two are good girls, and you're worried about Catherine, but you should be staying out of trouble. Things haven't been quite right in Ashfall lately. Only a few days ago I was called in for one of the sickest murders this town's ever seen…. Did you two hear about Father Gutierrez?"

"Yes," Abigail said.

Beverly nodded.

"Maybe I should have a look around this place." Officer Daniels moved a few steps past the girls. "Do you two girls know any room in particular that Catherine might've slept in? Anywhere she might've kept her personal belongings?"

"She mentioned the attic, sir," Beverly said.

Officer Daniels led them back to the spiraling stairway. The girls trailed him as he went up. They passed the steps where Abigail had sat down and written to Helen only minutes before she killed Cat—it was all flooding back to her mind, every single feeling she had that day, every single noise she heard. It was eating away at her soul and she couldn't stand it anymore—she needed to come clean, needed to admit it, and her lips and tongue were ready to say the words, but she clenched her jaw shut as tight as it could go, grinding her teeth against each other.

On the fifth floor, Office Daniels said, "Which way to the attic? Either of you two know?"

"Right over there." Abigail pointed. "There's a dropdown."

Two halls over they found the dropdown stairs. Abigail knew that Cat's body wouldn't be up there, but she had a sick, sick feeling about going up. Officer Daniels shined his flashlight through the attic opening and called for Cat. There was no reply—of course there wouldn't be.

At first Abigail and Beverly stayed at the base of the dropdown, but when Officer Daniels disappeared through the entrance, they decided to go up too. Abigail flashed the light ahead of her but couldn't see Officer Daniels until she was fully through the opening in the floor and found him looking at the pentagram and candles on the ground and the roadkill Cat had nailed into the wall.

"Were you two doing this with her?"

"Nuh-no," Abigail said. "I didn't know about any of this."

"I've never seen this before in my life. I swear."

"How'd you know where the dropdown was?"

"Be-because—because Cat mentioned it."

Officer Daniels looked Abigail in the eye then Beverly. "What have you girls been messing with?"

"Nothing, we swear, sir."

"I think you two girls might know a little more than you're letting on."

Something behind officer Daniels moved and Abigail thought it might have been Cat's eyes again until she saw the feather fall, and knew that it was the bird's wing that had moved. Her mouth went dry and she inched closer to Beverly.

Officer Daniels moved a small step nearer. "Look, neither of you are in trouble. But I need to know what you know. It'll help us find your friend. Don't you want Catherine to come home?"

Abigail's attention was split between him and the dead birds and the dead cats. Something was wrong with them.

The wing twitched again.

Abigail was chilled. She felt the room getting colder.

Then one of the cats opened an eye, and Abigail staggered backwards. Her hands trembled and she dropped the flashlight; Beverly picked it up without a word.

"Something wrong, Abigail? Something you want to say?"

Abigail couldn't answer him.

A black cat opened its mouth and hissed, and all eyes in the room were turned to it. It hissed again, a gravelly hiss that was deep and guttural and sickening. The cat had tire tracks imprinted on its side where it had been split open and all its guts had poured through on a road somewhere. Its neck turned with a snap and its unnerving yellow eyes sparkled under the thin wisp of flashlight that came its way and passed over its face quickly, then passed over the black cat's acquaintances.

CAW! CAW! CAW!

Across the room hidden by a lush shadow a raven was hung by its throat on a string. Its wings had been twisted and mangled and its beak was chipped and split, but suddenly it was alive and angry, rocking furiously on its string until it was broken loose and swept across the room. It landed at the center of the pentagram in front of the roadkill that had all been reanimated; they were all hissing, cawing, straining against the nails. In a sudden flash the candles were lit.

Beverly was the first one to run, then Office Daniels grabbed Abigail's arm and shoved her to get her moving. She rushed to leave the attic, catching one final glimpse of the animals breaking free of the nails, squirming free and leaving little trails of flesh behind.

On the fifth floor everybody ran, but there were footsteps behind them, and the soft growl of an invisible monster. Abigail forgot which way they had come from—couldn't even remember what was right and what was left, were they on the first floor or twentieth floor? Everything was a blur, and nothing was real outside of the dizzying footfalls.

The growl of the monster was becoming louder and wilder, ringing through the empty halls of the dreaded house, and its pouncing steps were catching up with them. Abigail imagined that at any moment prodigious claws would sink into the soft skin of her back and—

Don't think about it.

It seemed like a year until they found their way back to the spiraling stairway. Before they could descend, the monster roared and came into view; both flashlights turned to uncover the beast. All the pieces of the dead animals had converged into one misshapen beast; it was like a bear in its outline, with the beak of a raven and the skin of dead cats. Globs of flesh were merging and shifting and falling, leaving behind a slimy trail of guts. It raised its claws high and let out a great scream, then ran on all fours at Officer Daniels; Officer

Daniels drew his gun and a bullet zipped through the behemoth in an instant.

In total he put four bullets through the thing, and none of them had any effect.

The monster grabbed Officer Daniels in two gigantic paws and lifted him high above a gaping mouth with rows of teeth ready to devour. Officer Daniels slid an arm free and aimed his gun at the beast, shooting it through the eye; a mist of blood was released in every direction and covered Officer Daniels, and the great beast let go in a natural instinct to wipe its eyes from the blood.

Officer Daniels screamed at the girls to run, and they moved backwards down the steps, watching the monster run straight for them. Officer Daniels emptied his final bullets into the monster, getting it in the chest, but there was no reaction—it slammed its claws into Officer Daniels, and with the last flash of his life, Officer Daniels let out a hideous scream that was so deafening Abigail couldn't hear her own steps or her own cries.

One final glimpse of the monster; it receded into shadows with Officer Daniels in its paws.

Abigail and Beverly went out the front door; black birds were massing in the sky over the Engstrom place. Abigail needed desperately to stop running and take a breath, desperately needed to rest her strained legs, but the girls didn't stop, no matter how far away they were from the Engstrom place and the farm.

Raindrops fell, and Abigail realized that somewhere along the way, she forgot her umbrella in that sickening house.

24

Helen picked up the pen her father made, opened her journal, then the door opened. It was Agatha, weeping, as pale as a plucked flower. She was shaking. Helen rushed to Agatha and put her hands on Agatha's shoulders.

"Agatha? What's wrong?"

"Timothy fell down the well."

"Where's Father? Where's Mother?"

"Mother and Father went into town this morning and have not returned. I need your help. Hurry."

The wellhouse sulked as if an unclean spirit lingered within it. There was something unusual about it today, something that Helen could not place, but she had no time to try and figure it out. She hurried to its door and swung it open. Inside, Joyce and Thaddeus were looking over the side of the well, panicked, never looking up to acknowledge Helen in her rush.

Peeking over the edge she saw nothing.

"Timothy?" She said, then turned her attention back to Joyce and Thaddeus. "He's not in there."

There was a noise behind her; Agatha shut and locked the doors. Timothy was next to her, lifting a Holy Bible above his head. Helen shielded her eyes from the powerful shine that only seemed to bother her and not the others, as if the others could not see it shining like she could. She stumbled backwards and fell.

"Get it away from me." Helen didn't recognize her voice that was full of menace; the voice wasn't her own but came from her lips. *"Get it away or I'll kill you."*

She shut her eyes; Thaddeus and Joyce were behind her, wrapping a thick rope around her hands and tying the other end of the rope around the base of the wellhouse seats. In a split second they were in front of her, wrapping rope around her legs as well. She strained to loosen herself, but all power was being drained from her body as long as that blinding Holy Bible remained above her.

Helen's eyes were rolled back in her head and darkening.

Agatha double checked with Joyce and Thaddeus that the ropes were on tight, and Timothy held the Holy Bible over Helen's squirming body. Suddenly there was a chill in the room and Agatha saw her breath. A shadow passed over the sun so that shade was spread throughout the wellhouse, and a shadow of gloom lingered over Helen.

When the sun came back, the chills didn't end. Agatha shivered. Thaddeus opened the cabinet across from them and pulled out the blue bottle and brought it to Agatha; Agatha unscrewed the lid with an unsteady hand. Then Thaddeus brought out wooden crosses—crosses he had found around the house—and distributed them so that each sibling had one.

All the Engstrom children gathered around Helen with their crosses raised. Agatha splashed Holy Water on her restrained sister, and Helen let out a scream that pierced the chilling air of the wellhouse violently.

Helen's lips curled into an unkind smile. *"Rot in hell."*

Agatha splashed Holy Water again. *"Get out of my sister's body."*

"The whore is mine."

With all their crosses raised, the siblings said together: *"Our Father, who art in Heaven, hallowed be Thy Name."*

Helen hissed.

"Thy Kingdom come, Thy Will be done—"

"Each of you will rot in a shallow grave." The creature that had once been Helen pulled against the ropes.

"On earth as it is in Heaven. Give us this day our daily—"

A gust of cold air blasted through the wellhouse. The siblings suddenly shut up. Helen was rising off the floor. Agatha was transfixed; her sister rose six inches off the ground, then a foot—the highest the restraining ropes would let her go—and she hovered in place, screaming, *"Each of you will burn in hell, each of you will melt in the lake of fire."*

A chill slithered up Agatha's back and shook her; the Holy Water slightly slipped in her hands and she clasped it tight. She sprinkled more Holy Water on the floating creature that had once been her sister, and puffs of smoke uprose when it made contact with her reddening skin.

"*Give us this day our daily bread,*" Agatha said. Then her siblings repeated it all at once, lifting up their crosses higher.

Helen descended. "*Satan will make slaves of all of you.*"

"*And forgive us our trespasses, as we forgive those who trespass against us.*"

Helen shook violently; her head slammed into the floor. Her arms strained so powerfully against the ropes that her skin was cut and she was bleeding. Agatha was terrified of what Helen might do if she broke free of those ropes—that was all that separated Agatha and her siblings from certain death.

"*And lead us not into temptation—*"

"*Agatha you'll be the first to die.*"

"*But deliver us from evil. Amen.*"

"*Rot in hell.*"

The siblings moved closer, pressing their crosses downward toward Helen's body. Helen pulled hard on the rope and it came free; Thaddeus dropped his cross and rushed to tie the rope back to the base of the wellhouse seat.

Timothy opened the Holy Bible and read, "But Paul, being grieved, turned and said to the spirit, I command thee in the name of Jesus Christ to come out of her. And he came out the same hour."

"*If you couldn't save John, Timothy, what makes you think you can save your sister?*"

Timothy stepped backwards, tears dripping from his eyes.

"*You should have been watching him, Timothy. Father said so.*"

"*Shut up.*"

"*John's in hell because you didn't watch him.*"

"*I can't do this.*"

Agatha shook him by the shoulders. *"Keep reading, we need to save our sister."*

"Your sister is mine, the filthy whore is mine."

"Don't listen to it, Timothy." Then Agatha turned her attention to Joyce and Thaddeus, who were kneeling on the ground at Helen's sides, lifting their crosses over her face. *"None of you listen to it."*

"Untie me and Satan may spare you."

"Don't listen."

Joyce set down her cross, then her hands hovered over the knots that bound Helen. *"I don't want to go to hell."*

"Joyce you're going to ruin it. Pick up that cross."

Joyce reluctantly picked it up again.

"Now read it, Timothy."

"John died because of you, Timothy. Now he's rotting in hell for eternity."

Agatha joined Joyce at her side, and held her cross over Helen's face. Helen's eyes shut at once.

"The Lord is my shepherd, I shall not want." Timothy read. "He maketh me to lie down in green pastures: he leadeth me beside the still waters. He restoreth my soul: he leadeth me in the paths of righteousness for his name's sake. Yea, though I walk through the valley of the shadow of death, I will fear no evil: for thou art with me; thy rod and thy staff they comfort me."

The creature that was once Helen hovered again inches from the floor, and Agatha and Joyce and Thaddeus backed away. Timothy was frozen in place, all color drained from his cheeks. His sullen eyes dripped tears again. Helen violently pulled on the ropes midair, bobbing with each pull. The ropes miraculously stayed in place; Thaddeus must have tied a good knot.

"I'm gonna dig a grave of brimstone for you Timothy, right next to John's so you can hear him screaming forever and ever," Helen said. She opened her mouth and the painful cries of a child emerged despite the smile that played on her face. They were John's screams.

"Don't listen." Agatha burst into rapid tears. *"Please don't listen, it's not our sister, it's not her. It's not our sister talking, it's a liar."*

Timothy was shaking; Agatha thought he was going to faint. Ignoring the hovering creature, Timothy finished the passage from the book of Psalms: "Thou preparest a table before me in the presence of mine enemies: thou anointest my head with oil; my cup runneth over—"

"I'll drag every last one of you into the lake of fire."

"Surely goodness and mercy shall follow me all the days of my life: and I will dwell in the house of the Lord for ever."

Agatha unscrewed the cap on her bottle of Holy Water, and wound her hand back to sprinkle more when Joyce put her hands on her and stopped her from bringing it down on the thing that had once been Helen.

"Don't hurt her."

"This is how we save her."

"When I get out of here, Agatha, I'm gonna tie you up by this rope and hang you from the stairway for all to see."

"You are not Helen." Agatha pulled her arm free from Joyce and brought the Holy Water down on the creature's skin. Smoke uprose again. *"You are not my sister."*

"I was the one who killed John. I was the one who pushed him from the roof."

Agatha sprayed her again. "That's not true, Helen was with me when that happened."

"I killed him and I'll kill every one of you."

Timothy read more: "And Jesus rebuked him, saying, Hold thy peace, and come out of him. And when the unclean spirit had torn him, and cried with a loud voice, he came out of him. And they were all amazed, insomuch that they questioned among themselves, saying, What thing is this? what new doctrine *is* this? for with authority commandeth he even the unclean spirits, and they do obey him."

The room was abruptly colder—so much so that Agatha thought she felt frost forming over her skin.

Helen violently hovered and fell, hovered and fell, beating her arms and legs up and down, and a thin mist of blood came from her mouth. Helen hissed and screamed wickedly. Agatha grabbed Joyce by the hand and pulled her away. Thaddeus stepped away too and collapsed in one of the wellhouse seats. But not Timothy. Timothy came forward from across the wellhouse where he had been reading the Holy Bible and set the Bible on Helen's chest. Immediately the creature sank back to the ground, no longer hovering whatsoever, and violently shook, trying to shake the Bible from its body, but the Holy Bible did not budge.

"Come closer," Timothy said to his siblings.

They were hesitant. They exchanged doubtful looks. Then they obeyed and came closer. Timothy and Thaddeus on one side, Agatha and Joyce on the other. All their wooden crosses were held out toward Helen.

"I charge you, Satan," Timothy said, "enemy of human salvation!"

Agatha clutched tightly to her cross in response to Timothy's admonitions.

"I charge you, Satan, prince of this world!"

Helen's wrists twisted in her restraints.

"I charge you, Satan, deceiver of the human race! Acknowledge the justice and goodness of God the Father, who by His righteous judgement has damned your pride and envy. Depart from this servant of God, Helen, whom the Lord has made in His own image, adorned with His gifts, and adopted as a daughter of His mercy."

A strong ray of sun came in from the window behind Agatha, but the chills never left the room. She could still see her own breath. And she thought, *We're never going to get out of this, we're never going to save her. Oh my God what's going to happen to us? What are we going to do? God help us.*

"Helen I know you're in there," Agatha said. "Helen talk to me."

Helen's eyes opened and flashed completely black, then they were back to being rich blue eyes.

"Help me." Helen shook, and her eyes shut, and her voice changed into a guttural hiss: *"She is mine."*

The ceiling of the wellhouse cracked and a spray of dust descended on the ritual. The cabinet where the siblings had hidden the Holy Water and crosses swung open and banged shut repeatedly. All the children were frozen, continuing to hold hands, with no idea what to do or say.

"Helen will rot in hell with John."

"Acknowledge the power and strength of Jesus Christ, who defeated you in the desert, who overcame you in the garden, despoiled you

on the Cross, and, rising from the tomb, transferred your spoils into the kingdom of light—"

"I'm the devil and I've prepared a grave for each of you in my kingdom."

"Depart from this creature Helen, whom Christ by His death purchased with His blood."

The creature that they surrounded twisted violently against its restraints, and at once it came free. The Holy Bible still weighed the monster down. Everybody let go of each other's hands, and Agatha was the first to pick up her cross and hold it between her and the monster—the monster whose eyes flashed black again, and whose hands were not hands anymore but vicious paws with pointed claws. The features of Helen's face were suddenly changing so that she wasn't Helen anymore, but becoming something *Other*. A contorted face with misshapen eyes and irregular features.

With the restraints fully released from Helen's wrists, she reached for the Bible on her body but instantly pulled away and shouted that it burned—and for one moment, perhaps even less, Agatha heard Helen's real voice seeping through, and her real eyes flickered between long moments of pure blackness.

Joyce suddenly was moving the Bible from Helen's body, and Agatha jumped to pull Joyce away, but it was too late—the creature that had once been their sister was free. It towered above everybody and grinned hideously. The cabinets were still opening and shutting on their own, splintering the wood, and at any second they'd break off entirely. The room was so cold that Agatha could hardly breathe.

Feebly she picked her cross back up, having dropped it when reaching for Joyce, and held it feebly in a trembling hand between her and Helen. She had no words—her mouth opened and shut and opened again and shut again. Helen picked up a rope and looked Agatha in the eye.

"I told you Agatha, I told you you'd be the first to go. I'm going to hang you for all to see. Your grave in hell awaits."

"Helen this isn't you."

Joyce stepped between them then hugged Helen as if there was nothing wrong with her; as if she hadn't become a monstrosity. *"Hurt me instead, not Agatha."*

At that moment, Thaddeus and Timothy each grabbed one of Helen's arms and pulled her back to the ground. Thaddeus slid the Holy Bible back over Helen to keep her suspended; to keep her from floating or moving.

Agatha stood up then leaned over the side of the well. What were they going to do? What was going to work? They had tried the crosses, tried reading scripture, tried Holy Water, tried everything that they could collectively think of. What was left? Were they defeated? Agatha frowned. Her tears fell from her eyes into the well.

While the boys were scrambling for their crosses, Joyce crawled to Helen's side and hugged her. *"I love you Helen."*

"I… love you… too…" Helen said in a voice that was naturally her own. Her eyes were blue and normal, despite the irregular structure of the sickness the demon had curled Helen's face into. Then, in the demon's cruel voice it said: *"It almost hurts that I have to kill you."*

The boys stuck a cross on each of Helen's cheeks.

"Acknowledge the Spirit of truth and grace," Timothy said, *"who repels your attacks and confounds your lies."*

The demon hissed and its jaw moved unnaturally wide. Its long black tongue stretched forth and moved in fast bursts from side to side. Its face was struck with agony.

"Go out from Helen, this creature of God, whom He has signed with a seal from on High."

Helen's body convulsed worse than ever before, and suddenly her arms and legs stretched straight in every direction.

"Depart from this woman."

A massive cloud of gloomy smoke pushed from her mouth and eyes and massed at the top of the wellhouse.

Agatha looked from the cloud back to her sister. Her face was completely her old self again, but her eyes were closed and she was still, her body limp, her skin reddened in the places where Holy Water had stung. Was she still alive? Could anybody survive that display of power?

All her siblings screamed and caused her to look back up. The smoke formed into the hideous silhouette of a demon's face; the irregularly shaped eyes that had overcome Helen's face, and the devious smile that had seldom left Helen's lips—Agatha had to look away; there were hidden dangers and demons within the smoke, and Agatha thought if she looked at the sickening face for a second longer she'd die.

The cloud suddenly swirled around the wellhouse, not as a face, but as a serpent, spiraling around the brick walls. Agatha's hands tightened on the edge of the well, and Thaddeus and Timothy who were nearby came to her side as well. In the commotion, Agatha hadn't noticed Joyce—she had been focusing on holding on to the edge of the well so that she wouldn't slip with the great gusts of winds, and was focusing on Helen, whose slumped body had been turned over, and for a second Agatha was distracted by the continually slamming cabinets that were about to be thrown loose.

Joyce stood at the doorway, hands over her face, and everything stopped. The smoke gathered into a face again and was gliding toward her. Agatha moved with a jolt of terror and ran the short distance from the well to her baby sister at the door and grabbed her in one quick motion as they slammed into the hard ground. The Demon Smoke passed an inch in front of them, only separated by the wooden cross that Joyce held up and between them.

Then, suddenly, the smoke passed through the wellhouse door and moved completely unseen. The wellhouse was already warming, and while Agatha's siblings were gathering together, checking on each other, and checking on Helen, she couldn't help but worry about the Demon Smoke, and where it had gone, and who it would devour next.

25

THE ASHFALL HISTORY MUSEUM must have been the smallest museum building in the world. Cramped, redbrick, and almost hidden away by the obscuring shrubs and bushes in front of it. The sign at the top of the museum was withered and rusted.

Beverly's car was one of two in the parking lot. She took a deep breath before opening her door and stepping out. She needed answers, but was there anything she could find here that could help her? She thought about all of Cat's warnings and everything Cat had said about the possessed girl named Vanessa Gannon, and thought about everything that had happened since the day Cat had given Beverly the book.

She could still hear the fright in Cat's voice when Cat had tried to warn her, *I told you the next thing was that she couldn't walk past a crucifix, now look at her. Who knows how long until she's completely taken over…*

As much as Beverly wanted to keep denying it, there was something hellishly wrong with Abigail.

Cat I wish I listened to you. I wish you weren't missing. I want to tell you how sorry I am that I didn't listen to you. I could really use your help right now…

The book Cat had given Beverly was basically useless. It contained no answers. The Vanessa girl had completely vanished from the face of the earth. How could Beverly save her friend without knowing the solution? How could anybody save a possessed person? Beverly was desperate for an answer—desperate for anything that might help.

Beverly pulled open the museum's front door and entered. The last time she had been here was in elementary school when doing research for a school project. It looked exactly as she had remembered it—the plants in the pots near the entrance were dying, the carpet was old and ugly and needed to be replaced, and the plastic shelves of brochures were packed full as if nobody had ever taken any of them.

She went to the museum's archive room. The wall opposite the entrance was long and packed full of old books and binders stuffed full with papers. On the right wall were bins of old and yellowed newspapers and magazines; the left wall was a toss up of various books, newspapers, documents, and microfiche. Along the left wall also was a counter where an employee was sorting files and arranging them in their proper places along the wall. He hadn't noticed Beverly walk in.

Beverly traced her hand along the spines of books, searching for anything that could be useful. Perhaps in another book by this same author—James McDowell—she could find out more about possession, she thought. Or perhaps there were other books on possession. Or books about the Engstrom place in general. She wasn't going to leave any stone unturned.

When she couldn't find any of the books she was looking for, she said, "Excuse me sir."

The employee was startled and dropped his file; sheets of paper spread across the room.

"I am so sorry," Beverly said. She went across the archive to help him collect the papers. She noticed the guy's collar was upturned, so she fixed it. "I didn't mean to make you drop all these papers. Sorry again."

"Not a problem," the man said. He was in his late fifties probably and looked like Ichabod Crane in the Sleepy Hollow cartoon that came on TV every October. Lanky. Brown hair in a ponytail. A pointy nose. "What can I help you with, young lady?"

"I'm not sure what I'm even looking for to be honest, it's not your average subject matter really."

"Well, I've worked here many years, I know the books along these walls like the back of my hand."

"Really? I thought you looked familiar. I haven't been here in… since elementary."

"Well, neither have many others. We haven't seen much in the way of visitors these days. Mostly I just spend time dusting the displays and waltzing these halls."

"Well I think you've done a fine job maintaining its integrity, Mr.…."

"Thistlefoot. But you can call me Cornelius."

"Cornelius. It's wonderful to make your acquaintance. I'm Beverly."

"Charmed. Now what can I help you find, young lady?"

"Well I'm trying to do some research on the occult. For—for school."

"Oh. Not too often I get requests for that. But I think I have a good start for you."

"Thank you kindly, Cornelius."

Cornelius went across the room and scanned a certain shelf looking for a book. "I thought the schools around here still had a couple more weeks left of summer."

"I like getting a head start."

"Uh-huh," he said, pulling a book off the shelf. "Here, this is rather intimidating but likely more information than you'll actually need. *The Secret History of Magick.* This book covers practically everything." He handed it to Beverly. "Myths, spells, demons, black magic, curses—just about everything you might need."

"Oh, this is perfect. Thank you. Thank you again."

"It's no trouble. If there's any more I can do for you, I'll be right up there." He pointed at the counter. "Don't be shy."

"Hey is there anything in this archive about the old Engstrom place?"

"Now nobody's asked me about that rotten place in a while, but I know I've got a book or two around here somewhere. We were planning a whole exhibit about that house, but way back when—much before your time, I'm sure—there was a bit of a mishap that… shut down the idea."

"Huh? What happened?"

Cornelius leaned against the countertop. "Twenty-something years ago some folks paid a visit to the Engstrom place. They were spending a few weeks there doing research. They dropped like flies. Lord I remember it like it was yesterday."

"I never knew about that."

"It was real bad. The whole town was shook up."

Beverly brought out *What Walks Unseen* from her purse. "Do you have any books from this author? McDowell?"

"He was one of 'em who died." Cornelius tapped his finger on the cover. "You know I knew him."

"You did?"

"Guess I shouldn't say *knew him*. Rather I met him. He came to town a few days, maybe a couple weeks, ahead of his investigations in that house. He did some research here in the library's archive—I had only just started back then—and here's this renowned investigator that I got to show around the museum and be sort of his assistant."

"And he died in that house?"

"Along with his acolytes."

"What was he studying there?"

"There was a car crash about a year before McDowell came by. Maybe you should be writing some of this down for your report, Miss Beverly."

Beverly tapped her head. "It's all up here."

"This lady and her husband were coming through these parts during a terrible storm and crashed into a tree. They took refuge in the Engstrom place for the night, and the lady came out alive but her husband went missing. McDowell was writing a book on the topic, but he died before it was completed. Guess that's the risk you take when you play with fire."

"Uh-huh," Beverly said. "I have so many questions about it all."

"This *is* for a report, isn't it, young lady? You aren't planning to do anything foolish, are you?"

"No, sir. I'm curious is all."

"You seem like a nice girl, Miss Beverly, so I'm inclined to believe you. But I'm just telling you that if you are thinking about setting foot anywhere near that old mansion, don't do it. Because this stuff is dangerous and it's real."

"Yes, sir."

"You know the story about the Great Flood?"

"Yes, sir."

"You know that there are similar stories about great floods in Japan, Mexico, Ireland, Australia, Poland, Peru, China, from one end of the world to the other there are untold stories of catastrophic floods. It's incredible. In Iran there's a story of a great flood where a man takes two of each animal onto a boat. In India the story's identical. In all of these countries the stories have their differences, sure, but in all of these countries the stories are all... derived from something. Are you following me?"

"Yes, sir."

"Civilizations that had never existed for one single moment at the same time as each other, civilizations that existed on opposite ends of the earth, different people from different spectrums of time—there were similarities in all of their flood stories. Because it had really happened. Maybe I don't know which legend is closest to the actual flood, but we can't deny it actually happened."

"But what's that have to do with the Engstrom place?"

"I've read McDowell's books. I've read books about demons and everything associated. There's stories like it in every culture from all around the world, from every time period that's ever been record-ed. You take the haunted house for example. There are legends of haunted caves. Haunted forests. Sickly lands that were considered cursed or evil because spirits lingered there. Naturally these legends developed into haunted houses."

"Well—well, Mr. Thistlefoot, um…"

"Yes?"

"In all those stories that you've read about, how do they help somebody that's been possessed?"

"Well typically there's an exorcism."

"What happens when an exorcism… let's say doesn't work?"

"Sometimes they'd trace it back to the start. McDowell himself wrote about a village where a boy was possessed. He had gone up to the mountains with some friends and brought back a statuette. After all the horrors that followed this boy, the only way to cure him was to return him and the statuette back to the cave where the boy had discovered it in the first place."

"So you really believe in these things?"

"Well, history has a way of exacerbating things. But most folklore is rooted in some semblance of truth. After all, the truth is told by those who win. Take that for what it's worth."

"Yeah, I suppose that's worth something."

"Is there anything else I can assist you with?"

"I think I've got everything I need. Thanks again, sir."

"Any time," he said.

Beverly walked out of the archive.

"Young lady?"

She turned in the doorway to face him. "Yes, sir?"

"Don't forget what I said. There really had once been a great flood."

"Yeah," Beverly said. "And there have always been demons."

26

It was eating Beverly up inside to know that something had happened to Officer Daniels. His picture in the newspaper dispenser stared up at her; he was in uniform, smiling, and Beverly hated looking at it, but morbidly couldn't take her eyes away. He was dead, she knew it, Abigail knew it, and nobody else did. What if somebody were to put it together and discover that the girls were there that night? She shuddered—but how would anyone put that together? Regardless, she couldn't shake the dirty feeling—couldn't wash it away. It clung to her like dirt clings to the filthy walls of an old building.

"Excuse me."

The words of the stranger didn't register with her, and she kept on looking at Officer Daniels's picture. His screams still rang in her ears, and she still had the image of terror on his face permanently in her mind when she shut her eyes.

"Excuse me."

She glanced up then down. A guy was holding a stack of papers and a stapler. She moved a step to the side and turned her attention back to Officer Daniels. He might have had a family—and if she read the article, it would say, but she felt too guilty to read about him since she knew the truth—and didn't they deserve to know what happened to him? Didn't everyone deserve to—

"You know it's free." The guy opened the plastic window and grabbed a paper for her. "You don't have to read it through the glass."

Beverly took it with a shaking hand and saw that the stack of papers the guy was holding had Cat's face all over them. He stapled one to the pole. It must have been the only pole she had come across in Ashfall that didn't have Cat's face on it already.

She vaguely recognized him from that day she met Cat, and Bruno had come out of the house. "Wait a second, you're Bruno aren't you?"

"Are you a friend of Cat's?"

"Yeah I'm Beverly. She probably mentioned me."

He gave her a few of the posters. "Hand these out, will you?"

Beverly accepted them. "Have you had any luck?"

"What do you think?"

"I'm sorry, I was only trying to be…. I miss her too."

"She was the love of my life."

"I'm sorry."

Suddenly Bruno was hanging his head. "I shouldn't have mis-treated her. I should have been good to her."

Beverly put a hand on his arm. "She really loved you too, Bruno. She told me so. Trust me, she loved you."

"Cat wouldn't have run off like this. Something happened to her. I feel it in my gut."

Beverly gulped. "What do you mean?"

"I don't know… but I have this feeling…"

"Uh-huh?"

"The day I talked to her last we were supposed to meet up like usual at the old Engstrom place. When I got there I couldn't find her, so I went upstairs to check if she was asleep in the attic. As soon as I reached the second floor I heard somebody running down below. I hurried down to see what was going on, but whoever was in the house with me ran away too fast." Bruno took a deep breath. "I assumed the worst, assumed somebody else broke in and hurt Cat while I was gone, but I searched that mansion high and low. She's not there."

A couple tears formed in Beverly's eyes. "I'm sorry," she said. "We'll find her, all right? I know we will."

When they parted ways, she had a sick feeling in her stomach. There were only four or five people in town who had any reason to be in that house: Bruno, Cat, Officer Daniels, herself, and Abigail...

...and Beverly could eliminate herself and Office Daniels right away.

There was something chilling about St. Dymphna Catholic Church, as if it shouldn't have been open to the public ever since Father Gutierrez died. Beverly was uncertain about entering but went inside; the church was eerie and quiet. A few people awaiting confessional were kneeling in the front two rows of pews.

Beverly was chilled. The church couldn't even be bothered to replace the confessional the priest was murdered in.

Beverly knelt in the pew furthest from the altar. Nobody acknowledged her. On the back of the pews she found worn hymnals and Holy Bibles with black covers and golden letters. She grabbed two bibles then stood up, walked across the church, and found a picture of a saint at one of the stained glass paintings. She didn't know which saint it was, but any of them would do.

Next she reached into her purse and pulled out an empty bottle of nail polish. She dunked it in the container of Holy Water that was in little bowls near the entrance. Little air bubbles popped at the surface. She double checked to make sure nobody saw her, then screwed the lid on and put in her purse with the bibles and the random saint.

In the very back of the church lobby, there were candles burning, and there were little statues of the Virgin Mary. Beverly took two unlit candles and shoved them into her purse as well, then pulled one of the rosaries off the Virgin Mary and put that in her purse too.

At the door, Beverly turned back around and opened her purse one more time. There were two twenties and a ten in her wallet; she put the money in an empty donation basket then exited the church. Was it going to be enough?

A chill passed through Ashfall when Beverly left the church. She thought again about Father Gutierrez, and everybody still using the same confessional he had been killed in. He had died strangely… and Cat had gone missing when Bruno heard a stranger in the Engstrom place…

Beverly felt like she was going to go crazy. She didn't want to have the suspicions but her stomach was full of nerves and she couldn't shake it no matter how hard she tried; there was a connection her best friend had to both Cat and Father Gutierrez.

Back home, Beverly laid out everything she bought on her dresser. Would it work? Would it be enough?

She picked up one of the posters of Cat. "Oh Cat, what happened to you?"

Beverly thought she was home alone, so she snuck into her parents' room and found the key for the liquor cabinet in the sleeve of a vinyl record. She opened the cabinet and was pulling out a big glass bottle of whisky.

"What's you doing?"

Beverly almost dropped it. "Judy what are you doing home?"

"Uh, I live here."

"Whatever. I need to be alone."

Judy crossed her arms. "No."

"Don't tell Mom and Dad I was in the liquor cabinet."

"I could have told them last year when I caught you if I wanted to, but that's the last thing I care about. What's wrong? Why are you drinking? Why do you look so sad?"

Beverly poured herself a drink then poured one for her sister. "I can't tell you everything, Judy. Just… I have something to do and I'm not sure if I can do it."

"But what do you mean? Tell me."

"I can't."

"But I'm your sister."

Beverly poured another drink. "Didn't I tell you I needed to be alone?"

"Sure. So?"

"Judy please…"

"But Bev."

"Want another?"

"Sure."

Beverly poured her sister another one. "I've got a big decision to make."

"What about?"

"It's about Abigail."

"How is she? I haven't talked to her since she came over for dinner last month."

"She needs help."

"Is there anything I can do, Bev?"

"I'm not even sure there's anything *I* can do about it."

Judy didn't know what to say.

"Everything always works out for the best, right?" Beverly said after a sip.

"I guess you can say that."

Beverly poured another drink without a word.

"Keep pouring and I won't even need to say a word to Mom and Dad about the liquor cabinet, they'll find it empty themselves."

"Yeah. Sure."

They were silent until there was a knock at the door.

"Are Mom and Dad back already?" Beverly asked. "Where are their keys?"

"Funny thing," Judy said. "I won't tell about the liquor if you don't tell them Oliver came over."

27

Abigail passed through the sliding glass door into her back yard, bringing with her Helen's journal, the pen with the unique plexiglass window, and one of the cigarette lighters her parents left on the kitchen table.

It was a bright beautiful day. Birds were humming and the sky was empty of any clouds. Abigail could have enjoyed it if it weren't for the feeling that she was being watched. She furtively looked over her shoulder to see who was there, but nobody was in sight. She was all alone.

Abigail set her things down then dragged the grill to the center of the yard. A cheap little charcoal grill that had started rusting a few years back. She lifted the lid and picked up the journal. She had filled up about half of it talking to Helen—it hadn't felt like that much, but she could see where the untouched pages, although slightly water-damaged, met the pages that were wrinkled from writing and turning.

Abigail ran her left thumb over the lighter's wheel and button. A precious flame vibrated gently as a breeze passed. Abigail put the flame to the corner of the journal then dropped it when pain stung her right wrist.

Abigail ran a finger over her scar, puzzled as to how such a small flame could seem so hot on her arm from across the entire length of the book's spine. Any pain was gone instantly. Sweat rolled down her forehead; Abigail wiped it away with the back of her right hand. She inspected the journal but couldn't find the corner of the page she had started burning. As far as she could tell, all of the pages were unscathed.

The flame swayed again. Abigail set it against the first page of the book, awaiting the flame to engulf the old pages; she was excited to watch the journal burn. A piercing abrupt pain emerged in her right hand in a sudden violent pulse, and she dropped the book again.

Her right hand reluctantly closed around the journal once more, moving it closer to the flame of her parents' lighter. As soon as the pages met fire, a blazing pain seared into her skin; and yet she was unmarked, unchanged, and the shock of burning left as quickly as it came.

Helen's book was not changed by the flames in any way.

Abigail slammed the journal on the backyard table and opened it up one final time. She wrote: *WHAT THE FUCK DO YOU WANT FROM ME?*

Abigail wanted the pen to snap as she placed it in her left hand. Helen had been eager to write for a long time, and Abigail had been ignoring her. The pen guided her left hand: Set my soul free. That's all I've ever asked.

Leave me alone.

Cat's here with me. She wants to know why you killed her.

Tell her the truth! Tell her you killed her!

Abigail shut the book for the final time.

241

Abigail rubbed her right hand. There were no burn marks on her skin but her hand pulsed as if it had been seared by the hot metal of the lighter. The things were in her bag and she went on her way to Beverly's house, tears blurring her vision until she wiped them away.

A gust of wind dragged leaves through the air, and was shaking a sheet of paper from a streetlamp; the tape at the bottom of the paper had come loose and it was about to fly off. Abigail pulled it down and found that it was one of the posters Bruno had set up all over Ashfall; he must have put up so many that there wasn't an inch of town left uncovered.

Abigail crumpled it up and threw it at her feet. She was tired of seeing the posters. Tired of seeing Cat everywhere. Tired of seeing Cat's dead body every time she closed her eyes. Tired of feeling guilty.

Sometimes when she thought about it hard enough, Cat was in her hands again, under her touch, and she could feel the lifeless body as she dragged it through dark hallways, dragged it down to the basement, and pushed her into the Wet Room. It was a hideous memory that Abigail wanted to erase from her mind, but knew she'd never forget it.

At Beverly's perfect house, everything lovely and new, the only lawn without a single leaf on it, Abigail wondered if she was making a mistake, and for a brief moment hesitated at the gate. Considering everything that happened, this must have been the only option left.

The gate creaked open. Abigail went up the path to the door and knocked softly. Her left hand stayed in a fist even after Beverly answered the door.

"Hey Abby."

"Are you busy?"

"No, what's up? Come in."

"Is anybody else home? We need to talk in private."

"Judy just left. I'm home alone."

Abigail sat at the dining room table. "I need you to help me." Beverly watched Abigail's crestfallen eyes divert from her. Why couldn't Abigail look at her directly?

"Anything."

"We need to go back to the house."

Beverly stiffened. Her purse was on the table, and she stood between it and Abigail. Maybe Abigail wasn't affected, Beverly thought, because the cross and Holy Bibles were hidden in the purse. Beverly knew if she were ever going to help Abigail, it would require going back to the Engstrom place—but she hated the thought of ever being in there again.

"Why do we need to go back?"

Abigail opened her purse and held up Helen's journal. "We need to burn it. I need you to burn it for me."

Beverly thought about the things Cornelius Thislefoot had told her, like the possessed boy who was only cured when the statuette was taken back to the place where the demon originated from; and Beverly was certain that Abigail's demon came from that damn journal.

"Are you sure you want me to burn it?"

Abigail cried. *"Yes. Yes. Please."*

Beverly hugged her. *"Breathe. Breathe. You'll be all right. Breathe."*

What if I'm wrong? Beverly wondered. *What if what I'm doing is going to hurt her? What if—no, I saw it with my own eyes. Something is wrong with her. And Cat knew it.*

Cat…. What happened to you?

Abigail sobbed. *"Thank you so much."*

"Let's get you some water. Or something."

"I don't want anything."

Beverly put the back of her hand on Abigail's forehead. "You're burning up."

Abigail opened her purse while Beverly went into the kitchen. At the bottom was the Navaja.

I don't remember packing this.

Looking at her own eyes in the shine of the knife, she didn't know who she was anymore. Could she still call herself Abigail Martinez, or had she changed so much in the past few months that she was somebody entirely different?

Beverly returned with a cup of water for each of them. Abigail's left hand didn't want to let go of the blade. In the back of her mind was a voice screaming so loudly that it drained Beverly out: *Cut her throat. Cut her throat. Do it now while you have the chance. Cut her throat and hide her like you hid Cat.*

"Are you feeling any better?"

Abigail's hand unclenched the knife, and she shook as she grabbed the cup in both hands.

"No," Abigail said. "Not at all."

28

THE CHEWED WORMS FROM Mother Raven clung to Helen's mind like the sky clings around earth.

The night was full of strange dreams, and Helen was back in the cemetery again, chased by Mother Raven, moving too slow. The forest had changed with eternal darkness, and its trees pressed closer to Helen, their branches reaching for her like sickly bent arms.

Earth slipped away from Helen. Everything in her vision blurred. Sudden pain jolted her body. Helen had been thrown on her stomach over a dense sweep of roots. Her left hand searched for something to support herself on so that she could stand, but Mother Raven walked on Helen's fingers and stood on the back of her wrist, sharp talons burrowing into her skin. A sharp cry was stuck in Helen's throat.

CAW! CAW!

At a distance there were cries; hushed at first, then a symphony of unbroken screams.

From the indistinct shadowy spaces of the woods came baby ravens. Bones extended through their flesh. Their heads were crooked. They croaked hideously unpleasant screeches as they stepped closer to Helen, beaks snapping in excitement for their revenge.

Mother Raven stepped off Helen's hand, tracking blood as she went to her babies and kissed them. The eyes of the grotesquely misshaped birds went from Helen to their mother then back to Helen. All at once they rampaged for Helen's body, plunging jagged rows of teeth deep into Helen's flesh.

When she awoke, she was curled into a tight ball, and tried to sleep again, but the nightmare had shaken her so bad that she was fully conscious, fully awake, and could not sleep again, even when she shifted into a more comfortable position.

There were steps in the hallway. Helen wondered who was awake. She tiptoed from her bed, grabbed her candle from her dresser, and realized she had no lighter. She crept to her door, then opened it and crept into the hallway with a whisper.

"Who's there?"

Nobody replied; the steps creaked again from far away. Helen followed their direction.

She didn't like the way the house felt at night. She could have sworn that there was somebody with her in the cavernous shadows that painted every hall; could have sworn that something was deeply wrong with the house at night, as if it became sort of misshapen, or became a completely different house altogether. And after what she had been through, and what her little siblings had to do to save her, she wouldn't put anything past this house. Why was it so weird? There had to be a reason.

In the kitchen she found a lighter, and put the flame to her candlewick. Then she steadily walked back through her home, as silent as a mouse, and had completely lost track of whatever footsteps she had heard when she had left her bedroom. Walking curiously up and down each hall, studying the strangeness of her house at night, feeling as if eyes were always watching her, she came to the hall of her parents' bedroom, and their light was still on.

She tiptoed to their partly closed door and crouched behind it and listened. She was curious how people talked when they thought they were alone.

"It was on the bottom of the cellar stairs," Mother said. *"I don't feel safe in my own home."*

"Shut up," Father said.

They were both silent. Helen wished they'd both explain what they were discussing. What had Mother seen? Why had it made Father mad? Helen hovered a hand over the flame, feeling its warmth, and suddenly she had to sneeze. She rubbed her nose and held it in.

"And what Julia said she saw in the wellhouse. A severed… oh God."

They were both silent again. Helen didn't like it. What could her mother have possibly seen?

"People in town have been whispering about our home."

"What do they say?"

"They say—they say John died because we're cursed. Why do they say we're cursed?"

"There are things about my family I never told you."

Mother was crying.

Father said, "Many many years ago, Adolph Engstrom settled on this hill and owned the whole expanse. Over time the pieces of land where that old farm stands now were sold off, but my family kept the rest. Adolph Engstrom farmed tobacco and that's where our wealth originated.

"Adolph built a cabin, and that's where hell reached up from down below and touched my bloodline. A drought came to Ashfall and money wasn't good. Adolph Engstrom worked hard and did everything for his family. Each day Adolph prayed the drought would end. Well, weeks dragged on by and there was no end of the drought in sight. You can imagine how desperate someone might be...

"Mabel Engstrom invited the devil himself into that cabin. Adolph never learned how all it started but over time things that weren't quite right popped up in the cabin. Adolph moved a cabinet and found the symbol of the devil scraped into the floor, or found that somebody tuned the crucifix over his bed upside down. Then one day..."

Helen's mother was sobbing, and Father waited until she calmed down a little bit before he continued.

"Then one day he finds Mable in the fields, she's naked and unconscious near a fire. Adolph swore he had heard other voices with her when he saw that billowing smoke rising up, but Mabel was alone.

"Maybe that don't sound like much, sleeping nude in a field, but after that... only two days later... one of Adolph's little ones died. Then Adolph was in an accident that broke one of his arms. And Mabel... Adolph noticed Mable at all hours of the night peeking out the window as if she were waiting for something, or scared of something that might come.

"As the story's been told to me, one of Adolph's brothers ran off with a large sum of Adolph's fortune and donated it to the church to try and atone for Mable's sins. Adolph was at the end of his rope and couldn't pay any of his debts, nor could he pay his taxes, and so the constable comes to collect.

"Adolph had been building the house that used to stand where this very house is now. The constable came and made his threats. Adolph… wrung his neck. He dumped the constable's corpse in the woods where it was eaten by the wildlife. The only witness was a squatter who had taken to living in the house's unfinished structure. Adolph, you see, couldn't take the chance that anybody would tell.

"Then came the damn day, a Sunday, when Adolph was out in the field and heard gunshots. He ran up to the cabin and found that his children had been taken out back by a strange man, five of his children who still lived in the cabin and hadn't moved out, none of 'em older than age thirteen. It had been payback by the squatter's lover for her death.

"Innocent blood was shed on our land. All of them buried out back in the Engstrom Graveyard in our forest.

"Adolph's kids, the three oldest children who hadn't been living in the cabin at the time, took over the family business. There were other houses built on our land, some of them around the area where our house stands now."

Quietly Helen stood, then she tiptoed away, the voices of her parents becoming a distant fuzzy noise. She went to the door that led into their dreamlike basement, and found that it was already open. She shuddered thinking about the cistern within.

Silently she moved through the threshold and descended the stairs. With every step she imagined a hand would reach out and pull her down. At the bottom she crouched, peering over the railing at an indistinct glow across the basement. For a brief moment she considered turning back, but floorboards in the halls above her creaked, and somebody was awake, and she changed her mind about leaving the basement because she didn't want to be caught. She moved off the final steps into the realm of unknown that was her basement; the realm that was a living breathing nightmare—an existence with a mind of its own.

Helen moved in such small steps across the basement that she was hardly moving at all. Closer she came to that dreaded glow of candles, and strange shadows spread across her body and reflected off the cluttered spaces of the basement.

A chilling moan uprose from the cistern. Helen thought her heart was going to explode. Something was moving within. And at that moment she knew immediately that she had been right, there had been a hand down there. And in this strange place that seemed set apart from reality, she couldn't begin to imagine the things her mother might have seen too.

Her eyes were chained to that dreaded opening on the floor, and she tiptoed a little closer, moving less than an inch with each movement, worry blooming in her heart, and sweat rolling down her forehead. And when she was finally close enough, she couldn't see anything but an indistinct shadow, an amorphous movement in the deep darkness where the glow of candles did not extend, and the dreaded deathly moans continued to rise.

In a split moment, whoever's eyes were below in the cistern must have caught hers, because while she could not see them, she felt them, and somebody knew she was above. The moans paused. Then, after complete silence, came a whisper.

"…Help."

"I'm sorry."

Helen backed away and all noises ceased.

As she turned toward the direction of the stairs, the floorboards creaked above her again and she was frozen. They were coming nearer and nearer toward the door. Helen moved backwards and urgently looked for a hiding place, and found a heavy wooden bed-frame whose cracked structure allowed her to both completely hide and yet also glimpse into the basement and observe the flickering candles.

Somebody was down here with her. Somebody was moving or dragging something. Helen pulled her face away from the crack in the structure; then, grotesquely curious, looked through it immediately. Nobody was there yet, but her own terror had filled up the room and lingered, and she was afraid that whoever was with her might know she was hiding.

Helen was on her hands and knees, adjusting herself, when she felt something cold and painful under her palm. And then there was a rag. And as she fidgeted around with them, she realized it was a man's shirt, and smelled of powerful cologne, and accompanying it was a wristwatch. Helen slipped the watch into her pocket.

A guttural deathly growl. In her mind Helen pictured a tall bear with wide jaws and endless teeth, and paws that would rip her in half like tearing paper. Looking through the cracked structure once more, the first thing she saw was a naked body on its back, the radiance of a dozen candles washing over it to reveal a servant's outfit that was torn off. It was one of the servant women, although Helen couldn't see the lady's face, and Helen's father was kneeled over her with a knife in his paws.

His hands were changed so that they were completely animal; prehensile claws that gripped the knife tight as he raised it above his head and buried it into the servant woman's corpse. Light glimmered against his eyes so that Helen saw they were completely black. He was excited, growling again, and a long tongue slid from his mouth and licked his lips.

Father—or what had once been her father—growled again; that awful growl that made her guts squirm.

SPLASH!

A descent into the cistern.

In a split second, Helen made a run for it across the dreaded basement. Heavy footsteps chased her. Her heart felt as if it were going to stop dead. Helen turned around when the person chasing her had stopped. Her father stood a few feet away, and his blue eyes flashed grotesquely black.

When morning came, his eyes were blue again. He was standing over her with a cup of water and a bottle of medicine. He was smiling, and any of the terror from last night had not carried over, because it had not been real.

"Good morning, pumpkin. Here."

Helen took the medicine from her father's hand and swallowed it, then drank half the cup of water. Her throat was dry and it all stung on its way down. Father took the cup and set it on her nightstand next to her journal, then he left her bedroom with the medicine bottle.

Last night's dreams flowed in her mind again; her father in the cistern, the knife in his paws...

Helen's hand slipped under her covers into her pocket. She pulled out Mr. Carter's discarded watch. It was as if pulling an object from deep within a dream. Helen had the watch with her because last night had been real: she had hidden from her father. He had been taken over by an unclean spirit.

"Where did you find that?"

Helen jolted and dropped the watch on her lap. She hadn't noticed Father come back to her door. He came across the room and picked it up. Helen was frozen as he looked it over. At any second, she was sure, his eyes would turn black.

"I don't know."

Father put it in his pocket, then put the back of his hand on Helen's forehead. "You're burning up."

Helen slid her covers off. "It's too hot under these covers."

She wanted to be away from him, and stepped past him toward the door. She was halfway into the hallway when Father put a hand on her shoulder. "Breakfast is on the table."

Helen shuddered from his touch. "Thank you, Dad."

Somewhere down the hall she lost him.

Helen needed to be protected so she snuck into her parents' room and found her mother's golden cross necklace. She put it on then hid the cross in her shirt. She grabbed Holy Bibles and crosses from around the house and put them together in a cardboard box.

When Helen heard somebody in the hallway heading toward her room, she quickly pushed the cardboard box under her bed. A split second later, Agatha opened the door without knocking and came in.

"Hey, Helen?"

"Yes?"

"Can I talk to you?"

"What is it?"

Agatha stepped over to the window and looked outside. "Why you?"

Helen came to the window as well. The wellhouse was brooding in the back yard. Helen didn't know what to say.

"How did it happen? And why you?"

"I don't know." Their eyes held each other's. "I don't know."

At night, Helen looked over her box of crosses, Bibles, and Holy Water. She took off her mother's gold necklace and set it down in the box. Then, after hiding the box in her bedroom closet, she went to the foot of her bed and kneeled for a prayer.

Dear Lord, please help me.

Helen laid in bed, but she was too afraid to be alone. She kept thinking of the servant that had died, that must have been in the cistern. She tiptoed from her bed to her doorway, looked both ways as if crossing a street, and went through her home to the ground floor to Agatha and Joyce's room.

Helen tried to hide the terror on her face. She wondered if Agatha or Joyce suspected anything.

"I had a bad dream... can I sleep with you two tonight?"

"You can sleep in my bed Helen," Joyce said. "But I'm so cold. Can you bring another blanket?"

"Of course."

Helen stepped out of the room and through the shadows that were so thick they had texture to them. Across the hall was a stairway that went up to the second floor; Helen ascended, and halfway up heard heavy breathing.

At the second floor she opened the storage closet that had extra blankets and pillows. She grabbed two blankets then closed the door. Her father was there.

Helen stepped back.

"Hi Helen. Why aren't you asleep?"

"I had a bad dream."

"Uh-huh."

Helen cried. "Was it a dream, Dad?"

"Was what a dream?"

"We were in the basement and you hurt somebody. A servant woman. You dumped her body in the cistern."

"Yes, that was only a dream. You don't think your father would hurt anyone, do you?"

"No, Daddy, but it felt so real."

"Would it make you feel better if we went down and checked? If I showed you that the cistern was empty?"

29

THE GIRLS WENT UP the hill. Abigail felt bulging eyes were chained to them. She opened the gate, and Beverly followed her through. Walking into that damn place was like walking back into a nightmare; walking back into the night she killed Cat.

They sat together in front of the fireplace; it was full of ashes. Abigail removed the journal and lighter from her purse and gave them to Beverly. Beverly ran her thumb over the lighter's wheel and button and the flame emerged.

"I've tried. It doesn't burn."

Beverly brought the flame to the edge of the book. Blistering torture ran the length of Abigail's scar. Beverly held the book still, waiting for it to ignite so she could throw it into the fireplace. The torment in Abigail's aching wrist grew, and instantly she reached up to Beverly's hand and pulled the book away from the flame.

"We need something more powerful. I brought lighter fluid with me from my garage."

Beverly set the book down in the fireplace, while Abigail pulled out the small white bottle with a red cap from her purse. Abigail smiled as she doused the pages with flammable liquid; it would be a pleasure to watch it burn.

Beverly tried to light it but it clearly wasn't catching fire, so Abigail took the lighter from her friend and ran her thumb over the wheel and button. Abigail lowered the flame to the edge of the book, then pulled herself back instantly when sudden heat flared in her palm.

"Ouch."

"Are you okay?"

"I don't think my scar likes the heat." Abigail pulled her sleeve back a little so that Beverly could see.

Because the book wouldn't burn they went outside and nearby the gate found twigs. They brought them back into the house and spread them in the fireplace over the journal. Then, once they were set, just to be sure, Abigail wet them with lighter fluid.

Beverly set them on fire. The flames raged across the twigs in a swift wave of fiery scarlet, immediately changing the twigs, and stretching the flames as far as they could go in the confines of the fireplace. Abigail choked as she watched a flurry of smoke uprise from the flames, putting her hands around her neck. She was burning up. Sweat poured down her head, and swaying dizzily, she staggered away from the fireplace and bumped against the living room table. She tried to keep her balance but fell. Abigail clutched herself on the floor. Heat flooded over her.

"It burns it burns it burns make it stop it burns make it stop make it stop."

Her eyes darted toward Beverly, her vision obscured by smoke, and Beverly was shaking, moving ancient items from the shelf over the fireplace so that she could hopefully find something to remove the book with. She couldn't be moving any slower.

"Beverly." Abigail coughed. *"I'm burning."*

"I-I'm trying, I'm trying."

Her mouth tasted like smoke, and flames spread closer over her body, entangling her, twisting around her like a devious serpent that was ready to sink its fangs into her neck. Abigail's vision was darkening, but for a hideous second she saw that blisters were emerging on her hands.

Everything was black and Abigail was lost in the flames of the fire. Wretchedly they consumed her soul. Higher and higher the colossal waves of smoke gushed until she could no longer breathe at all, and everything that filled her lungs was a thick smoke; thick smoke filling her body, pumping in and out of her lungs.

Gradually the cruel flames receded, and Abigail was brought out of the haze of smoke. Across from her were burning twigs; she shielded her eyes from them. Beverly stood with a fire poker over the journal. The damn thing hadn't burned at all.

A second later Beverly was kneeling at Abigail's side, helping her sit up, and shuffling through her purse for a water bottle. She twisted off the cap and helped Abigail sip it; it felt pleasant going down the burning walls of her throat.

Abigail examined her hands; there were blisters on the back of them, as if fire had been pressed directly against her skin.

"How am I gonna explain these scars to my parents?"

"We'll think of something."

Abigail's left hand was burning with a desire to write. Helen wanted to tell her something.

She ignored the urge.

Her eyes swept the living room. There was so much to discover in this house. There was endless history here, endless possibilities;

fragments and remnants of families who had been dead for a long, long time.

"Let's go."

Beverly went to the front door.

"No, into the house. I need to do it. I need to find Helen's body. It must be the only way that I can get rid of her once and for all."

Beverly removed a flashlight from her purse. One of the few things—including a couple water bottles—that they had brought with them in preparation for this. "Which way?"

There were so many corners they could turn right now, so many levels they could go to, so many stairs they could choose from; stairs, which, according to legends, people had ascended and were never seen again.

Abigail was chilled.

"Which way?" Beverly asked again.

"To the right I guess."

She led them under the gigantic spiraling staircase made of aged wood; it spiraled tightly, like something out of an old castle in an old picture book. The house smelled ancient, like an antiquarian library. Through a few oddly placed windows—windows at odd heights and angles and corners—they had a little light to illuminate their impossibly dark path through the hall, and for one brief second Abigail caught Beverly's frightened face. Her friend was shaking. Abigail had to pretend to stay calm, because one of them had to be, but being in the Engstrom place meant certain death—it had meant that for the Engstroms and the Blochs and for Cat and for Officer Daniels. Why should it be any different for Abigail and Beverly, Abigail thought.

The hall turned abruptly, and spanned probably the entire length of the house. The floor creaked under every step. There were many places to hide a body, many places for Abigail and Beverly to search if they could survive the torment that this house brought upon every soul who entered. Had Helen ever given a hint? Had Helen ever explained? There must have been a reasonable place for Abigail to start—if she searched blind, and searched all night, she'd be done with half a hallway by morning.

Then Abigail was abruptly jolted from her thoughts; she and Beverly jumped at a screeching on their right; when they turned, the leafless contorted branches of a tree neighboring the house scraped against a window.

Abigail's hand flexed and burned. Helen wanted desperately to say something. Abigail had no intention of letting Helen ever use her left hand again to transcribe her messages from beyond the

grave, but temptation was strong, and Abigail felt weak in this house; felt, at certain moments, as if she was dissociated from her body, as if her spirit was drifting.

The hallway curved into another entrance at the left; the big window that ended the hallway had its curtain drawn so that only small sparks of light leaked through and illuminated that other entrance. Here at the center of the hall there were stairs; darkness was chained above them, so that Abigail could not see where they led, and the thought of illuminating it with the flashlight startled her, because she had a strange feeling that there was something hiding in those shadows, something lurking, something that would reach its hands out and grab her and Beverly.

Five rooms at the center of the hallway on the right, Abigail instinctively reached for the middle door. It creaked loudly, chilling Abigail and pulling her lips into a grimace. She took a step into the doorway, then turned to see her friend suspended in place; Beverly hadn't moved since she opened the door.

"Coming?"

"In there?"

"Yeah, in here."

"Abby…"

"Yeah?"

Beverly didn't say anything else, she finally stepped forward and entered the room. The curtains were blue, just as Abigail had pictured them, and she set her purse down on the second of the two beds that were separated by a small nightstand with a lantern on it. There were no trees behind these windows, and it allowed for sunlight to fill the room perfectly, so that it didn't matter that the switch that was over by the door wouldn't work.

Abigail's heart rushed; something flowed through her veins, something foreign, something she hadn't ever felt before, something she had no words for. Her hand turned into a fist, reminding her that Helen wanted a chance to speak.

Her left hand curled around the pen.

Welcome back.

30

Beverly's lips were pulled into an eternal frown. "We should go. We should forget everything about Helen and this house and never come back."

Abigail held the flashlight ahead of her, grabbed Beverly's hand, and led her through the doorway out of the bedroom. It shut behind them. One step into the hall, enchanted by darkness, there was a whisper. Abigail held the flashlight to her left in the sound's direction. Thin light fought against coiling darkness. It revealed nothing.

"What was that?"

Abigail bit her lip, unsure what to say.

"Did you hear that?"

"Somebody's here," Abigail said, listening to the whisper float through the hall again—so low and soft that it was indistinct; so strained and weak that it was impossible to decipher.

The house was endless; the whisper could have come from anywhere. The house was like an eternal archaic maze that had twisted over itself time and again, so that way it was easy for anybody unfamiliar with the house to get lost. The girls walked close to the wall, light shining against antiquarian architecture.

There were at least a dozen, maybe more, rooms in the hallway, and there was the other hallway that connected at the very end by the window, and there was a flight of stairs leading to the next floor, and if they went back the way they came, they would pass the gigantic spiraling staircase that was old and pretty.

"Help me."

The girls exchanged a frightened look. The voice was nearer; coming from the stairs. Abigail's grip tightened on Beverly's hand that was slick with sweat and hard to hold on to. The walls of the stairway obscured all vision until they were past the final step; then they were on the second floor balcony—endless rooms, endless halls, plus a balcony—and together they looked to the main floor, leaning over the edge, and old dusty belongings were scattered below them.

Abigail shivered. What happened to that whisper? Who was it?

Goosepimples rose on Abigail's arms. The girls went around the balcony, taking in pictures and paintings framed on the walls that were packed tightly together, as opposed to the spaciousness of the photos and paintings in the front room. There were statues too; a tree and a knight.

Around the balcony, a big doorway took them to another part of the second floor, where there was no balcony but endless halls full of uncountable rooms. There was a little cabinet oddly placed near them, and Abigail had a compulsion to push it to the side to find something behind it, but resisted the urge. The girls went past it, down to what might have been the shortest hallway in the house—at least, the shortest one Abigail had seen—and to the room at the end.

The door opened with a squeal; its hinges were rusty and its wood was rotting. Walls were packed tight with books, so much so that Abigail wondered if there was really any 'wall' behind the shelves at all, or if the shelves were the walls. Under their steps, the floor screamed loudly, and Abigail feared that there were gaping holes under the rug, and that she might slip through to some other place.

"This house is ancient," Beverly said, "I can't imagine how old these books might be too."

Dust was attracted to the endless books like magnets. Abigail wondered if the person who primarily owned this library ever had enough time to read all the things in here. How long would that take? Probably more than a lifetime.

Some spines didn't have titles or author names, and she wondered what could be inside of them. Abigail grabbed one from a random shelf at eye-level. "Let's see what this is."

The opening pages were blank, and still felt as crisp as if the book were fresh off the printing press. After the blank pages were illustrations of dissected bodies, torture devices she vaguely recognized, like the piece of metal sharp on both ends that was strapped under somebody's neck so that their head was tilted back—a 'Heretic's Fork', Abigail scanned the page for its name.

Right away Beverly said, "Put that disgusting book back."

Abigail flipped through two more pages then put it back on the shelf, wedging it between the other books and sticking it out a length so that she would know which book to return to if she ever had the chance.

Abigail moved over to the desk where Beverly was standing looking out the window. Abigail saw there was some extension of wall above and below the window, so she knew that the walls weren't made of bookshelves after all, and that regular walls did hold up the ceiling.

The moon was out in daytime; Abigail caught part of it between high branches. She was going to comment on it, but was interrupted by the whispers again.

"Beverly help me."

Beverly tensed. *"Cat."*

Horror hovered with batwings over the room.

The girls locked arms. In the hall Abigail flashed the light around and revealed nothing. She shivered. Whose voice were they hearing? It couldn't have been Cat, she was dead, Abigail had thrown Cat's corpse into the Wet Room.

She didn't want to move any further but Beverly was pulling her through the hall, leading them closer to the whispers, calling Cat's name repeatedly. Abigail shuddered thinking about what the house was capable of, like the *thing* that killed Officer Daniels. She shuddered thinking of the legends about people who had been found in *pieces* here, or were never found at all. What had become of those vanishing people? Abigail hoped she and Beverly would not find out.

"Where are you?" Beverly led them around a corner. *"Cat? It's Beverly, where are you?"*

But the whispers had stopped dead, and the only noises were the sounds of their beating hearts. The girls were still, flashing the light down the hall, and Abigail dreaded what might be revealed at the other end.

Beverly suddenly pulled on Abigail's arm and led her down the hall.

"Do we have to search the whole house in five minutes? Slow down."

"There's five floors, Abby, that's only a floor a minute."

"Well one minute is a long time in this place."

Partway through a corner, deeper and deeper into the house's intricate maze of halls, Abigail was uncertain which hall led which way. Her mind rushed, and it was getting harder to breathe, and she was so nervous, so scared, so trapped. Was there still a way out? She bit her lip, and panic slithered through her mind.

"Abigail help me."

Abigail was frozen. She thought she was going to have a heart attack. It was Cat's voice—exactly Cat's voice. A voice that was soft and cold and scared and lost. The water in the Wet Room had probably shriveled her skin, had probably made her skin purpled and deformed, and Abigail pictured Cat coming through any of the adjacent doors with her neck bent at an impossible angle, hands outstretched for Abigail so she could hurt Abigail in the same way Abigail hurt her, and Abigail would be the next corpse to be thrown into the Wet Room.

There were eyes watching from every corner; hands waiting to pounce.

Abigail and Beverly took two small steps to the right, coming closer to the cries, coming closer to the whispers.

"Help! Help!" Cat's voice turned from a whisper to a scream.

"We're coming," Beverly said, moving faster.

Abigail's mind spun, her thoughts were changing. Something pulsed inside of her; something different, something strange. Her left hand twitched.

"Abiiiigaiiiil…." Cat dragged her name out hideously. *"Bevvvverl-lllyyyy…"*

Chills crept on wildly beneath Abigail's skin. Her body pulsed with that new feeling she had only recently felt; she still had no name or words for it. Gooseflesh rose on her arms. Far away doors opened and shut under an unseen hand. Cat's corpse was looking for them.

"Aaaabiiigaiiil…. Bevvverlllyyyyyy…"

The shadows that filled the windowless corners of the hallway were deep and cavernous, and prodigious streaks of cold crawled spider-like up Abigail's back when she thought that if she took one misstep, she'd plummet into the world of shadows.

With every step into darkness, the house was becoming colder, and the voice was becoming louder. The thought of Cat's reanimated corpse dragging her into the Wet Room surfaced again; for a brief moment an image of a nightmarishly misshapen face with sunken red eyes and twisted hands with sharp claws appeared in her mind, and she was absolutely certain she was going to see that monstrosity reaching for her with decaying skin dangling from the corners of its lips. Another chill slithering serpent-like up her spine snapped the image away from her mind.

"Help me!"

Abigail regretting coming to this sickly cursed place. She wanted to turn around and leave. But her body refused to listen to her. A streak of light flashed across the hall at the girls. Just then, that new feeling was pulsing through Abigail's body once more. She wished she could begin to tell Beverly about it, wished she could put it into words, but there were no words for this type of feeling, as if something was *stretching* inside of her skin, as if something were *growing* inside of her body.

"What are you two doing here?"

Abigail pushed herself away from the bright light. Putting her hand in front of her eyes, she squinted over her fingertips and saw that it was Bruno. He lowered the flashlight so that it was aimed at their feet.

"We were looking for Cat," Beverly said. "She—she was calling us."

"Cat? She's here?"

"Didn't you hear her?"

"I heard your steps. I thought you were Cat."

Bruno looked from Beverly to Abigail. Abigail tried to stay calm and said, "She's up here."

"Well then where the hell is she?"

"We have no idea. She was screaming for help."

Bruno hurried past them, around the corner from where the girls came. "There's one room up here where she might…"

The girls followed to a hallway on the other side of the second floor balcony, a hall that flowed with primordial chills. They had never been to this hall either. At the very end a door towered over them; it was painted red, the only painted door they had seen so far—all the others were unpolished wood.

The girls shivered as they followed Bruno.

Abigail's body pulsed, and something twisted beneath her flesh. She looked at her friend to say something, but couldn't find words, and turned back to the dissolving light that illuminated their dusty path to the door at the end of the windowless hall.

A soft coldness passed over the girls; Abigail waited for it to pass, for summer warmth to come back, but it never did, and she wondered if warmth ever existed at all. For now, all she knew was coldness.

Cat wasn't in the room—but Abigail already knew that.

The flashlights revealed what Abigail first thought was an empty room until further investigation revealed a makeshift wooden altar with three smooth stones on either end of it. Laying on the floor in front of the altar were about a dozen black candles.

"What exactly did you two hear? Huh? Tell me."

Abigail wasn't sure what to say. Thank God Beverly answered Bruno's question: "We already told you, she was calling for help. But that was all we heard. I don't know where she is."

"Is she hurt?"

"I'm not sure."

"Well what the hell are you two sure of?"

"Excuse me, creepo?" Beverly put her hands on her hips. "Where do you get off yelling at us when we were trying to help you?"

Bruno ignored Beverly and pushed past her out of the room.

"AHHHHH!"

Everybody was jolted.

It was Cat's scream.

31

ABIGAIL RAN, FOLLOWING BRUNO'S lead, and they went to a hall on their right, where the scream was coming from, and went down a stairway. They were on the ground floor when the screaming stopped, and Bruno was opening doors and shutting them, looking for Cat, calling her name repeatedly, but Abigail leaned against a wall, her guts twisting at the fact that they were hearing Cat's voice from beyond the grave—how could it be possible? How could they hear the cry of a dead girl?

Bruno was all the way at the other end of the hall, his flashlight shining into another room, still calling Cat's name, and Abigail realized that Beverly was no longer with them. She looked left down the other end of the hall, then looked the other way back to Bruno. No sign of Beverly—how had she gotten separated from them? Had she seen something? Had somebody grabbed her? Was it Cat? Or was there something else in here with them? Her heart was beating fast. It was getting harder and harder to breathe. Suddenly Abigail noticed Bruno was in the hall over. She followed his footsteps. She didn't know him at all but was too scared to be left all alone in this house.

"Abigail…"

The disturbing call made Abigail freeze. Cat's voice drifted from behind her and sent chills digging into her flesh, running along her spine like the soft fingers of ghosts tracing up and down.

"I need to get out of here."

Abigail horrifyingly turned her neck to look over her shoulder. The awful door that led to the basement, the door she had dragged Cat's corpse down, creaked open on its own. With Bruno's steps drifting further in the background, drifting out of reality, Abigail went through the door. The steps creaked with every touch. Abigail's hands gripped the railings tight. She wished Beverly had given the flashlight back to her, because she was moving blind, moving by memory alone.

A small wisp of light pushed through the basement, giving Abigail partial vision, but walking through here was like walking through a place she had only seen in dreams; walking through a dreaded nightmare that she prayed every night would go away.

"Cat?" Abigail couldn't believe the words coming off of her lips. She was trying to talk to a dead girl. *"I-I didn't mean it, Cat. I didn't want to hurt you. It was an accident."*

"Get me out of here."

Tears stained her eyes and muddied her vision. She walked across and came to the tile that led down into the Wet Room. Abigail moved the tile away. Complete darkness below. Even after she wiped her tears, all was darkness below.

"I-I don't know how to help you. I thought you were... I thought I..."

"Abigail I'm dying. I'm not dead yet." Cat was crying. *"The water down here is freezing cold and I—I lost all feeling in my hands and feet. I can't stand up. I need your help."*

Abigail said nothing.

"Abigail please get me out of here. For the love of God please help me."

"You're not Cat!" Abigail slammed her fist. *"You're dead! This isn't real, you can't be real, I saw you die. I... killed you."*

Silence. Only silence.

Darkness from the abyss drifted up and engulfed Abigail. She was so guilty for what she had done, so damn guilty and there was nothing she could ever do to make it right. So damn guilty and didn't deserve any forgiveness.

"Abigail I'm begging you to help me. I don't want to die down here. I forgive you, Abby. Please come get me out of here. I forgive you, all right?"

Abigail leaned closer over the entrance. There was nothing to see but a crypt. A big dark tomb that she shouldn't be entering. Cat's resting place. Abigail looked over her shoulder then straight back into the abyss. Abigail wanted this nightmarish reality to end.

"Cat I am so sorry I hurt you. I don't deserve your forgiveness."

"It's all right Abby just—just huh-hurry please." Cat was crying worse than anybody Abigail had ever heard. *"I don't know how long I can last in this freezing water."*

One last look over her shoulder, then back into the entrance, and Abigail shifted her body so that she could go down feet-first. She was trembling. She dropped down and was instantly wet. A thin streak of light that trickled from the window above the entrance to the Wet Room didn't really help at all; she was blinded almost completely, but as her eyes adjusted to darkness she could tell that the torso across from her was Cat. It was still slumped in the corner but had moved—and Abigail shuddered to think about the corpse drifting with the flow of water. Cat's corpse had been turned to its left side, her chest facing the wall, but her head was twisted completely backwards so that between long clumps of black hair, her eyes watched Abigail.

Abigail staggered backwards into the wall of the Wet Room. Her mouth was open but her scream struggled to find a way to escape. She trembled watching ripples of water brush against Cat's corpse. Obviously Cat dead but—but whose voice had she been hearing? Abigail let out an insane, continuing scream that burned the walls of her throat.

The screams left her lips without end, especially when somebody else descended down into the Wet Room. She backed away further into the corner, aching scream after aching scream filling the hidden room, and suddenly there were hands on her shoulders telling her to shut up.

"What's going on?"

It was Bruno.

"I didn't mean to hurt her, I didn't want to hurt her, I don't know why I did it, I don't know why I did it."

Bruno pointed the flashlight across the Wet Room. Abigail shut her eyes so she wouldn't have to see Cat's rotten body. Bruno walked to the other wall. There were sobs. Abigail wanted to explain to Bruno what happened, but there were no words. How could you put something like this into words?

"What did you do?"

"It was an accident Bruno believe me."

Bruno came across the Wet Room again and smacked Abigail across her face.

"Bruno don't hurt me it was an accident, it was an accident, I can't explain—"

He smacked her again.

"I can explain! Listen to—"

Bruno grabbed her by the shoulders and slammed her into the wall. *"You bitch."*

Abigail put her hands up to stop him from hitting her; his fists came down on her arms then punched her once in the stomach. A jolt of terror ripped through her heart; would she make it out of the Wet Room alive? Bruno was beating her, and she was begging him to stop, but his punches kept coming.

I'm gonna die here. I'm gonna die and rot next to Cat.

All at once the punches stopped.

Bruno was looking over his shoulder. From his flashlight's shine, Abigail saw that a long plant was extended through the overflow pipe; a long ugly hydrilla. It slumped down from the end of the pipe and sank into the watery floor. In an instant the hydrilla jerked and Bruno fell down. The flashlight landed so that it was aimed at Bruno and illuminated it all. The hydrilla was wrapped around his ankle and yanked again, dragging him through the room.

The hydrilla crawled further up his body and tangled around his leg. The plant moved in one quick motion up the wall to the overflow pipe, and Bruno's legs were impossibly crammed through the eight-inch tube. His screams came to an abrupt end as he was pulled little by little, his body condensing and stretches of skin tearing around the edges of the pipe and dropping into the water. His shoulders were stuck, but one last big tug sent them through, peeling skin effortlessly, removing his face from his skull—his skull, all that remained of him, stuck to the pipe. His jaw was slack and open, and through them hung the end of a hydrilla dripping Bruno's blood.

32

BEVERLY WANTED MORE THAN anything to find Cat—and she needed her help—but she couldn't forget why she had come here in the first place. If there was a demon inside of Abigail like she suspected, she needed to banish it to the place it came from. She needed to banish it to the Engstrom place. And what better room to conduct her ritual in than this one that already had an altar and candles? Beverly shuddered to think what rituals had happened in this house before—there were rumors, many of them, about certain rites and rituals taking place in this wicked home. Many people had suggested that that was why the house was so cursed. But Beverly didn't know what to believe about the house's shadowy past and the many rumors surrounding it.

After initially running with Abigail and Bruno through the hall, she returned to the room with the red door—the only door that was different in all of the house—and arranged the black candles that had been left here. Their purpose, and the altar's purpose, she wasn't sure of, and wondered if Cat had something to do with them, since Bruno had suggested Cat might have been in this room.

Cat, I need your help. What am I going to do without you? I can't do this alone... can I?

Beverly opened her purse and was shifting through it all when she heard Cat's voice.

"Beverly please help me."

"Cat? Where are you?" Beverly walked out of the room. *"Cat? I'm right here."*

"I don't want to stay dead."

"Huh? Cat?"

No response.

Beverly went to the balcony. Her flashlight revealed nothing new. She didn't like standing there alone. She wished she knew where Cat was, or Abigail, or Bruno, but all sounds had stopped, and there were no footsteps, no shouting, no whispers.

"Hello? Where is everybody?"

Goosepimples rose on her arms. She was all alone.

She followed in the steps that Abigail and Bruno had gone, but she couldn't figure out where to go once she came into that hallway adjacent to the room with the red door. She moved carefully, hardly breathing, and was afraid that something was watching her.

"Abigail? Cat? Bruno? Anybody? Can you hear me?"

Beverly came upon a stairway and went down nervously. She felt all alone in the archaic house—only her and the eyes of a stranger. Even on the ground floor, the eyes that were watching her never stopped. They kept their hold on her, digging deeper into the back of her head, and any time Beverly turned around, there was nobody there behind her. She went up and down the hallway that the stairs led to, which was a hallway that practically spanned the length of the house, and moving from passageway to passageway, passing under darkened arches, she wasn't sure which direction she was going in anymore.

Her light was fighting against a new type of darkness that was so strong it seemed to overtake the delicate light from the skinny bulb. It was sick cavernous darkness, and Beverly was extra careful to avoid stepping into any shadow that looked so endless and deep.

Beverly moved directionlessly through untraveled halls until she made her way through the other end of the maze and came out under the gigantic spiraling staircase. From there she went to the front room, and from there outside. The sun was setting. Had everybody left her alone? No, they wouldn't have done that. But then, Beverly thought, why didn't she hear anybody? What was everyone doing? She had an awful feeling that something bad had happened to Abigail and Bruno and Cat. She had an awful feeling that everything was going wrong and her whole world would collapse.

A strong wind passed and chilled her.

"Abigail? Cat? Can anyone hear me?"

All alone.

Then Beverly walked up to the gate, thought about leaving, and her hand hovered hesitantly over the latch. She lowered her hand then turned back. She couldn't leave Abigail in there, she couldn't leave without her friend.

The Engstrom place was even more hideous as night was approaching; the last glimpse of brightness was getting further and further away in the sky. Beverly looked from the horizon, which was jagged with trees, to the top windows of the house, and there she saw a flash in the window; a girl moving. It was quick, too quick to tell if it were Abigail or Cat or just who it was, but somebody was up there in the house.

Beverly waited to see if the person would come back to the window or move to any of the other windows. Whoever the girl was, she never did come back. Beverly went back inside the house, chills pinching her skin, and set off to find where everybody had gone. Maybe, she thought, they had all fallen through a trap door. Maybe they were shouting from a hidden unseen place, and she couldn't hear them because they were impossibly far away.

"Where is everybody?"

Beverly nervously went up the spiraling stairway, finding it odd that she suddenly knew a bit of her way around the place, and was able to come right back to the room with the red door, where she had desperately hoped Cat would be waiting for her so that they could banish the spirit from Abigail.

Beverly thought about that day at Abigail's house with Cat. Abigail's eyes had changed and were black, and her hands had changed into paws, and Beverly knew she couldn't do this without Cat's help.

Was there any way out of this now?

"Cat?"

Nobody said a word.

And where was Abigail? Where had Bruno taken her? Beverly shivered.

She didn't want to assume the worst, but thoughts were crawling into her mind. She never did trust Bruno, she shouldn't have believed him when he seemed so upset about Cat—maybe he was acting, maybe it was all a show, maybe he had done something to her, maybe he had hurt Abigail, maybe—*No, no, stop thinking that way. If he hurt Cat and Abigail, why isn't he after me?*

"Abigail? Where are you?"

Beverly walked across the upstairs balcony again, going to her left, going back to the library room. Was Abigail back there? Beverly nervously entered, and the room was empty. She even checked under the desk. Nobody anywhere.

Back in the tangle of hallways, she was crying as she searched for them. *"Please Abigail where are you?"*

"I don't want to be dead anymore."

Cat's voice. She was near. She was crying. Her voice was full of pain, and it sent immense shivers along Beverly's back. What did she mean she didn't want to be dead anymore? Beverly wanted to scream.

"Can I have your body, Beverly?"

Beverly said nothing.

"I need a new body, why can't I have your body?"

Beverly stood with her back pressed against one of the back walls near a window. She was too terrified to move, too terrified to look away from the hall straight ahead that was strangely dark; oddly full of the kind of darkness that people disappear in. Cat's voice came from within, and carried with it an otherworldly tone that Beverly could not describe.

"I can't walk around looking like this. Please understand. I need your body. I need it really bad."

At the edge of darkness was Cat's deformed face, half hidden by the grip of strong shadows. Her skin was pale as sickly death, and her lips were pulled into a tight frown. Her hair was gathered in odd clumps dripping water. For one brief second Beverly saw light come across Cat's face and completely reveal its hideousness; there was nothing behind those cold eyes. No soul. Nothing left.

Beverly ran.

It was the last thing she remembered.

Abigail rubbed her eyes. She was laying a few feet away from the entrance to the Wet Room, and her body was still a little wet. Prodigious streaks of cold washed over her and the room. She rubbed her eyes and climbed the stairs. There was no light at all coming in from the tiny window above the Wet Room entrance. There was a flashlight in her pocket, but her hand didn't respond when she told herself to grab it.

Beverly was dead.

She was at the bottom of the stairs.

Abigail kneeled at her side. There was a pulse. Abigail had been wrong, her friend was fine.

She was so peacefully asleep, and Abigail didn't want to wake her. She carried her the short distance to the front room and laid her on the couch.

Kill her, Abigail thought, and her hands slid around Beverly's neck.

She looked at her friend's sleeping face. She couldn't do it. Why did she want to do it? Why were her hands here? Abigail slowly slid them away. What was she doing? She backed away from Beverly, wiping her tears, and left the front room.

Then Abigail finally turned on the flashlight and crept alone, and went all the way up the spiraling staircase back to the second floor.

Back in the library, Abigail grabbed the nameless book she had left partly sticking out, and took it to the desk. She used her flash-light to read, but there was a little bit of moonlight, and that helped her too. She flipped through pages, clinging to every word and every illustration.

Thus was the first night in the Engstrom place.

33

THERE WAS NOTHINGNESS; ONLY a dark haze. She didn't know who she was or where she was, or what the pain in her back was, or why her body felt as if something were stretching inside of it. This body did not feel like her own, and for a while, she thought she was only a floating consciousness. It wasn't until her body convulsed against the chilled floor did she realize she was in control of the body, and she realized she was staring up at the eldritch darkness of the ceiling. Still, for a while, she laid there, trying to remember her name. It was on the tip of her tongue, and she shivered again, and her head hurt, and her body twisted, and something inside of her was pulsing with the beat of her heart.

Who am I? Where am I?

Minutes ticked by before she had the strength to move her hand to wipe sweat from her forehead. Grasped in her hand was a circular piece of metal that jingled keys. She held it back, trying to study it through the murky cloak of blackness around her, but its outline was jagged and difficult to decipher. She took a deep breath, then sat up, and her body lagged behind her thoughts and commands as if it were her first time ever controlling a human body, as if she had never been alive before now, as if she had just been born, a teenage girl, just a moment ago. As if she had never been Abigail Martinez until this very moment.

Abigail, that's my name, her thoughts came between brief stabs of pain. Everything hurt, everything was sore. *How did I get here? What's going on? Bev—Beverly? Where is she?*

Abigail's eyes searched the hall, but it was so dark that she couldn't tell which hall she was in. It was cold, she was tired, she was lost, she didn't know where her friend was, and her last memory was opening the door to the library. What had happened since then? Had she made it past the door? Had she gone inside? What book did she read?

Suddenly she had an image in her head of her hands around Beverly's neck.

Did I hurt her?

Her mind strained to remember what had happened, but no thoughts could be conjured up past the immense pain in her skull. Maybe she had fallen, she thought, but she had not remembered ever walking through this hall, and had no clue what she could've been on her way to do... what was with the keys? Where had she found them at? What did she want to unlock with them? And more importantly, where was her flashlight? Abigail felt her lap and her pockets and felt all around herself, patting up small clouds of dust but there was no sign of the flashlight.

"Beverly? Beverly can you hear me?"

She inched to the nearest wall, braced herself, and wobbled up. She wiggled side to side fixing herself and finding her footing. Her body felt so alien to her, but the more she moved it, the more normal it felt, as if she had to get used to her own body again, as if it were forming itself around her spirit. Her joints felt *loose,* as if they hadn't been constructed yet, or were in the intricate process of reconstructing; the regrowth of her body was strange, and it was only by analogy that she called it *regrowth* at all, because it felt as if it were the first time she ever existed. Part of her soul felt missing, along with all her memories.

The keys jingled again—had she been opening a door or locking something away?

"Beverly?" Abigail called again. "Bev? Bev?"

No answer.

Abigail took a step. As if relearning to walk, her body wobbled, and pain shot from her feet to her knees, and screamed from her knees to her hips. Pain flew down in white sparks from her wrists and disappeared around her elbows. Her next step was more balanced, but a few more paces and she was leaning against the wall again.

"Beverly?" Abigail screamed against the pain. *"Oh… where are you?"*

She shivered. At the end of the hall, there was a passageway left and a passageway right, and no sort of exit that would take her into any place other than this jumbled maze. There were many, many doors and statues surrounding her, and as she looked over her shoulder occasionally, she was certain that some of the statues had moved, or shifted position, or shifted in size, and some of them that she saw hadn't been there the first time… but that all could have been her imagination, she thought, and that her mind was only playing tricks on her.

Dizzyingly, she thought, *I'll never get out of here.*

"Bev?" Abigail whispered as she walked through halls. It was all she could think to say. "Bev? Bev? Bev? Bev?"

She slumped against a wall to catch her breath. Walking, even only short distances, was exhausting.

Maybe this was the afterlife, she thought, and she was doomed to walk and walk and never find her way out; every turn there'd be more halls, more statues, and she'd always think, *I know where I am, just a minute longer and I'll be out,* but 'out' would never come, and she'd be on the brink of coming close to the exit forever and ever.

Forever and ever, she thought, so weird to never have an end. Everything had a beginning and an end—everything in this house, all the people that had been inside of it, and everything on earth had a beginning and an end, but eternity had no end, and the thought of being alive for all existence and never coming to an end bothered her.

Turning a corner, dizziness erupted and pumped through her body so strong that she felt the end would never come.

God please get me out of here.

In a certain hall, a cabinet was pushed back to reveal a short door behind it whose knob was chained shut. As she reached for it, fists banged behind the door. Abigail screamed and backed away, her grip tightening on the keys. Her body felt more natural now, and felt as if it had stopped regrowing itself around her.

"Beverly? Are you in there?"

As soon as she spoke, the knocking stopped.

Suddenly footsteps raced up and down *inside* the walls, and Abigail bolted away from it, hoping that she'd not be turned around and find her way back to this very hallway. She had no idea where she was going.

Running turned into a walk, and Abigail caught her breath, resting against a wall.

"Oh Beverly... Beverly where are you?"

Abigail listened to the open house, waiting for a reply from her friend. There was only silence. She thought she would hear those steps in the walls again, behind that chained door, but there was nothing stirring.

God help me, God save me.

Abigail ended her break and moved again until she came to a stairway that ended a hall. It could've brought her anywhere, but it was better than being up here with whatever was threatening to break through the hidden door. How long had that *thing* been in this house? And why was the cabinet moved? Was somebody trying to open that door? How long ago had they tried? Had... had Abigail been the one trying to move it? There were the keys in her hand, the keys that she didn't have any idea where she found them... was she trying to open it?

Abigail shivered.

The wide stone steps echoed under her touch.

It went straight down, with only one small twist in their structure. When she came out the bottom, there was a faint light in her peripheral vision; she turned to see Beverly looking out a window, with Abigail's flashlight held lazily in her hand pointing at the ground.

Abigail ran to her. *"Beverly! Oh my—"*

Beverly shut the curtains. *"Don't look."*

"What?"

"Don't look out there."

"What do you mean?" Abigail finally was standing next to her. Even through darkness, and with her hair all messed up from sleep, Beverly still looked as beautiful as she always did—but her frown was so tight and her eyes were so full of fear that Abigail was chilled.

"Don't look."

Abigail reached for the curtain and pulled it back; moonlight revealed part of the back yard, but in the moment before Beverly grabbed the blind back and shut it, Abigail saw nothing out of the ordinary.

"We need to leave. Come on."

"Is this a dream? Beverly what happened?"

"Come on."

Abigail grabbed Beverly's hand but stayed in place and didn't move when Beverly tried to walk away. "Tell me what you saw."

"I can't."

"Why not."

"Where were you, Abby?"

Abigail shut her eyes and squeezed Beverly's hand, trying to remember. "I was following Bruno. I don't remember what happened after that."

Beverly gulped. "We just need to leave. Come on."

"We can't go, I need to put Helen to rest, I need to get her out of my life once and for all."

"We need to get out of here now," Beverly said distantly, as if she were standing ten feet away.

Abigail opened her eyes to see that her friend *was* ten feet away, and she screamed. Whose hand had she been grabbing?

Shivers climbed her body. Abigail ran.

Footsteps slammed behind them, and chills slithered further over Abigail's body.

Cat's whispers followed. *"Aaaabigaiiiiil… Beeeeverlyyyy…"*

Beverly led the way, turning a corner, and no matter how fast she and Abigail ran, Abigail felt they were putting no separation between them and whoever was chasing. Tears swelled in her eyes, making the already faint light even more difficult to keep track of through coiling darkness.

"I need your help."

Abigail's body pulsed again, and her head felt like it weighed one hundred pounds, and she leaned against a wall, then fell on her side. Something flowed inside of her; something was happening, and she wanted to get out of here this very second.

Abigail pulled herself up then slipped back down.

The light was gone. Had Beverly realized Abigail wasn't behind her anymore?

No footsteps ahead of her, no footsteps behind her. Abigail laid down in pain, all alone and crying, until a hand grabbed onto her own. She did not scream, did not flinch, did not pull away; she allowed herself to be pulled up.

Abigail stood over the balcony on the second floor, watching Beverly. Beverly was shining her light around, unaware that Abigail was above her. Abigail's lips curled into a smile.

"Beverly help me."

Beverly screamed, shining her light up. *"Abby!"*

Abigail ran around the balcony for the main winding staircase and ran down as Beverly ran up. Beverly shined the light at the steps as she ran, and they met each other partway to the bottom of the stairs.

Beverly wrapped her arms around Abigail. *"I didn't know I lost you. I am so sorry Abigail, Abigail please forgive me."*

Abigail grabbed Beverly by the shoulders. *"The girl is mine."*

A shadow of terror crept over Beverly's face. *"No."*

Beverly stepped down. Abigail descended with her. *"This body is mine. It belongs to me."*

Beverly raised a fist and hit her, but it didn't hurt; Beverly wasn't strong at all. *"Get away from me."*

"I'm going to kill you."

"Abby snap out of it, it's not you."

"Beverly?" Abigail looked at her friend confused. How did they get to the stairs? Why was she looking at her like that? What was happening? "What's going on?"

"It's this house, it's not you, this house—"

Abigail grabbed Beverly's wrist in a tight grip, then pulled her up the stairs with her. Abigail dragged her in one hand, keys jingled in the other, and she listened to Beverly's beautiful screams. Her lips pulled into a smile from a frown.

"Abigail stop it, this isn't you."

Abigail laughed.

Beverly screamed; she clawed at Abigail's arms, but the pain did not phase her.

Abigail dragged her through the second floor, down two halls until she came to the room that had the altar and the candles. She shut the door behind them, and pushed her friend into the center of the room.

"What are you going to do to me?"

"Beverly?" Abigail said breathlessly.

"Yes, it's me, it's Beverly."

"Beverly…"

"Yes, Abby?"

"Run."

34

THE FIGURE IN DARKNESS ran to the door and opened it, and all she could do was watch the girl leave. Two different thoughts from two different voices screamed in her mind dizzyingly, and she wanted to move, wanted to chase, and it wasn't until one of the voices overpowered the other that she finally felt the urge to move, and her joints hurt as she ran, and she was near the other girl—*What was her name again?*—and tried to grab her.

The girl, just out of reach, slipped past her hands, and Abigail tumbled down and bumped her head against a wall. Pain pulsed. The girl was stampeding, putting so much distance between them both, but instead of following her, Abigail went down a small stairway, one she had not remembered seeing previously, which led her quickly down to the main floor in time to step into luscious moonlight and startle the girl—*Beverly, that's her name*—and her raised hands twisted, ready to grab the girl by her long blonde hair and rip it from her scalp, but another voice in her mind, a much more hushed voice that she struggled and strained to hear, told her not to, and took control of the hands. She lowered them.

"Something's happening to me," Abigail said. It was hard to finish the sentence when something stretched in her soul, filling her, overtaking her.

Beverly stepped away, but with listless sullen eyes said, "I want to help you."

"How can you help me?"

The two minds in Abigail's skull fought against each other; one whispered that Beverly should live, the other whispered that we needed to use her, then she would die. Abigail's mouth opened, and she wasn't sure which mind's thoughts to speak.

Beverly took another step away, then ran, and Abigail thought about chasing her, but didn't. She wasn't in any hurry. The night was very young.

Drenched in darkness, she thought that tonight would last forever. The longest night on earth. It was all hers and she was in control. And somewhere far, far into the house, the girl was crying, and her footsteps echoed empty halls.

"Beverly I don't want to hurt you."

But one of the minds told her: *That is not true. We want to hurt her. Very, very much. Once she helps us.*

Then she thought, *No, Beverly is my friend, we don't want to hurt her.*

Yes we do.

No—please, I can't hurt her, why should we hurt her?

There were steps behind her, and she thought that maybe the girl had gone around her and gotten to the door, but there was nobody else here in the living room but her. Then she went to the window and took a peek outside; nobody was there, Ashfall was still, and night was heavy, and everybody must have been having pleasant dreams on such a night as this.

Keys jingled on their chain. *Raise those keys in your hand and slam them down on that girl's head. Do it until she's dead.*

No, no, no.

Do it.

No. I can't.

Yes you can.

Shut up.

I am your conscience. You cannot shut me up.

Get out of my head.

But I'm you. You can't get out of your own head, Abigail.

Shut up.

I'm you, you want this to happen, you want to kill her.

Shut up shut up shut up shut—

Raise the keys and bring them down on her big fat head.

Abigail lost control of her body, and as coldness slithered tightly over her skin, she was moved like a marionette, and her movements were not her own, and yet they felt natural, as if this is how she always should have been moving, as if something else should have always been in control.

Abigail was a floating consciousness in her head; Something Else had taken control. She couldn't move her arms or legs the way she wanted to; something else, the *Other Voice,* was moving them for her. She strained to take back control, and felt that flexing feeling, that feeling of her soul stretching, acting in reverse, and she was the one stretching inside a body, trying to fill it with her spirit.

Somewhere, Beverly was moving.

"Come out come out wherever you are."

Calmness. She waited for something to stir.

Abigail was chilled, and fought against her legs that were marching up another staircase, marching towards the third floor.

She must've gone up as far away as she could get from us. We'll find her. We'll kill her.

No please you can't do that, you don't understand, she's my friend, I don't want to cause her any harm. I don't want to hurt anybody. Leave me alone.

This is what you always wanted to do.

"Beverly you were right." Abigail forced the scream past her lips. Her soul stretched until she was in control again. *"We need to get out of here. I have the keys, the fence is locked."*

There were no sounds in the house, and Abigail wondered if Beverly even existed at all; but she had remembered the girl, had remembered looking into her eyes, had remembered walking with her, talking to her, grabbing her hands, burning a book with her, putting her hands around the girl's throat. Hadn't she been real? Hadn't she run? Hadn't she seen her eyes shining in faint moonlight?

At the end of the hall she looked into a mirror hanging in a silver frame; she looked as pale as a gleam of moonlight. Her eyes were still the same, her hair was still the same, but was she still the same person she always thought she was? Thick and dark hair, full hazel eyes, and a rather pale face. Abigail Martinez looked like a cheap imitation of Abigail Martinez. She lifted a hand and touched the glass as if it were a portal to another earth—maybe that was where she was, another earth where nothing made sense, and Abigail was not herself.

Abigail shivered.

In her mind, the two voices fought continually, and that made it hard to decide where to keep going. Where was she again? The third floor? The fourth? Was she still headed up? Where was Beverly? She was soundless—maybe she turned into a spider and was crawling her way out of here and past the gate.

"Come out come out little spider. I promise I won't step on you."

Abigail wanted to scream something out, but didn't know what to say, and any minimal control she had gained for a minute or two had receded, and she was slipping away into the depths of her own mind, sinking into her brain, and her *Other Voice* was in control, pulling the strings that hung from her marionette arms and legs.

"Where can a spider be in such a big place?"

At another stairway she went upstairs until she was at the fifth floor. Adrenaline pumped through her body; if Beverly had come all the way up here, she was closing in on her, and she felt a rush and a thrill. And with so many rooms, where to begin?

"Spider?"

A smile crept across Abigail's face when she heard running coming from downstairs.

35

ABIGAIL'S MIND WAS SO hazy she couldn't focus on her surroundings, and moved as if in a dream. Her surroundings seemed to be shifting or turning, but her eyes couldn't focus on them; there was only the haze, and only the idea of her body moving, and she somehow moved between statues and corners and things unscathed. Behind certain doors things rattled and whirred, and when she was near enough to the chained door, fists pounded again, and she became faintly aware of the keys still in her hand, and thought about unlocking its door, but something else in her mind told her to catch Beverly first, and that they needed her, and that the keys on the ring would bash in her skull. Then another part of her mind told her that that wasn't what they were going to do, that Beverly was her friend, that they needed to leave with her, that there was no point in being here, and they never should have come.

Moving by somebody else's control, Abigail wondered if any of the things she was seeing were real or not, because there were whispers in the halls, there were darkened faces hidden by draping shadows, and hands reached for her but never touched her.

You're gonna kill her.

I don't want to hurt her.

We are going to bash her brains in.

Somebody walked behind her, but she was passing through hazy darkness like a puppet being pulled by its thin strings, and couldn't convince her body to turn to see who was there. Abigail dropped back into a little floating spirit in her mind; the *Other* was in control, and Abigail struggled again to regain her body.

She panicked. She felt as if it were impossible to reach her soul back into her arms, and that she was frozen like this. Stuck forever. Stuck while she had to listen to those sick, sick thoughts from the *Other Voice.*

Tell me who you are.

You know who I am.

Do I?

I'm you.

Her hand flexed; it had something to write, but there was no time to stop and write. Abigail—or, rather, her body—descended wide steps, and on the second floor she heard slamming footfalls again, and near the balcony she saw the outline of the running girl.

Keys raised, Abigail brought it down on the girl's chest, then stared into blankness. There was no girl there at all.

She turned in each direction to find her, but the girl wasn't there. And while her guard was down, her soul stretched, and she retook the body, and the other voice in her head became its own floating consciousness, and all it could do was listen to her, and watch her as she regained control, relearned how to move her arms and legs, and set out to find Beverly.

"Beverly I—I need you to help me. Where are you?"

Abigail went through the hall that led to the library; she walked there without a second thought, as if something else were guiding her. She pushed the door open; Beverly stood by the table, looking for something in her purse.

"What's happening to me?"

"Please don't hurt me." Beverly backed away. "Please don't hurt me, please don't hurt me."

"I'm not going to hurt you. I don't want to. It's the *Other Voice* that wants to hurt you. Not me."

Beverly said nothing.

"There's someone else in this room with us. They're in my head. I need to get it out before it hurts you. Sometimes they take control of me and I can't do anything about it. They want..."

Beverly was frozen.

"They want to kill you."

Beverly stepped to one side of the desk, then Abigail stepped in that direction as well.

Abigail fell to her knees. Her body pulsed with irritation, and the *Other Voice* was growing, stretching inside of her, regaining control, pushing itself into her mind, extending itself through her brain and body, receding anything that was Abigail Martinez into an abyss.

"Help me." Abigail whispered before it took full and total control.

Beverly foolishly leaned down to give her a hand, and Abigail pulled Beverly down with her. Abigail's wrist strained as she held on to the body, then Beverly pulled her hand away and smacked Abigail across the face. Pain burned in her cheek.

Beverly rushed away from Abigail and opened her purse to bring out a crucifix; Abigail's eyes immediately were repelled, and Beverly came closer, pressing it closer and closer to Abigail, until she was close enough so that Abigail was able to grab Beverly's arm and sink her nails past the skin; soft blood trickled thickly and warmly over her fingers. Beverly recoiled, dropping the cross, and moonlight flashed on her face, and Abigail snapped out of it. She was sobbing, she didn't mean to hurt Beverly—it was the *Other*.

"*I'm so sorry. It wasn't me.*"

Beverly held her bloody arm. She left the room. Abigail wanted to tell her to stay but she couldn't bring herself to do it.

How can I fix this? Isn't there something I can do?

Abigail was in control over the *Other Voice*, and was startled at every shadow that moved. The halls were wide and empty, and stretched for unusual lengths.

Something stalked her.

Eyes burrowed into the back of her skull, and she hoped it was Beverly, but she knew better, and she knew how the eyes of a friend felt. Turning around to look back the way from which she came, something was approaching the corner.

"*Oh Abigaiiilll…*"

Cat's dead voice chilled her. Abigail opened a door and slipped through.

The room had one little window displaying the side of the house; leafless branches scratched the window, making a very unpleasant noise that made her cringe. The room at first glance was empty, until she noticed a little wooden piece in the wall that shifted eagerly under her touch. She moved it back and forth gently, then opened it fully. The length and height were big enough for her to slip through, and as the footsteps approached, she was tempted, so she crawled inside and shut the sliding wood.

Just as it closed, the doorknob across the room opened, and Cat was coming into the room—how did Cat know she was in here? Had Cat seen her? Abigail was chilled. Listening to the unseen steps of the dead girl in the adjacent room, her body convulsed and threatened to scream. Cat must not have noticed the sliding piece of wood, because Abigail heard her steps walk right out, and Abigail was relieved. Then, when Abigail reached for the sliding wood, she discovered that it would not budge.

She had no idea if she should scream or not, for fear that *Cat* would find her. Fidgeting with the strange set of keys, she realized that the wood had no lock, so none of them would be useful to her at all.

With what little room she had to work with, in the place that was so dark that even the smallest step could send her plummeting into decaying darkness, Abigail backed up a little bit, then ran at the wooden door and kicked it.

It did not budge—not even a crack.

She wound back, careful not to go any length further than she had already gone, and kicked again, and yielded no results.

Abigail faced unnerving darkness and prayed that God was listening—that even here in depths so far away from the world, that He could hear her—and prayed that He could rescue her from this nightmare, from this hell she had been thrust into, that He could make the voices in her head stop, but they just wouldn't stop, and the two voices intertwined and crisscrossed in her skull, and one of them wanted to kill Beverly, and the other wanted her to live, and she was to the point where she couldn't remember which one was *Abigail* and which one was *The Other.*

Looking into the open vastness of darkness, what archaic realms could possibly lay just beyond her reach? A part of her mind hinted at ancient evils, and about things locked away, and about certain rites and curious rituals that might have happened here, but the other part of her mind was reluctant to think that such things had ever happened, especially just out of reach of where she stood.

In desperation she tried knocking on the wood again; it was flimsy and old, but it acted as if it were new, as if it were enchanted not to break. It had moved so easily and softly on the other side, but on this side it did not move at all. She set the keys down, and with both hands tried to angle it so that it could slide open if perhaps it were stuck on a certain groove, but that did not improve the situation whatsoever. She picked up the keys again and wondered what she should do. There was a whole world on the other side of darkness, a world where she could be one of the only people to ever visit, but it would take her further away from where she needed to go—she needed to go get to Beverly, she needed to get out of this prison, she needed to find a way to separate herself from the madness seeping into her brain, overpowering her, taking control of her, making her forget who she was.

Here in darkness, she thought, *This is what it's like to be dead.*

Abigail shivered. Darkness was tempting. She gave in and moved forward as softly as she could, stretching out her hands to grab on to smooth walls which then gave way to rough rocky structures. Her weary eyes tried to make sense of darkness, but this darkness was so unnatural that nothing could be seen through it.

Eventually the walls tightened. As they closed on her body, she had to stand sideways to keep going. One of the voices in her mind told her to keep moving, but the other told her turn around and try the piece of wood again—it was only a piece of wood, a thin old piece of wood she should have been able to kick down without any effort...

...but all her efforts had been useless. It wasn't going to budge.

Going deep down into the unknown was the only thing she could do.

36

MANY RUMORS ABIGAIL HAD heard before about what went on within the walls of the Engstrom place—rumors of voices on the other side of walls, things moving within them, and subterranean passageways and strange caverns of untold depths. If any of these things were true, Abigail was horrified of what she might discover when traveling through these walls blind without a flashlight or lantern or candle.

Abigail shuddered. It reminded her of the other Ashfall legends, that people who had never seen light were lurking underground in tunnels that were haunted by the spirits of human offerings used to summon Satan himself, but there were so many different rumors about those tunnels it was hard to keep track. Supposedly those tunnels were deep under the forest area behind the house and leading toward the farm and beyond.

Abigail pressed her ear to the structure and listened. Maybe she would hear Beverly—*Oh Beverly I miss you*—and maybe that meant she could talk to her, and have her get to the room and open the door, but all was silence. Perhaps the walls were too thick to let sound through.

Her breaths came shallowly, and all her fears tumbled through her head. She was absolutely helpless, wasn't she? Tears poured suddenly, and her heart was beating at tremendous speeds. What if she became like those people lost in darkness, she wondered. What if she became like one of those hideous legends about people lost in underground tunnels?

She tried to think pleasant thoughts, or hum her favorite songs, but no matter how many times she tried to cheer herself up or calm herself or remain hopeful, her breaths felt as if they'd never leave her lungs, and every part of her body was tense, and she felt her consciousness slipping away, and the other part of her mind was taking over.

Get the hell out of my head.

I can't do that, Abby. You're the one in my *head.*

Get out! Leave me alone! Leave me alone already!

Don't you understand anything, Abby? You're the intruder. 'Abigail' isn't real at all. You made her up.

No.

You wanted so bad to stab your parents. You wished that car had run over Beverly when you pushed her into the street. You killed the priest. You killed Cat. You know you have a sick mind that's capable of taking somebody's life with no remorse. You made up this other personality to have another person to blame it on—just like you always blame your problems on somebody else.

Was the voice right? Was she the intruder? Was everything Abigail knew about herself a lie? Was she evil? Did she really want to harm her loved ones? She grabbed her head with both hands, keys softly scratching her cheek, and pulled on her hair. She wanted to explode—it was killing her, she was torn, she wanted both voices to shut up and stop arguing, but both of them were fighting for control of her body, and she had no earthly idea who it belonged to anymore. Was she real? Had Abigail Martinez ever existed at all?

I don't believe anything you're saying. You're the reason I've done all those things. You're the one who wanted to kill my parents. You're the one who made me push Beverly in front of that car. You're the one who—

Soon you'll find out just how wrong you are, Abby.

Her name sounded sickening the way it rolled off the tongue of that other voice. Her hands clenched into fists. She despised it. She wanted to reach into her mind and pull out that other voice and strangle it.

Hideously her body pulsed, and she leaned against the wall trying to stop that all too familiar feeling, trying to stop what she knew was coming. The other voice stretched inside of her, filling its soul and spirit into every last part of her body, relearning how to move it and how to make it function. Her hands fit the other voice's spirit like a glove; it stepped into her feet, adjusted to the shape of her torso, and when her heart beat, it beat for the *Other.*

"Help me. Somebody help—"

At first, Abigail thought these were her own words leaving her lips, then she realized they were coming from somewhere else—it was Beverly, and she was distant, yet her strained screams traveled very, very far.

Abigail slammed her hand on the wall, using all the force in her body to push past the grip that the *Other Voice* had over her. *"I'm coming."*

There was no reply, only shouts, and Abigail knew that Beverly hadn't been near enough to hear her, and she hadn't been loud enough either. Or maybe sound only traveled one way in here; maybe everything moved differently in the dark, and the rules of the universe need not apply here, because anything could happen here, anything could exist, anything could be lurking, and anything could be watching her.

It was almost better not to know, she thought, or she'd be even more frightened.

Abigail took a step, her soul fighting with the intruder. Where was the exit? Where did this place lead to? Surely there was a reason for this chamber to exist, for somebody to construct it, and to have that little sliding piece of wood put in.

You're going to die in here.

No I'm not.

You deserve it for all the pain you've caused.

I didn't do anything, it was all you.

Cat's family can never get her back and it's all your fault, Abigail. They can't even have a proper burial because you hid away her body to rot.

I—but I—

You killed the priest. You're nothing but a murderer.

He—but I—I didn't—

You tried to steal my body, now give it back, Abigail.

Abigail didn't know what to believe. Her mind was swirling. Which voice was right? Whose body was it? Had she stolen it? Maybe she had. Maybe she was the intruder. Maybe the voice was right and she needed to give it back. She wasn't sure anymore which voice was right and which voice was wrong; they were blending closer and closer so that it was becoming harder to tell them apart.

Abigail tiptoed again, frantically searching, frantically shifting her hands up and down looking for any latch that would give, or any knob that would turn. Sliding her hands against the rough surface, she came to a loose section of wall by accident as she readjusted herself and held on to keep balance. It moved under her touch. A large section of wall receded, allowing light in. Before crawling out, Abigail watched faint amounts of light fill spaces that must not have been illuminated in a lifetime; she wasn't sure what the source was, but there was just enough to reveal two other paths she could have gone down. There was no time to wonder about the stygian worlds that lay just beyond this view, and where she might have ended up had she not accidentally found her escape.

Leaving the hidden space in the wall, she shut the piece of wood, and found that she was stepping out basically at the same spot where she had been when she first heard Cat's steps a little while ago. The wall slid back perfectly into place so that she could not really notice any seams unless she looked very closely.

"Beverly?" Abigail whispered.

A scream came from outside the house.

Abigail ran to the direction of the screams, and from the window saw Beverly rattling the gate.

"Somebody, anybody, please help me—"

Abigail watched her.

Beverly shook the fence furiously under a tight grip, then gave up and let go and fell on the ground. She sobbed. Watching her hopelessly try to escape made the *Other Voice* smile.

Abigail floated away from her body, floated out of control, and hung like a cloud in her head. That other voice was in control again, looking viciously at Beverly with sickening thoughts about hurting her.

Please don't do anything to Beverly.

We're going to mutilate her corpse beyond all recognition.

She's my friend I don't want—

Yes you do want to. Think about it, can't you feel it? Can you feel how badly we—how badly you want to hurt her?

I don't want to hurt her. I'm not you. I'm me.

I'm going to bash my friend's head in. I'm going to kill her.

Yes…. Yes I am.

Beverly looked up to find Abigail in the window. Their eyes locked, and Beverly screamed.

37

Everything was blurry behind tears that erupted in Abigail's eyes. Her body moved as if reality were on fast forward, and it was under the control of that hideous *Other Voice,* and she thought, *I'm never going to have control over my body again.* Abigail was a marionette, and her body moved with every pull of its strings.

Her body was becoming more foreign with each passing second, but then again maybe it had never been her body at all. Maybe she had never been Abigail Martinez and that was all a lie. And if she did return to control of the body, she thought, she'd never know how to move it. How did legs move? Where did movements start—the toes, the knees, the hip? These hands were too big for her spirit, she'd never fit all the way through them, like putting on winter gloves that were too big for her hands.

The house was a glowing darkness; a hazy silhouette. Everything blurred as flowers did when observed from the window of a speeding car. Shivers traced Abigail's spine. Beverly was screaming somewhere, and her screams were soothing and relaxing, and Abigail felt her consciousness slipping deeper and deeper into her brain, becoming replaced by that other voice telling her that this was right, this was the way things should be.

The front door had opened—Abigail's hands had done it, but she hadn't felt them move—and she had to cling to what little aware-ness she had left, or the invader would win. Abigail was so tired, so drained, absolutely powerless, absolutely helpless, and so weak—so absolutely weak—that she couldn't fight back against the invader in her body who was approaching the girl. The girl she had once recognized as Beverly, who was now as pale as Abigail had been in the mirror, as pale as a plucked flower, was pressed against the fence, and blonde threads of hair fluttered against cold breezes of wind.

"This isn't you." Beverly looked deep into her eyes. *"Abigail snap out of it. This house is ruining you. Give me the keys—give me the keys right now so we can get out of here."*

"Here you go," Abigail said sweetly, smiled, and held out the keys. *Don't listen to her, don't grab them. Beverly please don't do it.*

Beverly nervously inched forward. Abigail wished to part her lips and scream for her friend to stay away, but she had no power here anymore. This body was not her own—no longer could she take it back over... if it had even been her body to begin with.

Beverly stood as far as she could while still being able to reach for the keys. Her fingertips brushed against them, then Abigail grabbed Beverly's arm and pulled her near. Abigail slid her other hand over Beverly's throat. Beverly dropped the flashlight and dug her nails into Abigail's hand.

Abigail's hand recoiled from Beverly's throat; suddenly Abigail was in charge again of one arm and only one arm, and used it to hold her other arm away from Beverly. The other spirit inside of her body fought for its control again. During Abigail's struggle with the *Other*

Mind, Beverly picked up the flashlight and ran across the yard to the front door.

"Nothing in there will save you."

Don't listen to her, Beverly, it's not me.

Beverly crossed the threshold back into the house.

Abigail slowly followed. Beverly was gone.

There are things I need, Abigail thought. She wasn't sure which of the voices had put the notion in her head—they both sounded so alike that she could not tell a difference between them.

We're going to kill her.

Do I want to kill her?

Yes you do.

I do?

Yes.

Why?

You want to crack her head open.

Suddenly, through the haze of merging voices, a thought was trying to surface. Abigail was trying to remember something. Something Beverly had told her not so long ago. Something important—something that could save them from all of this. But what had Beverly said?

The memory just couldn't form.

It was the key in all of this, Abigail was sure, to remember what Beverly had told her. It was something so small, but now her brain was trying to explain to her what it meant. Abigail prayed she could remember before it was too late.

The thing controlling her body took her through the ground floor, leading her past the spiraling staircase into forbidden areas of the house. All her thoughts were telling her don't enter, but her body continued to move.

We're going to kill her.

Yes, we are.

We're going to crack her head open. We're going to bury her with Cat.

No—no, stop it, I don't want this.

You do, Abigail. You want this. Because I'm you.

You're not me, you're an imposter.

I'm you and we are gonna kill Beverly.

We're... we are going to bash open her skull.

I can't wait to see the terror in her eyes.

Don't lay a finger on her I don't want to hurt her.

The way the two voices talked, the way they sounded, they were both her own voice. There was no difference between them at all anymore. This brain and body shared them both equally.

There were things Abigail knew she needed to find, things she needed to get. The *Other Voice* was leading her body, while the little piece of Abigail that was left was trying to figure out what the important thing Beverly had said was.

What could help me now?

Forget about Beverly. We're going to kill her. Didn't we agree on this?

No I am not.

But you want to, Abigail. You are the one thinking it. You are the one who wanted it.

Abigail could see the *Other Voice's* thoughts clearly—Beverly's face misshapen with terror as painful screams left her lips, Beverly thrown on the grown and gushes of blood escaping her torn skin. And Abigail would be responsible for it all.

Abigail's soul pulsed, and as it pushed to overtake her arms again, that other soul pushed her out.

Amorphous shadows rose and fell on the surrounding walls, and Abigail wondered what cast them. Moonlight found its way in through a back window, or so Abigail assumed, but she couldn't control her face or neck to turn and see where the light was entering from. Her eyes were set on a staircase—it seemed as if the house had more staircases than rooms somehow—and the thing controlling her led her up.

And you thought it was fun killing Cat and killing Bruno. Wait until you see how fun it'll be to kill Beverly.

I feel so guilty about Cat. I didn't want kill her. And I didn't kill Bruno, it was the house.

You killed her. You put your hand over her throat and squeezed.

But I didn't want that to happen. I didn't want to do it.

Kill Beverly just like you killed Cat.

I'm not a killer.

Yes you are.

Abigail couldn't tell which level of the house the thing in her body had taken her to. It possessed her hands and moved them across a wall, pulling back a loose section, but she stopped abruptly and pushed it back into place. There were sobs and footfalls in the hall. Beverly must not have known Abigail was up here. Quickly Abigail retreated into a shadow and stood very still. Her friend walked past without a clue that she was hiding. Beverly looked both ways, and Abigail felt like a shark stalking its prey, or like a hidden spider.

This would make it all feel so much better in the end.

Beverly went around the corner, and walked distantly until she went up a staircase and disappeared. When she was completely gone, and Abigail was sure Beverly wasn't coming back, she moved out of the shadow and slid her hands on the wall again. It moved back to reveal a shelf. On the inside was a robe.

She crept to the mystical spiraling staircase. Joy was flowing through her veins.

I don't want to do this.

Then why am I so exited?

You're not me.

This is you. Haven't you figured it out yet? You want—I want this. Kill her.

She descended the stairs and came to another level of the house, still unclear where her body was being led, and came to a bedroom near the back of the building, near the windows of the long back hallway. In the dusty room, which must have been sealed for decades, she set the robe on the bed. Moonlight entered gently through the window so that she could see it more clearly; it was all white but had yellowed around the edges.

I want no part in this.

The *Other Voice* said nothing. It didn't need to. It had taken all it could from Abigail, and owed her no response.

Soon, Abigail thought, there might not be an Abigail anymore.

The thing in Abigail's head undressed her body. She was naked in the room, and for one brief second her soul flexed and stretched into the empty sockets of her hands. She held them across her body to cover herself, especially to cover her wrists, then as she reached back for her shirt, she lost control. The thing in charge of her body was not embarrassed by nakedness, but immediately put on the white robe. It stretched over her body perfectly, fitting her as if she had always been meant to stand here in this room with this ugly robe on.

Abigail collected branches then put them in the fireplace and lit them with the matches she had found in the kitchen. As she watched the tiny red and blue flame spread, she wondered where Beverly was and what she was thinking, and what she was up to.

Soon warmth spread around her. She rubbed her hands together over the flames, but had no time to waste. She lingered for only a minute, then set off into the house. There were things that needed to be put into place, starting with candles. She took the box of matches with her up to the second floor, then made a quick stop in the library.

Like returning to a place she had only visited in dreams, she was mystified returning to the shelves of books. She ran her hands on the spines, almost forgetting what she was in here for and what she planned to do.

Abigail searched all the shelves until she found the book she was looking for. Its cover was cracked leather and the book was significantly aged and was so fragile that she thought it might split apart in her hands and crumble to dust, yet the week spine held.

Tempted to turn the pages of the forbidden book, she resisted the growing urge. A ribbon bookmark protruded from the spine and was tucked into place right where she needed it; it would do. Abigail slid the book under her arm and left the library.

Upstairs a floorboard creaked. Perhaps it was Beverly, perhaps she was hiding, perhaps she had to shift balance or readjust herself; one small, small movement had given her away.

Abigail quickly went up the wide stairway and to the third floor. The room directly above the library, as best she could figure, was one of the bedrooms on her right. She tried a door but the knob wouldn't turn. Nobody acknowledged her knocks.

"Oh Beverly, I know you're in here."

She waited. No answer.

Another knock. *"Beverly?"*

Abigail walked away then stopped at the end of the hall, hoping that if Beverly were in there, she might open the door when Abigail was gone. After a while, when that did not happen, Abigail went around the corner, wishing she could bash Beverly's skull in.

From two halls over there was a sneeze. Was it Bev?

Abigail made no sounds as she edged closer, then hid below a small table in one of the halls. Eyes wide, she anticipated the steps that came her way. It was Beverly. She was unsuspecting and frightened, and at any moment Abigail could have reached out and grabbed her feet, but it was better to watch her be scared, watch her wander with her flashlight, looking for a way to defend herself, looking for her own set of keys to exit the house.

Abigail slithered out from under the table, and the hall was darkened because there were no windows near, so that moonlight could not penetrate the perpetually shadowy hall, and as she was halfway out, Beverly paused and turned around. Darkness blanketed her like warm covers, obscuring her from Beverly's vision, and while Beverly stared for a long while, she did not see Abigail whatsoever.

Beverly disappeared into the house again.

Abigail's hands were filled with the urge to raise the keys and bring them down on Beverly's pretty face.

Go get her, go kill her.

No I won't, I won't kill Bever—

Yes I will. I have to. I want to kill her.

As Abigail passed through strange shadows that were cast without a source, she leaned into them, resting on a wall, and was becoming one with the house. It felt alive and she was part of it. She was on the second floor, heading back to the red door.

The small windows in the room cast in a glow of light. At the altar's base, Abigail found a piece of chalk, and without thinking put it in her left hand. It moved in mysterious patterns, forming symbols she had never seen before—symbols which felt enchanted and forbidden.

Around the symbols, Abigail set up the black candles that were already near the altar. Each of them had a small metal piece at their bases to hold them up. She lit a match, lit the first candle, then blew out the match, and used that first candle to light all the others.

With the symbols drawn, the candles lit, and the book placed at the altar's side, she thought, she needed a few more things: Beverly, a knife, and the pen.

Abigail felt like an unnoticed fly on the wall when she stood in the doorway watching Beverly look through the knives in the kitchen. Beverly was unaware, and Abigail loved being there in secret, waiting for the perfect moment to kill her friend.

Down at the other end of the kitchen, there was an entrance to the dining room, and Beverly went through it with a knife in her hand.

Snap her neck before she can hurt you.

She doesn't want to hurt me.

That's why she has a knife. She does wants to kill me, that's why you need to kill her first.

Her hands were suddenly against the knife block. She inspected the knives, lifting them one by one, but none of them would do. It had to be a special knife.

"Abigail? Can you hear me?"

Abigail almost replied, but was hushed. Her lips pulled tightly closed. She listened to Beverly walk around, and floorboards creaked viciously below her.

After prolonged moments of silence, Beverly spoke again as if somebody had spoken to her: *"Abby? That you?"*

Abigail crept out of the kitchen the way she had come in from, floorboards screaming under her steps no matter how carefully she shifted her weight, and from a distance footsteps came her way. She hurried to the spiraling staircase, knelt at its lowest point so that she could be hidden, and Beverly came by, and Abigail wanted to laugh now because she was a spider and Beverly was a fly, and she had Beverly in her web, and Beverly could never break free.

Abigail rattled the keys.

A sourceless glow laid a hand on Beverly's cheek revealing terror in her eyes as Beverly jolted and raised the knife. Beverly stepped forward then stepped back. The flashlight shook back and forth, scanning the open area, but Abigail pulled back so that she was hidden.

"Abigail?"

Abigail remained quiet, holding in her laugh.

Beverly stepped away into the depths of the house. Abigail waited until she heard the footsteps travel far enough before she left her hiding place.

As she went up the spiraling stairs she shivered; she passed through coldness that was so heavy it was tangible. Abigail entered the library and found her purse next to the desk where she must have left it before blacking out and waking up in that random hallway.

She picked up her purse and set it on the desk. Inside was the Navaja knife.

Abigail ran a finger across the cold metal blade.

It was time.

38

THE CANDLES BURNED PROLIFICALLY and wax stained the floor. Abigail put the pen and journal on the altar, then left the Red Room with the Navaja raised. Creeping as silent as a shadow, Abigail went across the floor to the adjacent halls in search of Beverly.

"Come out come out wherever you are."

There were steps approaching her. Abigail turned to find Beverly pointing her flashlight at her, with a knife held in her other hand. Light reflected against Beverly's face to reveal her frightened reddened eyes.

"Let's stop this." Beverly stepped closer. *"We don't want to hurt each other."*

"Beverly." Abigail dropped her knife. *"Please help me."*

Beverly came closer. *"Do you have the keys? For the gate?"*

"I don't know. I can't remember. Beverly, there's something wrong with me. There's something in my head."

"I want to help you. Tell me what you need me to do."

"I need you to—to—"

Abigail fell to her knees. She slammed her head on the hard floor then put her hands on her head and yanked her hair; waves of torture pulsed through her head and spread through her body. The voices crammed into her head were fighting for control.

She glanced at Beverly who was inching backwards with tears running down her face. *"I'm going to kill you."*

Beverly didn't say a word.

Abigail was out of control of her body as she watched it chase after Beverly then slam her to the ground. She pinned Beverly down and grabbed her friend's throat with both of her hands. As she pressed, gently at first, then increasing the pressure, Beverly's right arm pulled free and brought up the knife. Abigail let go of Beverly's neck, reaching from the knife, but a sudden rush of pain made her recoil. Blood leaked from her hand and stained her pure white gown.

She was back to that awful day in the tub.

The bathroom was chilled and Abigail set down the pen and the note. She stepped into the tub then sat down. The chill of the razor-blade made her shiver. Gooseflesh rose on her arms. She held it in her left hand and brought it to her eyes, inspecting it through blurred vision, thinking, *Why am I doing this?*

Abigail brought it to her right wrist, pressing the cold sharp edge to her soft flesh. One pull and it would all be over with. She lifted the blade and hesitated. She had never wanted to kill herself, but the voice in the back of her head was screaming at her to do it.

No, no, I shouldn't be doing this.

Abigail brought the razor to her wrist again. She traced it across her skin, opening up her wrist. At first the pain was dull as blood spilled over the brim of her wound, then there were sharp threads of pain that shot from her wrist up through her arm.

The blade dropped from her hand. She reached for it but the tub was too red to see what was below the surface; the bottom of the tub could have been a mile away for all Abigail knew, and the blade was drifting away forever.

Her lips were pulled into a smile. A smile that wasn't her own.

"Abigail I'm so sorry. Abigail? Abigail?" Beverly was behind the bathroom door.

Abigail opened her mouth to answer, and was back in the dreadfully dark hallway, back on the floor in the hallway, vaguely aware of a pain in her hand, vaguely aware of pain flowing through her body, and hardly understanding what Beverly was saying.

Abigail tried to sit up, but the pain was too much.

"I didn't want to hurt you. It's this house—look what it's doing to us. I didn't meant to…"

Abigail was silent, then said, "Do you trust me?"

Beverly said nothing.

"Do you trust me?"

"I do."

"Then come with me to the Red Room."

"For what? Abby, for what?"

"To get it out of my head."

Abigail picked up the Navaja knife. Beverly backed away. Abigail stood up and held it out in her shaking hands.

"I need you to cut my wrists."

"What?"

"This is the only way to get it out of my head. That's how it entered the first time."

"Abby I can't cut you."

Abigail's left hand closed around the Navaja's handle, then with her right hand she grabbed Beverly's hair and tugged on it, sending Beverly falling to Abigail's feet and causing Beverly's purse to slip from her shoulder in the chaos. Beverly dropped the knife and flashlight, but Abigail had enough vision as she dragged her friend through the hallway because moonlight was coming through the windows softly.

She dragged her friend to the Red Room, where shadows were patterning on the ceiling and wax was dripping over the edge of black candles. Everything was ready. Abigail threw Beverly to the center of the markings she had drawn in chalk.

"Oh my God Abigail what are you going to do to me?"

Abigail opened the nameless book next to the altar. "If you move one muscle I'll—I'll…" The spirits inside of Abigail squirmed, pulsed, stretched, trying to regain lost ground. *"Beverly please I don't know what I'm doing. Please help me. Please cut me."*

Beverly stood up and backed away to the other end of the room. *"I can't cut you. I can't do this. I can't."*

"Beverly I need you to do it. I'm afraid. Please help me get it out of my head."

"I can't."

"You're the only person who can. It won't let me hurt myself."

"Abigail…"

"Do it. Please do it."

"I can't do it."

"I'm begging you to cut me Beverly. Cut me."

Beverly was trembling, stepping forward, and kneeling at Abigail's side in the middle of all the symbols. She took the knife from

Abigail, who then stuck out her wrists. Beverly held the knife over Abigail's soft flesh, candlelight gleaming off the metal, and brought the sharp blade down to touch her friend's wrists gently.

"I can't do it."

"Cut me."

"I can't do it."

"Cut me Beverly."

"Abby I can't do it."

"You can do it, you can cut me, it's the only way to get it out. Hurry."

"I can't."

"Hurry before it hurts you."

"I can't cut you."

"Hurry."

"I can't."

Both girls were hushed as footfalls echoed in silent halls. Their eyes held each other's, then they turned to the red door that creaked open on its own. Irregular darkness poured into the room, and from the other side came Cat.

Grey and cold and lifeless with a disturbingly chilling smile. Cat was dripping wet. Her hair fell over he face in dark black heaps. Her impossibly dark eyes were stiff, moving slowly between Abigail and Beverly.

"Beverly, it's been such a long time. I thought I'd never see you again."

Beverly was stunned. "Cat what happened to you?"

"Why don't you ask Abby?"

Beverly looked from Cat momentarily to Abigail who was backed against a wall, then back to Cat who had taken a step further into the room. "What is she talking about?"

Abigail sobbed. "Beverly don't listen to her."

"No reason to lie, Abby. Just tell the truth."

Abigail looked away from them both. *"I didn't mean it. I didn't want to do it. I swear to God I..."*

"Abigail what did you do?"

"Beverly it wasn't me. It was Helen."

"What did you do?"

"She killed me. She left me to rot in the cistern."

Abigail wiped her tears then turned her attention back into the room. The candles were flickering, and glimpses of light were running across Cat's lifeless face and lifeless eyes. It truly was the longest night on earth, Abigail thought. And there was a way to get out of it, she knew, if she could only remember what Beverly had told her that was so important.

"How could I live like this? I'm a freak."

Beverly stepped away without a word.

"You've got a nice body, Beverly, did anybody ever tell you that? I bet I'd fit inside it perfectly."

Cat was stepping closer to Beverly, who was stricken with horror, and Abigail crept from the wall, noticing that Beverly had dropped the Navaja in front of the altar. Abigail grabbed it then ran behind Cat, plunging it as far as it could go into her back. Cat laughed, turning, and not one drop of blood leaked from the body as Abigail pulled the knife out.

"Wasn't killing me once enough for you?"

327

"I… I…" Abigail took small steps away.

Cat's reanimated corpse followed her. *"Yeah? What? Are you just going to make another excuse that it wasn't your fault? That you didn't mean to?"*

"Cat, I'll give you my body." Beverly screamed. *"Come take it."*

Cat turned to find Beverly holding a crucifix out ahead of her, which blinded both Cat and Abigail. In that split second, Abigail made a run for the door at the same time as Beverly, and together they ran from the Red Room and through the top floor to the stairway.

"Where do you think you're going?" Cat screamed from behind them. Her voice sent sickly chills down Abigail's back.

"Where'd you put the keys?"

Abigail reached for her pocket then remembered she had set them down beside the altar. *"They're in the Red Room."*

"Fuck."

On the ground floor, Abigail and Beverly ran hand in hand around the spiraling staircase to one of the adjacent halls which spanned to the very back of the house. Cat's footsteps were still sounding distantly; she was coming down the stairway as they approached the back door.

Abigail twisted the doorknob and opened the back door. The girls exited and slowly closed it behind them, praying that Cat couldn't hear. Outside was a large expanse of a back yard with a shed, a wellhouse, and the practically endless woods.

Abigail and Beverly exchanged a worried look.

"Where are we going?"

Beverly shivered. "Who the hell cares?"

The girls ran together into the woods, kneeling at the undergrowth and low branches where they had a view of the back yard. How could they get out of this mess? How could they get out of here? Abigail shuddered when a chilling wind washed over them. It was so cold out—what she'd give to erase everything that happened today and be at home, in bed, warm under her covers.

"Beverly?" Abigail was scared to whisper, scared that somehow Cat could hear them from all the way inside.

"Uh-huh?"

"You told me something that could get us out of this. What was it?"

"What are you talking about?"

"I don't know."

The back door was opening.

The girls quickly took off and went along the path deeper into the woods. Following the path they came past a little river—a little stream of dark water in the woods—and past that, off the path, they were traveling deep into the unknown; deep into the mystical world of night, where anything could be lurking, anything could be real, anything could be following them.

Abigail looked over her shoulder. She had suspected somebody was watching her—had *felt* somebody was watching her—but nobody was there. Unblinking eyes sneaking closer, closer, about to reach with sharp claws for both Abigail and Beverly. Abigail was terrified, she wanted to go home, wanted to get out of here, but there was no going back through the house for the keys if Cat was still around.

They came past a tree that had fallen over rocky soil and was half-decayed. Past that was a rise in the ground, and coming down, Abigail and Beverly came to an old cemetery with chimes that screamed loudly, and a rusted gate that was falling apart, and whose door had fully been torn off. There were many, many graves, and Abigail felt the spirit inside of her body twisting.

"*Oh my God.*" Beverly stopped in place.

"*Do you think Cat knows about this?*"

"*She must know. All the time she spent in this place, what doesn't she know about it?*"

"Maybe if we go far enough…"

As the girls stepped past the rusted archaic gate, a primordial chill passed over the graveyard. The ground rumbled and vines fell from the surrounding trees and sank into the graves. The girls were motionless, completely frozen, watching as the vines lifted decayed corpses and whole skeletons from the ground. The vines swung them by their arms and legs, animating them like marionettes. The woods behind the Engstrom place was alive with dead bodies.

The girls ran. Directly ahead of them were swinging corpses. Decayed bodies were torn open by the pull of the trees, swinging torn pieces of flesh and dripping intestines inches from Abigail and Beverly. Black tongues hung limp between deteriorated lips. As they passed a skeleton, Abigail could have sworn that the hands had reached for them, and she let out a painful scream that burned her already sore throat.

Beverly was standing with one hand on a tree, out of reach of any of the corpses, watching them spellbound. Abigail joined Beverly, bewitched by what she was seeing. How any of this could be possible was beyond any human understanding.

Then Abigail glimpsed something moving between the trees from beyond the bodies.

She pulled Beverly away, hiding them from view if it had in fact been Cat she suspected she saw.

"I think Cat is here. I think I saw her."

The girls moved down between the trees. There was no clear path to travel. They could only go down and hope that they were getting further away from Cat and the hanging corpses. Abigail wanted it all to be over. Wanted to be back home. Wanted to never hear about Cat or the Engstrom place again. She thought about running away if they ever got out of here alive—running away to the furthest end of the earth.

The trees tightened. The girls could no longer stand side by side. Beverly was ahead of Abigail, holding her hand, leading her through the woods. Abigail felt the voices in her head screaming at each other, fighting for control, and she was afraid that the *Other Voice* would take over again and hurt Beverly here in the middle of nowhere.

Here in the Engstrom woods, Abigail thought, nobody would ever find the body. Nobody would ever come this deep into these woods. Nobody would think to look here of all places for Beverly. If Beverly's body was hidden here… she'd stay hidden until the end of time.

Suddenly Beverly stopped. She was out of breath.

Abigail put her hands on her friend. "Are you okay?"

"I'm—I'm exhausted."

"Keep going."

Beverly was crying. Abigail took her friend's hand and led her through the woods, going down this terrifying unseen world that seemed like a place completely outside of reality; there was no telling where they were going or what they would find or who they would run into. The woods were a portal into another universe. Abigail moved forward in a blur, moving almost by instinct around the branches and trees, scraping against leafless branches, traveling further into the heart of the unnatural. If she listened close enough, she could still hear the moving of the corpses along the vines.

Beverly was dragging, but Abigail couldn't blame her. Her own body was weak, she was tired, every joint ached, her feet begged her to rest, and she partially gave in, stopping for about fifteen seconds before continuing her slow jog through the mystical woods. Would this night ever end? Would they be chased through the woods for eternity? All they needed to do was get back to the Red Room and get the keys and unlock the gate—how could they get past Cat now, go back inside, and accomplish any of it? Abigail felt her mind was going to break in half—maybe it was already starting to snap, she thought. Maybe her worries and her aching body would kill her before Cat ever did.

They came to a slight rise, then the ground dipped down, and dodging branches, the trees parted, and they came to a large clearing. Straight ahead, the ground rose again, steeper this time, and Abigail thought that the cabin was a mirage at first, but upon closer inspection she was assured it was real. Moonlight shined precisely on the disgusting decrepit cabin. Moss clung to its sides and its windows were as darkened as the Engstrom place's so that it was impossible to tell what was inside. The cabin's door was cracked open an inch; there was no knob on it, and it moved with every touch of the wind. Grass had grown tall around the forgotten cabin, so that it took a lot of effort for the two tired girls to push their way through it.

Abigail listened. She couldn't hear the corpses anymore, nor could she hear anybody following them. Maybe they had lost Cat—maybe Cat had gone another direction, maybe she was looking for them elsewhere, maybe she went back into the house.

Abigail opened the door, Beverly shined her flashlight, and the girls went inside.

As Abigail shut the door behind them, she thought she saw something moving at the base of the miniature hill.

39

ABIGAIL PUT HER HANDS on Beverly and sobbed. Was there any escape from Cat? Was there any escape from the past? Was there any escape from the hideous things she had done and needed to live with for the rest of her life?

"I think she's out there." Abigail whispered.

"I think we can keep her out." Beverly shuddered. She moved away from Abigail to an open suitcase.

Abigail's flashlight followed Beverly through the short length to the suitcase, but Abigail was instantly blinded by the incredible shine erupting from within the suitcase and staggered back, pulling the flashlight away, rubbing her eyes until they adjusted to the creeping darkness that fought the feeble light from the tiny bulb. She inspected the cabin while Beverly moved in darkness. Abigail thought about looking outside but hesitated; she didn't want to see Cat's disgusting face and the terror of the longest night on earth.

The place was void, streaked with abundant dust that made Abigail sneeze. There was a small hallway and a small stairway, and here in the sitting room—which took up, it seemed, most of the cabin's ground floor—was an empty fireplace, and above it was an antiquarian painting of a man and his wife. His wife who looked exactly like Beverly to the final details—pretty blue eyes, long blonde hair, a smile that curved in the exact same way, and something else, Abigail thought, that she couldn't put a finger on. Maybe it was the way those eyes in the painting looked down on her; maybe it was the way that Beverly's soul looked through them at her.

Abigail shuddered.

"Beverly look. It looks just like you."

"Abigail, come with me."

"Where are we going?"

"There were crosses and Holy Bibles in that suitcase. I have to put them all around the windows and door so Cat can't get in. I've covered what's in here, so come with me to the back, we have to make sure she can't get in through another door."

The girls went through the hallway that stretched through uncertain darkness, and Abigail thought that at any moment hands would reach out and grab them and pull them apart into tiny pieces. If she had ever thought they were lost before, or were in the center of unreality before, now they truly were. This place was another existence, a place locked out of time, a place where neither Abigail nor Beverly's body would be found if anything happened to them. Nobody would ever check this cabin because this place did not exist.

Beverly squeezed Abigail's arm tighter with every step. Abigail felt a scream emerging in her throat and swallowed it. At the end of the hall at the back door, Abigail diverted her eyes from Beverly, because even in darkness she could see the glow of the Holy Bible. The girls turned around and came back to the sitting room, but the door was creaking open and shut an inch with continual bursts of wind.

There was a dirty old couch, a loveseat, and the girls pushed it together to the door to keep it shut, just as the door cracked open and Cat's lifeless eyes peeked through. Beverly held up a crucifix and Cat and Abigail were both repelled. Cat retreated from the door, moving unseen outside the cabin, and Abigail dropped to her knees crying.

"It's still in my head. I still need you to cut me."

"I told you I can't cut you."

"Yes you can. There's no other way."

"But I can't."

The girls sobbed alone, sitting next to each other on the cold floor. Abigail put the knife in Beverly's hand.

"I can't do it. I'm sorry but I can't hurt you."

"Please Beverly. For me."

"You're asking me to cut you open while we're in the middle of nowhere in the middle of the night. What if I cut you too deep? What if you lose too much blood? What if I kill you? I couldn't live with myself if something happened to you."

"I don't care if it kills me. I need it out of my head."

"There must be another way." Beverly held a cross, and held the nail polish bottle she had filled up with Holy Water; she had kept the bottle in her pocket instead of her purse. "Let me try it."

Abigail shielded her eyes. "What are you talking about?"

"There's Holy Water in this nail polish bottle, it's all I had to hold it in. Abigail, the other day... I don't think you remember... you called me screaming, and I went to your house with Cat, and the reason you were screaming was because you couldn't look at the picture of Virgin Mary in your closet. So Cat and I gathered the Bibles in your house and read from them and something… something started happening, but I was too scared to go through with it completely. I think I can help you."

"Then cut me."

"Listen to what you're saying. I'm not cutting you open."

"Just a little Beverly just a little cut."

"I'm not cutting you."

"But—but—"

The girls were silenced by a noise somewhere above that sent chills under their skin. The girls held each other, Abigail clutching her Navaja knife, and Beverly raising her crucifix. Then there was only silence; dead silence.

The spirits inside of Abigail were twisting, fighting for control.

"Beverly?"

"Yeah?"

"Maybe Cat won't kill you but I will."

Beverly pushed her away, and in the same moment Cat crawled out of the fireplace face-first, her body contorted into disgustingly uneven shapes. Her eyes glowed wickedly. A wide smile stretched on her lips.

"I'm tired of playing cat and mouse. Beverly, I want to be inside your body."

"Cat I'm sorry you… died but you can't—I can't give you—"

"I'm taking what I want. I want to be alive again."

Cat stepped forward with a wide smile that stretched from ear to ear. Beverly's hands shook uncontrollably as she held the cross out in both hands. Cat charged straight again for Beverly, and in that split second Abigail ran toward the reanimated monstrosity with her

Navaja and jammed it into Cat's side. Just like the first time, it had no effect, but Cat was distracted and pushed Abigail down.

Pain pulsed in Abigail's back. Abruptly Cat was on top of her with her sharp nails raised, and she brought them down on Abigail's chest before she could react—ten sharp nails pressing against Abigail's skin, threatening to break the surface.

"I'm sorry, Abby," Cat said with a smile. *"I didn't mean to hurt you. Can I blame this on somebody else too?"*

Beverly jumped on Cat's back and pressed the cross into Cat's face, sending up little billows of smoke as Cat let out gasps of pain.

"Why don't you die already?"

The two were struggling against each other, and Abigail felt the *Other Voice* surging through her mind, taking control, telling her to join Cat, telling her to kill her friend, telling her that there was another spirit that needed the body more than Beverly did.

Abigail had a little power left, a little strength, a little bit of control, and faced one of the glowing Holy Bibles. Momentarily it seared the intruder in her mind, and across from her she saw the nail polish bottle that contained the Holy Water.

It burned to grab it, searing her hand like Cat's face had been seared, and with pain consuming all of her body, she twisted the cap off.

Cat knocked the crucifix away from Beverly, and Beverly let out a horrific scream. Cat's hand was raised, all her sharp claws pointed down at Beverly. Abigail reacted suddenly, pulling Cat's head back and pouring the Holy Water into her mouth.

Cat convulsed. Abigail held her down with her hand over Cat's mouth, making sure all the Holy Water rushed down her throat. Then

Beverly was rushing to the door and windows, collecting the Holy Bibles and crucifixes and putting them around Cat's body. Abigail had to shut her eyes to avoid their burning brightness.

The body went slack under Abigail's touch. Was it finally over? Was Cat at rest?

As Abigail opened her eyes a sickly cold hand wrapped around her wrist. For one fleeting second Cat's eyes were her own again, and not the monster's, then they shut, and the creature was dead.

Abigail moved away from the body and stood next to Beverly who was breathing heavy by one of the windows which was letting in the first glimmer of sunrise. Abigail put an arm around Beverly then sneezed from dust that was uprising. The whole cabin was a mess. Beverly had set candles around Cat and had lit them and they were now dripping wax. The Navaja was on the ground at Abigail's feet. There were scattered Bibles and crosses that she couldn't look upon.

Abigail felt empty and lost. She could only guess how empty Beverly might feel. Months ago, when she had bought that damn pen from the thrift store, she never would have guessed it would have led to all of this death and destruction. Where was the good in the world?

Abigail picked up the knife. "Won't you cut me?"

"No." Beverly shook her head. "I can't. We'll find another way. There's got to be another way."

"Okay. What can we do?"

Before Beverly could say something, Cat laughed and stood up and every joint in her reanimated body cracked.

"I want my new body already."

Beverly lifted her cross. *"Go to hell."*

Cat staggered backwards then fell to her knees and her body convulsed. Beverly stood over her with the cross. Suddenly Cat's face was back to normal.

"*I'm all better now Beverly.*"

"*Don't listen to her.*"

Beverly said nothing.

"*You can put that down now.*"

Abigail stepped closer.

"*I won't hurt you Beverly. I think I'm all better now.*"

Beverly kept the cross raised. "I'm so sorry Cat."

Cat's body levitated a foot off the ground. Abigail stepped backwards, then took a reluctant step forward again. Beverly backed away from the floating corpse. It was convulsing midair, and the temperature in the room dropped so that Abigail and Beverly could see their breaths. The corpse did not breathe. It only levitated and struggled, then after a short while it descended back to the ground, and its face was Cat's regular face.

"*Beverly stop it stop it you're hurting me.*"

"*You can't trust it, don't listen to her Bev.*"

"*Beverly help me!*"

"*No we can't help her Beverly don't do it.*"

Beverly stepped away from both of them, splitting her attention between them uncertainly.

"*Beverly why would you listen to Abby? She's the one who killed me.*"

"*Beverly she's lying to you, she's dead, you can't save her.*"

"*Both of you shut up.*"

Everybody was silent, watching each other, then Beverly returned from the other side of the sitting room and stood at Cat's side. She lent her a hand to help her up. All Abigail could do was watch and increase the already painfully tight grip on her Navaja.

"Beverly no."

Cat smiled, putting her hand on Beverly's throat just as Abigail had done to Cat.

"Thank you, Beverly, for your sacrifice."

Abigail cried. There was nothing she could do to stop Cat.

Beverly screamed, then by sudden instinct raised the crucifix and jammed it into the hole in Cat's throat where Abigail's fingers had once pierced. The monster released her grasp on Beverly, and Beverly hurried away.

Cat fell backwards. The Holy Cross sank deeper into Cat's gaping throat so that only the very end of the cross was showing at all. Maybe this time, Abigail hoped, the monster was truly dead.

Beverly was crying.

Abigail put the Navaja in Beverly's hands. "You know what you need to do to me."

Beverly threw the knife on the floor. *"Stop asking me to do this already."*

Abigail smacked her. The unusual feeling of regrowth in her body was stretching, and the *Other Voice* was taking over.

Abigail struggled to move away from Beverly across the room.

Kill her now. Nobody will find the body.

No I won't kill her. I won't.

"Beverly. I know what it wants."

"What?" Beverly asked reluctantly.

Abigail lifted a finger to the painting. *"Don't you see what it's done to me? It wants to do the same to you."*

"I don't understand."

"The corpses we saw. That's what it wants. It wants to bring alive the dead Engstroms. It's not me it wants. It's you."

Beverly was silent.

"And what better bodies than former Engstroms? What better body than yours, Beverly?"

"I'm not an Engstrom."

"It only wanted my body because I was convenient. I was near."

Beverly was silent and afraid.

Abigail slid the Navaja across the floor to Beverly.

"I need you to cut me."

"For the millionth damn time, I won't cut you."

"That's how it entered the first time, Beverly. That's how I can get it to leave me."

40

PAIN BURNED LIKE FIRE then turned into icy numbness, and all there was was the void in front of her eyes, and Abigail was falling into the pit of a murky tomb. She gasped shallowly, her heart pumped, and her soul lifted and fell, ebbed and flowed, threatening again to leave her body. Suddenly breathing was impossible. Abigail choked, trying to force air back through her throat and into her lungs. She was falling—falling fast into a bottomless crypt.

All was darkness until a face appeared through the void—irregularly shaped eyes and a devious smile, the demon was all around, surrounding every small space around her, and Abigail suddenly realized she was *inside* her own body. She was inside of her mind.

Suddenly she saw Beverly at her side crying, holding a knife that dripped blood. Candles were flickering and casting amorphous shadows on the ceiling.

Abigail's heart was pounding violently, her soul was drifting out of her body, and the *Other Voice* was filling every inch of her. Abigail's soul was drifting toward the open wound, flowing with her blood. She would leak out of her body and be completely taken over by the *Other.*

Abigail sat up and snatched the knife from her friend.

"You can't save her."

Beverly ran for the door but the couch was still in the way, so she made the split-second decision to run for the stairway, since Abigail was between her and the hallway that led to the back exit door. It was the only place to go. Abigail chased her up the stairs, heart pounding with excitement, and Beverly disappeared into the upstairs hallway. But that was all right, Abigail thought, since the windows at either end, despite being obscured by tall branches and moss, were letting in light that grew in brightness with each quick moment.

Abigail's heart was beating fast. She loved the chase. She wanted to bring the knife down on Beverly's skull. Wanted to kill her. Wanted her body as a vessel for another soul to come back to life. It would feel so good dragging that knife across Beverly's throat and watching her bleed, watching the horror of death come over her soft blue eyes, watching her realize that this was it—her final moments.

"I thought we were done playing hide and seek, Bev." Abigail dragged her knife in her left hand across the wall.

Beverly slowly emerged from one of the rooms that Abigail had passed. *"Abigail stop this please stop this."*

"Abigail's not with us anymore."

Beverly ran back but Abigail grabbed her by the wrist and pulled her closer.

"Let go of me!"

Abigail brought the tip of the knife down on Beverly's skin until it carefully broke the surface. A drop of blood escaped and rolled down her skin.

"Abigail stop."

Abigail pulled the knife away and let go of her friend. Momentarily she was in charge of herself again. *"It didn't work. Cutting me open didn't work."*

Beverly ran down the stairs. Abigail followed slowly with vision blurred by tears. There was no hope, she thought. There was no way to get rid of the demon inside of her head. There was nothing she could do.

Back on the ground floor, Beverly had the Holy Bible open, flipping through the pages for someplace specific, and in her hands also held a crucifix. Abigail couldn't look at it; it burned to try. She looked at her feet and sobbed.

"It's not going to work." Abigail cried. *"We've lost."*

"Don't think like that. There has to be a way to help you."

Abigail was quiet.

Beverly read: *"Resist the devil, and he will flee from you."*

"I'm sorry Beverly."

Chills slithered on Abigail's back. The *Other* was stretching, filling her body, controlling her movements as she stepped forward. Beverly moved to the other side of the couch and pushed it from the door. Beverly wanted to say something but was silent; she watched her with crestfallen eyes.

With the Navaja raised over her head, Abigail ran for the door, but Beverly shut it just in time as Abigail slammed it down on the decaying wood. It went straight through but completely missed Beverly. Abigail tugged twice until the Navaja came free.

Instead of opening the door Abigail pressed the sharp edge of the knife to her throat. She was crying. One pull and the nightmare would be over, one pull and neither Abigail nor the *Other Voice* would have her body. One pull and Beverly would be safe.

"Don't do it Abigail," the demon said.

"Then neither of us can have my body," Abigail said. *"I'd rather be dead than give it to you."*

Her hand lowered the knife. She raised it up, started to open the door, then hesitated. The voices in her head were fighting for control. One was telling her to chase after Beverly, the other was telling her to end it all.

She peeked from the window and saw Beverly running down the base of the little hill. Then Beverly stopped and looked back up at the cabin. Abigail forced herself away from the window. She went to the candles, whose flames had almost completely melted away the wax, and held the knife with her left hand to her right wrist.

Abigail moved the knife away. *"I can't do it."*

"I knew you didn't have the guts."

Abigail cried and dropped the knife. *"Get out of my mind."*

The *Other* pulsed and grabbed the knife in Abigail's left hand, then stood up and left the cabin. Beverly was exhausted and wasn't getting very far. Abigail pushed through the tall uncut grass and through the vegetation and came to the base of the hill and through the forest, where she saw Beverly, out of breath, forcing herself to keep moving. When Beverly furtively glanced behind herself she saw Abigail and screamed.

"Bev I don't want to hurt you."

Beverly kept running.

Abigail ran to catch up with her friend, pushing her body through the slashes of pain shooting up from her feet through her hips and up to the rest of her body with every step over the hard rocky ground. Beverly tripped and laid in pain. She shifted to see Abigail coming up to her. Abigail keeled at her friend's side.

"Beverly I'm so sorry."

Beverly cried.

Abigail put the knife on her own wrist, and Beverly reached over to pull the knife from Abigail.

"I need to cut it out of me."

"It's not gonna work."

"We were close."

"No we were not…" Beverly couldn't control her tears. *"God look at all your blood. You've lost so much blood."*

"Don't worry about it."

"I wish it were me," Beverly said. *"I wish it were me instead of you."*

Abigail was brought back to the day at the farmhouse. The day she gave Beverly one cent and she threw it into the well.

What did you wish?

That your wish would come true.

All was darkness.

Abigail was back inside of her mind. The monstrous *Other Voice* pinned Abigail's soul. Abigail struggled against it, straining to slip her arms free, but the *Other* had a grip on her that was impossible to break free from. It laughed hideously and licked its lips.

"Goodbye, Abigail." The demon's lips pulled back to reveal rows of sharp teeth.

"I wish you would get out of my body."

Abigail's eyes shut and Beverly cried over her body. Abigail was getting cold despite the rising sun and the fresh rays of light that spread over them. Beverly's heart was beating with fear. She didn't want her friend to die.

"It should have been me. It should have been me."

Abigail choked and Beverly pulled abruptly back.

She choked again.

"Abigail?"

Beverly wasn't sure what to do but watch. Abigail choked again, her eyes flickered open, and from the depths of her body a thick black smoke emerged from Abigail's mouth and lifted far into the sky.

Beverly put her hands under Abigail's head and helped her sit up. They hugged each other tight and didn't let go.

For the final time, Abigail and Beverly went into the old Engstrom place. The keys were behind the altar in the red room. They hurried to find them and unlock the fence, then they left the keys behind and descended the hill. They stopped at the farm for apples and to rest. They sat in front of the well.

"Did you really kill Cat?"

Abigail couldn't look her in the eye. "Yes. Yes I did. I mean it was me but it wasn't me. It was—it was that thing in my head."

"Helen?"

"I think that was a lie. I don't think it was Helen. I think it only said that to trick me into going to the house."

"And Bruno?"

"The house got him like it got Officer Daniels."

The girls were silent for a while.

"Beverly?"

"Yeah?"

"I understand if you can never trust me again."

Beverly paused to think. "I don't know if I trust you or not."

"I never wanted to hurt Cat or anybody. I never wanted any of this to happen." Abigail was crying hard.

Beverly put her hand over Abigail's hand. "Abigail. How did you do it?"

"Huh?"

"When you… when you got rid of it. How did you do it? How did you get it out of your body?"

"Well, it was all because of you. Because you gave me your wish."

AUTHOR'S NOTES

I BEGAN WRITING THIS book because I wanted to write about a haunted house. It took me two years and seven drafts to complete. I owe a big thanks to two people: my editor Roy and my friend Andrew. Both of you gave me feedback that helped this book go from an awful first draft to a great final draft.

This was my biggest learning experience—along with my comic book CREEPSTERS—because I had a great editor named Roy who helped me learn what it took to write a great story. There were a lot of things in my head that weren't on the page, so when Roy read my books and asked, "Why does ___ happen?" or "Why did ___ decide to ___?" I would explain it to him, and he would say "But that isn't on the page."

Roy taught me a lot about showing my ideas on the page, and he also taught me about not being boring. I wrote this book for the first time in October 2020. I loved the first draft, but upon doing draft two, I realized it was boring. But I was stuck because I didn't know what to change. I'm known for being a quick writer and writing a first draft in two to four weeks, but I was not known as a guy willing to change his story. I guess if I was ever lazy in one area of my work, it would be in having the guts to come up with a different idea because I had this other one first, or because I'm married to an idea and setting it in stone—but that could really hinder a work of art. So when Roy read only the first three or four chapters of draft two and challenged me, it was really difficult to change things and come up with something new, but I like challenges and so figuring out how to change the story made me better.

Roy is very blunt with me when I'm being boring, and sometimes I know I'm being boring or that something is off, but I'm scared to admit it. We all need someone to be honest with us and tell us when our stories aren't working or when they're boring or when something needs to be changed. Thank you Roy for all the feedback and for taking the time to discuss the story with me and thank you for helping me fully realize my ideas and make them better.

My buddy Andrew read this book very close to the publication date and gave me last minute feedback that helped me, specifically in areas where I was not confident in the book. I was so nervous about a couple sections that I very nearly canceled the book because I was so afraid to publish something bad—I'd rather have three books out that I'm proud of instead of twenty that I'm embarrassed by or cringe at, and I did not want a book that's in the middle. I either wanted something I'm entirely 100% proud of, or nothing at all.

I can't thank Andrew enough for the feedback he gave me on the shaky chapters, and for his support and encouragement through this whole process. I also owe Andrew a big thanks for hearing me complain about this book for two years whenever a certain section was not going right.

It's good to have different eyeballs on your book and to get different perspectives on your story. I thought I had "don't be boring" figured out, but Andrew once again helped me to learn how to not be boring.

I completed draft seven of this book in October of 2022. You spend two whole years of your life with a story and it better be about something. Why spend all that time with it in the first place? Some people may say books need to only be about entertainment, or art for art's sake, and while I believe those arguments have their merits, I can't help but believe books need to have a moral to them or some type of theme or SOMETHING.

Originally I thought the theme was self-harm but it turned out that the theme—for me, at least—was friendship, but perhaps also being in control of your own life. I think part of this book is about not listening to the influence of another person—like an evil journal or evil pen or evil demon—and doing what you want to do with your life. The more I write, the more I find that the theme in practically all of my books comes down to "family and friendship."

The Bible says there is no greater love than laying down your life for a friend. While that did not entirely happen in this book, I think in some ways it did—Beverly knew how dangerous it was to go to Engstrom House, yet she was constantly trying to do what she could to help Abigail. Beverly could've died in a number of ways but stuck by her best friend's side. Even after all the awful things that happened, Beverly was still a good friend and helped her.

A big thanks again to Roy and Andrew for their help with this book and all the feedback and suggestions they gave me. This book would not have been the same without you guys. Thanks for helping me.

And thank you to everyone who bought this book.